# The Hillbrook Stash

## MIKE LYNCH

ISBN-13: 978-1492211686 / ISBN-10: 1492211680

*For Ian, Lucas, Eva, Mitchell, Brenna, Corinne,*
*Carissa, Ainsley, Nathan, and Cameron*

## Acknowledgements

Thanks to the people of Algonquin Area Writers Group for providing suggestions and support. Special thanks to Michelle Mathis for her editing help and story suggestions. She took the book from understandable to readable, and hopefully enjoyable.

Prologue

Everybody in Clear Valley knows about the Hillbrook stash. It's the biggest story in our little town. In 1937, a gangster named Jeffrey Hillbrook was shot and killed by federal agents in the woods west of town. The rest of the Hillbrook Gang was apprehended or killed in the days leading up to his death. So Jeffrey Hillbrook was holed-up alone in those woods during his final days.

During their reign of terror, the Hillbrook Gang robbed over thirty banks. It was said they accumulated hundreds of thousands of dollars in cash and other loot. None of the money was ever recovered. Since Jeffrey Hillbrook spent several days in the woods before his fatal shootout, everyone assumed he buried the loot somewhere in the woods.

Since then, just about everybody in Clear Valley has walked those woods with the hope of finding the Hillbrook stash. And the affair has become a huge part of our town's DNA. The woods west of town was renamed Bandit Woods. Our high school's sports teams are now called the Outlaws. City Park has a Hillbrook Gang Memorial that lists the banks that were robbed, the gang members and how they died, and law enforcement officers and civilians that were killed by the gang. Most of

1

the streets in town take aim at gangster-sounding names. Ammunition Avenue. Shooter Street. Getaway Boulevard. We even created a special holiday – Hillbrook Days – that we celebrate every year during the second weekend in July, that was the weekend Jeffrey Hillbrook was killed.

And then there's Jeremy Humphrey. He's Old Man Humphrey to us. He's almost as famous as the Hillbrook Gang. He was a fifty-seven year-old hermit living alone in those woods when Jeffrey Hillbrook was killed. He was supposed to have lived in a cabin that was burnt down by the federal agents during the man hunt.

Though Old Man Humphrey always denied it, people at the time believed that he harbored Jeffrey Hillbrook during his last few days. So everyone thought Old Man Humphrey knew where the stash was hidden. And they dogged him about it until the day he died. He was seventy-two when he died in nineteen fifty-two.

On his death-bed, his own brother grabbed Old Man Humphrey by the shoulders and shook him, shouting, "I'm your only family Jeremy! You've got to tell me where the stash is hidden before you die!" But Old Man Humphrey remained silent to his grave.

There was no evidence that Old Man Humphrey found or spent a penny of the stash. His spending habits remained exactly the same after Jeffrey Hillbrook's killing.

Wednesday

I'm not sure who started it but I'd bet it wasn't Tom. It really doesn't matter. My older brother's in a fight. That means I'll be in a fight too. I'm running now, trying to close the gap between us as fast as I can.

Our opponents are the Hinkle brothers. They're the bullies of Clear Valley Middle School. They've been picking on Tom and me ever since I can remember.

Tom's a good athlete but he's small for his age. He's thirteen. He makes up for his size with quickness. He's fast. I mean really fast. He can easily outrun the Hinkle brothers, so I'm surprised to see him fighting.

And me? Well, I've been called a bean pole. I'm over a year younger than Tom but three inches taller. And there is not an athletic bone in my body. Tom's size and my nerdiness make us perfect targets for the Hinkle brothers.

Ed Hinkle is the oldest. He's in eighth grade with Tom, but he's been held back twice. So he's huge. He's pretty fat so it's easy to get away from him. But if he catches you, watch out! Perry is in my class, seventh grade. He's okay if you get him alone. But he's different when he's with his brothers. And Larry. He's the youngest. He's only in sixth grade but he's scary. This one time, he cut the tail off of a chipmunk right in front of the whole school.

Tom is ducking punches pretty well. Playing basketball all winter with his taller friends has him in pretty good shape. But he won't last long. Not against the three of them. His long brown hair is already messed up and getting in his eyes.

I charge into the scene to ambush Perry. It takes my skin and bones running flat out to take him down. There's no muscle in my toothpick arms, so he easily absorbs my wimpy blows. But at least I got him away from Tom. I'm just about to punch him in the nose when BAM! – something hits the side of my head. Something hard. Something really hard. Then, everything goes black.

The next thing I know I'm flat on my back with my brother looking down at me. At least I think it's Tom. Everything's fuzzy. I remember the fight. Why doesn't Tom look beat up? And where did the Hinkle brothers go?

"Steve, are you okay?" he asks.

My ears are ringing like a church bell so I barely hear him. My jaw is on fire. My head aches. I ache all over. I'm cold, even though it's a warm spring day.

I give a weak nod, "I think so." My voice sounds strange, even to me. There's an odd echo, and I can barely hear myself over the ringing.

Tom reaches down and grabs my bony right arm at the wrist to pull me up. But my terrified scream stops him cold. "No Tom! Stop!"

He shudders as he lets go and staggers back.

I watch in awe as my right arm goes limp and droops down from somewhere between my shoulder and elbow. Even though I'm pretty

4

confused, I know it's not supposed to bend there. My arm falls limp like part of a rag doll.

Tom freaks when he sees my arm. "Oh God Steve! I'm sorry!"

His hand is shaking as he fumbles into his pocket for the cheap cell phone Dad got him just before he left for Texas.

About a minute later I hear the siren. It gets louder. And louder. So loud that my head feels like it's about to explode. Everything goes black. I don't remember the ride to the hospital.

\* \* \*

The hospital room is dark and gloomy. I can tell it's nighttime, but it probably doesn't look much better during the day. My mother, Annie Jones, is sleeping in a chair next to my bed. Her head is flopped forward. Her long blond hair fell out of its bun and is flowing down over her forehead, covering her face. She's wearing one of her work dresses. The tight blue one I think, but it's really too dark to tell.

I hear moaning. I tilt my head, and boy does it hurt when I do that. There's a curtain next to my bed, the moaning is coming from the other side. The deep moan tells me it's a man. I wonder who he is.

The bed sheets are tangled beneath me and my back itches. I rise up to change positions, but I forget about my broken arm, and try to use it to prop myself up. What starts as a whimper becomes an all out scream as the pain registers in my brain.

Mom wakes with a start. "Oh, you're conscious!"

The pain doesn't stop just because Mom is awake.

"Oh Mom, it hurts!"

Tears begin streaming down my cheeks. I feel like passing out again.

5

Mom rushes out of the room and returns right away with a nurse. The nurse sticks me with a needle and in less than a minute I'm unconscious again.

Thursday

The next time I wake up I feel much better.

It's morning and Mom is gone. She probably went to work. Her job is so very important to her, being a single working mom and all.

My broken arm aches, but the terrible pain that shot through it last night is gone. It's now propped up above my chest and hanging from two wires. The wires are attached to a contraption above my bed. A plastic cast runs from my shoulder to my wrist. A needle stuck in my left arm is attached to a line that runs to a bag of clear liquid hanging from a pole.

I begin wiggling body parts to see what hurts. I can move the fingers on my right hand without any pain, but the slightest attempt at moving the arm itself is unbearable. I can tilt my head from side to side but that hurts too. I can move both legs without any pain at all. And I can move my left arm and hand.

After checking myself out, I'm shocked to see Tom standing next to me. Has he crept in without me noticing? He's good at sneaking around like that. Or has he been there all along? If so, why didn't I notice him?

My startled brain causes my whole body to shudder. This triggers a jolt of pain in my arm.

"Tom! You scared the crap out of me!" I cry.

"Sorry Bro," Tom says. "I thought you knew I was here."

"Where's Mom?" I ask.

"She went to the cafeteria," Tom is looking down, apparently too ashamed to look me in the eye. He must feel like it's his fault that I got hurt.

"How are you feeling?" he finally asks.

"Awful. I can't move my head or right arm without a blast of pain. What the heck did they hit me with?"

Tom takes a quick look toward the door. "I'll tell you later. I told everyone you fell out of a tree. Don't mention the fight, okay?"

Tom is looking anywhere but at me.

"All right," I reply. "But I don't understand. How did those guys..."

I hear the clicking of high heels. It's got to be Mom. Sure enough, a few seconds later she bursts into the room.

"Oh Steve!" she shrieks. "It's so good to see you up. And talking too!"

She rushes the bed and crushes herself against me, giving her best attempt at a hug. She almost never hugs. Then she kisses me on the cheek. A mixture of perfume and cigarettes lingers as she backs away from the bed. She sits in the chair where she slept last night.

"Hi Mom," I say weakly. I put on a hurt face to make Mom feel sorry for me. I need some time to come up with a good story about falling out of a tree.

My stall tactic doesn't work.

"Is that all you can say?" she nearly screams, looking more upset than I've ever seen her. "I've been worried sick. You've been out cold

8

most of the night and doped up with pain killers. And I've had to take off work."

I think Mom is worried more about work than she is about me. But at least she's here. That's got to count for something.

I finally know what I'm going to say. I just hope it doesn't sound too corny. "It's embarrassing Mom. I feel pretty stupid for climbing that tree. It was strong enough for Katie's cat, but not me."

Katie is our next-door-neighbor. She's only eight, but she acts much older. We hang out quite a bit.

"You were trying to rescue a cat?" Mom asks.

She sounds suspicious, but that's just Mom. She's been suspicious of Tom and me ever since the divorce. She thinks we side with Dad too much.

"Sweetie, that was really dumb," she continues. "Cats will never let you get close when they're in a tree. And they always come down by themselves eventually. You should be old enough to know that by now."

Mom is lecturing like it will keep me from ever being stupid again. But at least it looks like she's buying my story.

"Well Katie didn't seem to think so," I say.

"Katie is only eight years old, Steve. But you're twelve. You should know better."

Her expression isn't anger. She looks like she feels sorry for me. And there is something else in her eyes. Disappointment at how stupid I am?

"She was crying Mom. You know how she gets."

Mom's expression softens and her disappointment fades away. "Well I'm just glad you're okay. Or at least that you're going to be okay

9

eventually. The doctor says it was a clean break and your arm will heal completely. He also said it was a good thing you got to the hospital so fast. You should be out of here in a day or two."

Mom starts fidgeting with her rings. It's one of her tells. She'll be off to work soon. At least then I can talk to Tom.

Tom is reading my mind. "Steve's being a baby, Mom. He'll be milking this for weeks. You go to work. I'll baby-sit him."

It hurts my feelings to hear Tom talk this way, but I know he's just trying to get rid of Mom.

Mom is already standing and rearranging her dress. She's probably trying to decide whether to go home and change before going in to work.

"Are you sure Tom?" she asks, but the decision is already made. "They miss me at the store when I'm not there. My cell phone vibrated three times this morning but I've been ignoring it."

Mom is talking more to herself now than to us. "I really should check in. I just know something bad has happened."

Yeah. Something worse than her kid breaking an arm.

"Sure mom. Go. We'll be fine. Won't we Steve?" Tom says. He winks from behind Mom.

"Yeah Mom, sure," I agree. "We'll be okay. You bring home the bacon and we'll fry it up in a pan."

Mom frowns but grabs her purse off the table next to my bed. This is a line she used on Dad when he was still living with us. She doesn't like it that Tom and I now use it so often on her.

"Well if you're sure." There is no hesitation in her voice.

Mom approaches for another hug and kiss, both are shorter this time. She's through the door without another word, cell phone already in her right hand, but her lingering perfume and cigarette odors remain in her absence.

Tom takes a seat in the empty chair and rubs his forehead. Neither of us wants to talk about Mom.

"How can I start?" he asks, more to himself than to me.

"The beginning is always a pretty good place," I snap back, though I don't think Tom is really expecting an answer.

"The trouble is, there's a lot to tell," he continues. "Let's see. You know about the Hillbrook stash, right?"

I can't help but roll my eyes. "Well duh. Of course I know about the Hillbrook stash. Everybody does."

"And you know the story of Old Man Humphrey?" he adds.

"Yeah, yeah," I respond. "That's old news too."

My brother takes a quick look toward the door. He turns back, leans in to my ear, and whispers excitedly, "What if I told you I found a note written by Old Man Humphrey? And there's a map!"

Now Tom has my attention. But over the years there's been a ton of bogus clues for finding the Hillbrook stash. And every store in town sells a fake map. It's a tourist thing. Tom knows this so he wouldn't be taken in, would he? But for the moment, my injuries are forgotten, along with our recent run-in with the Hinkle brothers.

"Where did you find it?" The skin on the back of my neck begins tingling as I feel myself getting sucked in. We'll be famous!

"I wasn't looking for it," Tom says. "I had to go to the library to get a book for school. You know how the history section is in the oldest part of the library, right? It's really dark and dingy back there."

The pitch of Tom's voice begins to rise. It's one of his tells. He's getting excited.

"I was looking for the book," he continues, "when I noticed something strange about the bookshelf. It was about twice as wide as others around it. After I pulled out a book, I looked through the slot it left. Something was back there. So I pulled out a few more books."

Tom's face draws even closer to mine. His nose is only inches from my ear when he starts to whisper.

"Sure enough, there was something there," he says.

"What was it?" My voice booms like a loud-speaker compared to Tom's.

"Hush," he whispers. "Indoor voice."

He continues in his hushed tone, "A cigar box. A really old one. I've never seen one like it. I grabbed it and stuffed it into my backpack. I could tell there was something inside. I put all the books back and got out of there.

"I ran to the Starbucks in town. I had the whole place to myself. The note was in the cigar box along with some other goodies."

He reaches into his back pocket and pulls out a yellowed sheet of paper. He puts it into my left hand, being careful not to interfere with the tube that's stuck in my arm.

"Read it," he demands.

The paper is about half the size of notebook paper. There are no lines. Writing appears on both sides. There's a drawing at the bottom of one of the pages.

I begin reading, which is difficult because of the shaky handwriting. It looks a lot like the way my grandpa writes.

*Consider this my last will and testament. I, Jeremy Humphrey, on this Saturday, June 23 of 1951 intend to leave my most prized possession to the finder of this document. Please do not consider this to be a kindness. The ownership of this possession has brought me nothing but grief and heartache for fifteen years. Now that I am growing close to the end of my days, it is time to pass this possession along to someone who may do better with it than I. But if you are of sound mind, you will heed my warning. Burn this document right now and forget you ever saw it.*

*You are still reading so I'll continue, but I refuse to make this easy for you. If you persist in finding the treasure which you know I have possessed, then you must be able to meet and defeat the challenges I have created – and even the least of these can place you in your grave. This is my final warning. Read on at your peril.*

*Are you still reading? Well, here is the first of your challenges.*

Beneath Old Man Humphrey's words is a map.

I look up to see Tom's face nose to nose with mine.

"Well, what do you think?" he says. "Isn't that just so cool?"

I'm not so sure. All those warnings sound pretty scary to me.

We're both startled by a nurse who marches into the room to check on me. I silently pass the note back to Tom. He folds it and puts it back into his pocket.

* * *

The nurse pokes and prods different parts of my body and takes my blood pressure. Then she removes the needle from my left arm, and pushes the cart hooked to the liquid-filled bag away from my bed. She reaches up to disconnect the wires from my cast and places my arm gently on the bed. She leaves taking the cart with her. She hasn't said a word the whole while she's been in the room.

The interruption has been a good thing. It's given me time to think.

"How do you know the note is real?" I ask. "I mean, anyone could have written it as a hoax."

Tom grabs his backpack. He pulls out the tattered cigar box and shows me the cover. On top are faded letters arranged in a circle. The upper half of the circle says 'Cuesta, Ray & Company'. The lower half says 'Made in Tampa'.

After giving me a few seconds to look, he flips the box over.

"Look how old this is," he says.

There's a date on the bottom. Nineteen forty-nine.

"If this is a hoax it's a really good one," he finishes.

He has a point. The cigar box is dated well before Old Man Humphrey's death. It's evidence that the note could be real.

"Why would Old Man Humphrey put his will in a cigar box and then hide it in the library?" I ask. "He couldn't be sure anyone would ever find it."

Tom shrugs. "I don't know. But it also doesn't make sense that he wouldn't tell his own brother where the Hillbrook stash was hidden. He might have been crazy or something."

I think about the broken relationship between Mom and Dad. Either of them would do just about anything to hurt the other. If the relationships in Old Man Humphrey's family were anything like Mom and Dad, Old Man Humphrey's actions would make pretty good sense to me.

Either way, Tom's explanation doesn't make me feel any better. We're about to go on a treasure hunt riddled with dangerous challenges created by a mad-man. Not my idea of a good time.

Tom stuffs the cigar box back into his backpack. While watching him do so, I think of something he said.

"What were the other 'goodies' you found in the cigar box?" I ask.

"Oh yeah." He grabs the cigar box again and holds it open so I can see. It contains three items. An old-style cigarette lighter. A short piece of string. And a key. He gives me a few seconds to look before he snaps the lid shut. He crams the cigar box back in his backpack.

"I tried the lighter but it doesn't work," Tom says. "I think it needs some lighter fluid."

"Have you studied the map?"

Tom shakes his head. "Not really. I haven't had any time to myself. I've been with you or Mom ever since the fight."

Oh yeah, the fight. With all this talk about the Hillbrook stash, I've forgotten all about the Hinkle Brothers. "Right. What happened after I got hit? You're usually so good at avoiding those jerks. Do you think they know about Old Man Humphrey's note? Or the cigar box? And how come you didn't get beat up too?"

The questions keep streaming out of my mouth, I can't seem to help it.

Tom waves his hand. "Slow down. One question at a time. On my way home I was distracted. I was thinking about the note. I looked up and there they were. I think they were just as surprised as I was. I'm sure they weren't in the library with me, so they can't know about the cigar box. And I don't think they were following me. They were just looking to raise hell and I came along."

Tom stops for a moment. "Come to think of it, how did you get there?"

I struggle to remember. Things are still pretty blurry. "I'm not really sure. I was just walking home from school and saw you fighting. I wanted to help. I don't think I did you much good though."

Tom twists a lock of his hair. It's another one of his tells. He's nervous. "Actually, you did great. You didn't move at all after you went down. That scared them. Perry yelled at Larry for using a baseball bat on you. And it didn't hurt that a siren went off a few seconds later. It was no more than a block away. They thought police were coming so they all took off.

"As for my not getting hurt..." Tom pulls up his sweatshirt to reveal a huge purple bruise covering his rib cage. "...They just hit me where it doesn't show."

Trying to remember the fight has left me tired. I think the excitement of hearing Tom's story is wearing off. Suddenly I'm exhausted.

Tom notices. "You look beat. Get some rest. I'll come back this afternoon."

I know Tom is going home to study the map but there's nothing I can do about it. I want to help but I'd be no good to anyone right now.

"Okay. Just promise me one thing."

"What?"

I look him in the eye. For the first time all morning he meets my gaze. "Promise me you won't go treasure hunting without me."

16

His expression darkens. He had other plans. Eventually he nods. "Okay, I'll just scope out the map and see what I can come up with. I'll wait for you before I do anything else. The stash has been hidden for over sixty years. I guess it can wait a little longer."

Tom leaves. I go out like a light.

* * *

I awake to clamoring. A pretty woman in blue scrubs is in my room. Her name tag says 'Jackie'. She's bringing in a food cart, it must be lunch time. Good thing because I'm starved. Did I have anything for breakfast? With all the excitement I don't remember eating anything this morning.

As Jackie prepares my tray, I notice the curtain is pulled back. I can see my roommate. It's hard to tell how old he is because of his condition. He's got the same wiry attachments I had this morning. But not just on an arm. Both of his legs and one of his arms are strung up. His face is bandaged too. One of his eyes is covered with a patch. I can't see the other. He's impossible to recognize. He could be my dad and I wouldn't know it.

I wonder why no one came to see him. Sure he's been unconscious, but shouldn't someone have come by now? I think about how lonely I'd be if no one came to visit me. I feel sorry for him.

I take an awkward bite of what looks like meatloaf. I'm surprised at how hard it is to eat with my left hand. I've never tried it before.

I can't stop thinking about my roommate. What could have happened to him? I'm betting on a car accident. It's impossible to tell if he is asleep or awake until a soft moan and a gentle twitch suggest he's out cold.

Jackie's cart has two trays. But when she looks at the man in the bed next to me, she frowns and pulls the curtain closed. I guess it's so I can eat in peace. She wheels the cart out of the room without saying a word.

I think about turning on the television, but I don't want to disturb my roommate. Instead, I eat lunch and think about Tom's story. It sure seems believable enough. This could be amazing. If we find the Hillbrook stash, we could help Dad. Lord knows he needs it. He lost his sports memorabilia shop just when Mom started managing the pawnshop in town.

Dad said the bad economy had everything to do with it. No one had money to spend on hobbies anymore. They were all selling stuff to pay bills and hunting for bargains on necessities.

So Mom succeeded while Dad went under. Dad looked for a job in town but there was no work. He ended up being a stay-at-home dad, and he wasn't very good at it. There were fights before Mom and Dad changed roles, but those were nothing compared to what happened after.

Dad eventually moved out and Mom filed for divorce. It all happened so fast. Within a month, they were divorced. Then Dad moved to Texas to find work. That was almost a year ago, but it still hurts.

Mom got full custody of Tom and me, though it doesn't make much sense. She can barely stand to be around us. But Dad can't wait to see us on those very few occasions when he's able to.

It doesn't help that Tom and I are always siding with Dad. And just about every conversation with Mom involves difficult questions about

Dad. Mom tries her best to change the subject, but kids can be pretty persistent when we want to be.

I'm sure Tom feels the same way. If anything, he'll feel even stronger about helping Dad. He's been around Dad for over a year more than me.

\* \* \*

After I finish eating, the items in the cigar box flutter back into my mind. An old lighter, a short piece of string, and a key. The lighter is made of a silvery metal. It has a flip top to protect where the flame comes out. Spin the small wheel and a spark ignites the flame. Tom said it was out of lighter fluid so it didn't work. I think we can get some at the hardware store in town.

The string is about four inches long and is much thicker than kite string. It doesn't look very flexible. Come to think of it, I've never seen any string like it.

And the key. It doesn't look like a house key or a car key. It's gold-colored and much smaller. It looks like a key that would open a briefcase.

I can't picture any situation that would require all three items to be used together. But Old Man Humphrey must have put them in the cigar box for a reason, right? They must be important.

Even the cigar box is pretty cool. I'd like to have one to store my school stuff in. Could the cigar box be part of the clue? No, I don't think so. When Old Man Humphrey filled it, cigar boxes must have been pretty common. They're only rare today only because people don't smoke many cigars any more.

After lunch, it gets pretty boring. I rethink turning on the television even if it means disturbing my roommate. As I reach for the remote hanging on the bed frame, I'm startled to see a policeman standing in the doorway. I drop the remote and it clatters to the floor.

He looks down at his notepad and then up at something on the wall outside my room. Then he looks right at me and strolls into the room.

"Hello," he says. "Is your name Steven Jones?"

I'm speechless for a moment. I finally nod and croak out a yes. He hasn't taken off his sunglasses so I can't see his eyes. His body is huge and intimidating. He looks like a football player. A really big one.

He senses my fear. I guess he's used to kids being afraid of him. And not just kids I'd bet.

"Don't worry son," he says. "You're not in any trouble. My name is Officer Grant. I just need to ask you a few questions about the fight you were in. Normally we just let these things work themselves out. But since a weapon was involved, we need to investigate further."

A weapon? Is he talking about the baseball bat? I'm not sure if he's expecting an answer. "Ah-huh," I mumble. Better to wait for a question before saying anything.

"You live over on South Seventh Street, right?" he asks.

"Yes sir," I say. Formal is best.

He stops, and smiles in recognition. He points his pen at me. "Hey. You're Dave Jones' kid, aren't you?" His voice is almost friendly.

"Yes sir," I cautiously repeat.

He smiles. "I knew your dad in high school. He was quite the wrestler. I was on that team too. But I wasn't nearly as good as your dad."

20

Dad took second at state in the 145 pound weight class his senior year. The school had never been very good at wrestling so Dad's success made headlines for weeks. He was a real celebrity after that.

I've always been jealous of Tom when it comes to Mom and Dad. Tom got Dad's athletic abilities and Mom's good looks. I got neither.

"Where's he now?" Officer Grant asks.

"Texas. Dallas."

Officer Grant sounds sincerely interested in Dad. "What the heck is he doing there?"

"Working. He couldn't find a job around here after his store closed, so…" My voice trails off. I don't want to talk about Dad with a stranger.

He pauses, and something changes in his expression. "Well, tell me about the fight."

"There's not much to tell. At least not by me. I was unconscious for most of it."

He begins writing in his notebook. "How did it start?"

I may as well tell what I know. I just hope Mom doesn't find out. Wait a minute! How does he know about the fight? Tom didn't tell anyone, did he?

"Well," I start, hoping not to stammer. "I was on my way home from school. When I turned onto Seventh Street, I saw the Hinkle brothers beating up my brother. I don't know how the fight started."

Officer Grant gives me a sympathetic nod. He knows all about the Hinkle brothers.

"They were all punching Tom at once," I continue. "I knew I had to jump in. But I had only thrown a punch or two when I was knocked out. I must have broken my arm when I went down."

"So it was just the two of you against the three of them?"

Is he questioning my story? "Yes. And if it hadn't been for that siren, Tom would probably be in here with me." I nod at the other bed in the room.

"The siren?"

Am I saying too much? "Yes. Tom told me that right after I went down, a siren went off about a block away. He said it scared the Hinkle brothers and they ran away."

Officer Grant looks confused as he studies his notebook. "Hmm. That doesn't sound right. There were no dispatches in Clear Valley yesterday afternoon except for the ambulance that was sent for you."

I'm confused too because I was unconscious the whole time. "Then I don't understand. Can I ask you something?"

"Sure."

"How did you know about the fight? We didn't tell anyone. We told my mom that I fell out of a tree."

Officer Grant takes off his sunglasses. He has a concerned look in his eyes. "Mrs. Hinkle filed a complaint. She claims your brother shot a gun at her kids. Does your brother have a gun?"

"No!" I scream. What the heck is going on? Neither Tom nor I have ever touched a real gun.

"Well, don't worry too much yet Steve. Mrs. Hinkle has been known to stretch the truth a bit when it comes to her kids. But I do need to talk to your brother. Do you know where he is?"

Officer Grant fixes his gaze on me.

"He was here earlier. But I got tired so he left. I think he went back to school," I lie.

Officer Grant nods and steps toward the door. He stops and turns back just before he exits. He pauses for effect. "I just have one more question Steve. Did your brother mention anything about a cigar box when he was here?"

I try not to let my astonishment show, but it's a lost cause because Officer Grant is watching closely for my reaction. "Ah, no, I don't think so." I immediately regret my weak answer.

He nods. But we both know I'm lying as he puts on his sunglasses and leaves my room.

* * *

The only other excitement for the rest of the day is a call from Dad. It's hard to believe that Mom called him to let him know I got hurt. But I guess even Mom is capable of a kind act once in a while. The conversation is short because Dad's on his break at work. We talk for less than ten minutes, but it's enough time to let him know I'm okay and that I'm going to make a full recovery. I leave out the part about the fight. And the Hillbrook stash. And Officer Grant. And that Tom may have a gun. And that we lied to Mom.

* * *

Dinner comes at five o'clock and I eat alone. Unless you count the moans coming from the bed next to me. When a nurse comes in, she gives my roommate a shot. Within minutes, he's quiet again.

Still, no one has been in to see him. I feel sorry for the guy. I want to do something. There's a drawer in the table next to my bed. I find a pen and paper. I slide the bed tray over and start on a home-made get-well card. It's not easy writing with my left hand, but at least my writing is readable. I think.

* * *

Boredom won out over my concern with disturbing my roommate. I've been watching television for over an hour. It's been a good distraction, but when seven o'clock rolls around, I start to worry.

Tom said he'd be back this afternoon. What happened? Did he go looking for the Hillbrook stash without me? Did he get attacked by the Hinkle brothers again? Did Officer Grant get him? And why hasn't Mom been back? Or even called? Along with the worry, I'm suddenly lonely and feeling sorry for myself.

At seven-fifteen I hear the tell-tail clicking of Mom's high heels. I'm actually glad she's coming for a visit. Maybe Tom is with her.

She breezes into the room. Tom's right behind her. She's still in her work clothes and she's wearing a thick gold chain around her neck. It looks like one that a man would wear. It was a gift from the pawnshop owner.

"Well Kiddo," she starts. "How was your day?"

"Boring. And that guy has been moaning non-stop." I nod in the direction of the other bed.

"Poor baby. At least you didn't have to go to school." Mom glances at the television. "And you've been able to watch T.V. all day."

She changes the subject. "I had a great day! We did our biggest week-day volume in the store's history. Marvin says it's all because of my new ad campaign."

Marvin Matthews is the pawnshop owner. Tom and I call him Mystery Marvin, since he's been in Clear Valley for a couple of years yet no one seems to know his history. We're pretty sure he has a thing for Mom.

Mom hasn't even asked how I'm feeling and she's already talking about herself. Her job. Marvin. That pisses me off. My loneliness and worry quickly turn into anger. Time for a little fun.

"Oh I forgot," I casually mention. "Dad called. We talked for hours."

Mom doesn't even hesitate. "I doubt that. He'd be lucky to get off work for ten minutes. And at his salary, he couldn't afford to talk for long."

She sees my face darken and her expression softens. Maybe she regrets her nasty response, but I doubt it. She starts fidgeting with her rings  Must be time for a cigarette.

Tom comes to my rescue. "Did you see where they put in a smoking section in the cafeteria?" he lies. "I thought we lived in a non-smoking city."

Mom brightens. "Really? I'll just have to go down there and check it out."

"Sure Mom," Tom says. "I can keep Steve here company for a while. You've had a hard day. You could use some down time."

It always amazes me when Mom responds to Tom's crap. But she does respond. She's heading out the door when she remembers that she hasn't said goodbye. She pokes her head back into the room. "Back in five."

Clicking from the hall fades a few seconds later.

"Piece of work, isn't she?" Tom chuckles as he shakes his head. Mom doesn't affect him nearly as much as she does me.

"Yeah. I just hope what she's got isn't hereditary."

"I don't think you have to worry Steve. I can't see you ever acting like her."

Tom takes a seat in the chair and we're quiet for a few seconds. I want to bring up Officer Grant. I want to ask about the gun. I want to ask if he's figured out anything about the note or the map. I just don't know where to start.

Tom starts for me. "Hey look. I've got to apologize. I'm sorry I lied about the fight." He's staring at the floor again.

This isn't what I expected. I thought he'd start with the map.

"I know," I say. "A cop was here. He asked me a bunch of questions, including where you were. I lied. I told him you went back to school."

"Well that didn't work. He found me. He was waiting in front of the house when I got home from the hardware store. Officer Grant. He said he went to school with Dad."

"He seemed like a nice enough guy. For a cop."

"Nice isn't quite the word I'd use to describe him. But I guess he was only doing his job."

I'm dying to hear the truth about the fight. But Tom seems content making small talk. I can't take it any more. "So what really happened during the fight Tom?"

"Well the part about the Hinkle brothers being scared off after you went down was true enough. But it wasn't a siren that did it. There was one more thing in the cigar box."

26

"A gun?"

Tom looks surprised. "Yeah. How'd you know?"

"Officer Grant told me that Mrs. Hinkle reported a gunshot. Then he asked if you had a gun."

"Oh. I should have figured that out I guess. Anyway, the gun was really small."

Tom holds up his right hand and holds his thumb and index finger about three inches apart. "I think it was a Derringer. I didn't even know it was loaded."

I wait. There's got to be more. Tom takes a deep breath. "The old lady at the library must have been watching me. She saw me put the cigar box into my backpack. As I started to leave, she began yelling for me to wait. So I ran."

That explains why Officer Grant knew about the cigar box. The library lady must have called the police.

"The gun was in the cigar box which was in my backpack when I ran into the Hinkle brothers," he explains. "Ed Hinkle was really starting to beat the crap out of me when Larry hit you. But the sound of that baseball bat hitting your head was really scary. It got his attention. And he froze when you stopped moving.

"But Larry didn't. He hit you again. Your arm. I'm sure that's what broke it. And he didn't look like he was going to stop any time soon. Since Ed and Perry were looking at you and Larry, I had time to open my backpack and get out the gun. They didn't react when I screamed, or even when they all saw the gun. But when I fired... Well, you'd think I'd lit a fire under them. They probably crapped their pants before they started running."

"What happened to the gun?"

"Officer Grant took it. He knew I had it."

"But why did you lie to me Tom?"

Tom hesitates. "The old lady at the library made me feel stupid for getting caught. I didn't want to admit it. But the gun? That's a different story. I hoped you'd never find out about that. I felt so guilty. And scared."

"But why Tom? You probably saved my life."

Tears are forming in Tom's eyes. "I shouldn't have fired that gun, Steve. I was so mad at Larry when he hit you that I wanted to kill him. I pointed the gun right at him when I fired. He was only a few feet away. I still can't believe I missed him. But two seconds later when I saw him running away… Well, I've never been more relieved in my life."

Tears are now streaming down Tom's cheeks. With Tom crying, I want to change the subject. I want to hear if he's figured anything out about the map. But I hear clicking in the hall.

Tom hears it too. "Shit!" He rubs his cheeks on his sleeve. He wouldn't be caught dead crying in front of Mom. "There's so much more I want to tell you. It'll have to wait until tomorrow when you get out of here."

I'm getting out tomorrow? That's news to me. Great news. I can't wait to see the map again. And to work with Tom to figure it out.

Friday

I'm released on Friday morning at nine o'clock.

As I get up from my hospital bed, I remember the get-well card. It's still on the table next to my bed. There's no sense wasting it. I pick it up and bring it to the table next to my roommate's bed. When I look up from the table, I'm startled to see him looking at me through his un-patched eye. I smile. He nods, weakly. Then he closes his eye and I walk out of the room.

My head doesn't hurt any more but my arm is still sore. The cast seems to be protecting it pretty well. I've bumped it a couple of times and no pain has come through. But it throbs if I try to use my right hand to do anything.

My biggest problem is just getting around. The cast holds my arm out straight. So if I reach for something with my right hand, I have to tilt my whole body. So far I'm not doing much with that arm so it really doesn't matter. But I can tell it's going to be a real problem in days to come.

Mom says I don't need to go to school today which is just fine with me. She stays with me just long enough to get me checked out of the hospital and bring me home. Then she's off, saying there's plenty of food in the fridge and grumbling something about problems at work.

Tom is at school today so I won't see him until after three-thirty. When I walk into my room, I find his note on my bed.

*What you're looking for is in our secret place.*

I guess he's worried that Mom will find the cigar box, so he's being all secret agent. Mom rarely comes into our rooms unless she wants to complain about how messy they are. So there's almost no chance that she'd find the cigar box. It could be sitting right on Tom's desk and she probably wouldn't notice it. But better safe than sorry I guess.

I go to the basement. Above what used to be Dad's workbench is a window-sized hole in the wall. It leads to a crawl space under the front porch. *Our secret place.* The floor is made of pee-gravel. Ventilation windows let in just enough light to see.

Years ago Mom and Dad stored a few plastic tubs in there. They contain long forgotten items. The crawl space is pretty dirty, so it would have been Dad who put the tubs in there. I'm sure Mom never crawled into our secret place.

I bring a stool close to the workbench and climb up onto it. It's not easy with my arm the way it is. What was Tom thinking? I use my left arm and legs to slither through the hole in the wall. When I'm finally in, my arm is throbbing. The cigar box is in the top tub. At least it's not buried somewhere at the bottom.

Back in my room, I empty the cigar box onto my desk. The string still puzzles me. It isn't string, exactly, that's for sure. It's more brittle. If I tried to tie a knot in it I'm sure it would crack or break. It looks familiar, but I can't quite place it.

I open the lighter and immediately notice an odd smell. A bit like gasoline. Tom must have bought some lighter fluid. That's right. He said he was stopped by Officer Grant on his way home from the hardware store. He must have gotten the lighter fluid then.

I flick the lighter and a flame dances to life. I flip the top down to put out the flame. I can't resist doing this several times. The magical appearance of the flame is mesmerizing. I could play with this thing all day. Very cool!

A memory hits me like a brick. I put the lighter down and pick up the string. When I was nine, Dad bought Tom a model rocket. They spent an afternoon building it. The next day they shot it off, only to lose it on the very first flight.

The string in my hand looks just like the fuse they used to set off the rocket. They even used a cigarette lighter to light it. But the lighter didn't look like this one. It was one of Mom's, a much newer cheap plastic model. But now I'm convinced that the string is actually a length of fuse. But a fuse for what? It's pretty old. Will it still work? Whatever the fuse is for, Old Man Humphrey must have intended that the lighter be used to ignite it.

That leaves the key. It's smaller than a house key and made of brass. It could be used to open luggage. Or a briefcase. Or just about anything. I study it for a while longer but I have no idea what it's for.

I read Old Man Humphrey's note again.

*Consider this my last will and testament. I, Jeremy Humphrey, on this Saturday, June 23 of 1951 intend to leave my most prized possession to the finder of this document. Please do not consider this to be a kindness. The ownership of this possession has brought me nothing but grief and heartache for fifteen years. Now that I am growing close to the end of my days, it is time to pass this possession along to someone who may do better with it than I. But if you are of sound mind, you will heed my warning. Burn this document right now and forget you ever saw it.*

*You are still reading so I continue, but I refuse to make this easy for you. If you persist in finding the treasure which you know I have possessed, then you must meet and defeat the challenges I have created – and even the least of these can place you in your grave. This is my final warning. Read on at your peril.*

*Are you still reading? Well, here is the first of your challenges.*

I'm convinced that our adventure will be a dangerous one. Tom doesn't seem to mind, but I'm worried. With my broken arm, what good will I be if something goes wrong?

The map is neatly drawn. It's quite beautiful, contrasting the shaky handwriting. Old Man Humphrey was an artist. It clearly shows Clear Valley as it was in 1952. The town is pictured on the right side. The town square is easy to recognize because of its shape. A few blocks to the west is City Park. Just where it is today. In the center of City Park there's a small solid dot. A straight dotted line runs directly west from the dot. Two numbers are placed under the dotted line and are separated by a dash. *2,250-50.* At the other end of the dotted line is an X.

I chuckle. Every treasure map has an X to mark the spot, right?

So our starting point will be in City Park. I'm pretty sure that the solid dot is the stone pillar for the Hillbrook Gang Memorial. Our destination is located in the woods west of town. Bandit Woods. But what do the two numbers represent?

I spend the afternoon thinking about the map. It's obvious that what we're looking for is in Bandit Woods. That makes sense because Jeffrey Hillbrook was killed there. And Old Man Humphrey lived there. It also seems fitting that our treasure hunt will begin at the Hillbrook Gang Memorial pillar. It's the biggest icon for the whole affair. But I'm still not sure what the numbers 2,250-50 mean, maybe Tom knows. I wonder if he's figured out that the string is really a fuse.

* * *

Tom bursts into the house at three-forty. He's out of breath. I think he ran all the way home.

"So, what do you think?" he asks, without even saying hello. He plops down on a chair at the kitchen table.

I'm on the couch watching an HBO movie. I raise the remote and click off the television.

"I think the map will be pretty easy to follow," I say, joining him in the kitchen.

"I think so too. It looks like we just have to walk straight west from the pillar in City Park, right? But do you know what the numbers mean?"

"Not exactly. They must be measurements of some kind."

"Yeah. Maybe in feet or yards?"

I shake my head. "Maybe, but who would bring a tape measure on a treasure hunt?"

"I don't know. I've seen some pretty big tape measures in the hardware store."

I'm still shaking my head. "It's got to be simpler than that. Maybe it's a number of footsteps. Or paces."

"That's got to be it!" Tom shouts. He races to the computer in Mom's office.

A quick on-line search gives us the length of a "pace".

"Here, look," Tom says. "According to Wikipedia, a pace is thirty inches, which is two and a half feet. We can multiply two and a half feet times 2,250 to come up the distance in feet."

I grab a calculator and do the math. "That's 5,625 feet." I point at the computer screen. "It says right there that a mile is 5,280 feet. If we're right, our destination will be just over a mile directly west of the pillar."

"That would be in Bandit Woods."

I nod. "But what do you think the other number means?"

Tom smiles. "There's only one way to find out."

* * *

We stash everything back into the cigar box. And Tom shoves the cigar box into his backpack. Then we head for City Park. It's about eight blocks away. The walk into Bandit Woods shouldn't take more than half an hour each way. We should be home long before Mom returns home from work.

Tom's walking pretty fast. He's almost jogging. Trying to keep up with him makes my arm throb.

"Tom. Slow down. My arm hurts."

Tom gives me a frustrated look but he slows down. When we arrive at City Park, we make a bee line to the Hillbrook Gang memorial pillar.

There's a clock on top of the pillar. It's four-thirty. Even with me slowing us down, we've made pretty good time.

But there's a problem. A *big* problem. The park pavilion is directly west of the pillar. The pavilion isn't shown on the map. It must have been built after Old Man Humphrey drew it.

We walk to the other side of the pavilion and discover another problem. Bandit Woods is still a long way off. Between the pavilion and Bandit Woods is a subdivision of houses.

Tom throws me a worried look. "This is going to be harder than I thought. We can't walk directly west from the pillar. So we won't know where to start walking in Bandit Woods. And we won't know how far we are from the pillar."

I shrug. "We need a GPS device. Mom's got GPS on her cell phone. We could use it to plot a course into Bandit Woods."

Tom's face lights up but then darkens. "That's a good idea, Steve. But Mom would never part with her cell phone."

Tom's right. Mom is addicted to her phone. Sometimes I think it's attached to her hand.

Tom pokes me in the side. "Your girlfriend has an iPhone." He's using a sing-song voice and there's a twinkle is in his eye.

Sally Alton is in seventh grade with me. We've been friends since kindergarten. We used to hang around a lot at school. This year's been different though. She's made lots of new friends so we don't hang out like we used to. Tom knows I still like her and he's always calling her 'my girlfriend'.

"That's true," I say. "But she's been different this year. I don't talk to her as much as I used to."

Tom ignores my concern. "Still, do you think she'd let us use it?"

"Never in a million years. She'd insist on *helping us* use it. That would mean we'd have to tell her about the map."

I think of another problem. "And she'd want to bring her cousin along."

Crystal Gent is in eighth grade. She's been living with Sally's family for almost a year. Her parents died in a car crash. Since Sally's parents are Crystal's aunt and uncle, they took her in. Now she and Sally are joined at the hip. Crystal is another reason why Sally and I haven't hung out much this year.

Having Crystal join us doesn't seem to bother Tom at all. In fact, he brightens at the mention of her name. "Well that would be okay, wouldn't it?"

I'd pictured this as being our own little adventure. Bringing two girls into it just doesn't seem right. But what other choice do we have? I don't know anyone else with a GPS device. "I guess so," I finally answer.

"So we'll ask them tomorrow," Tom says.

His decision sounds final. But I'm still trying to think of alternatives.

Our first attempt at finding the Hillbrook stash failed. But at least we've got a plan. Tomorrow is Saturday. We'll have the whole day to work on it.

The walk home isn't very exciting. We've had our hopes deflated a bit. We walk much slower and neither of us says much. I think we're both trying to come up with a way to ask the girls for help. I know I am.

We get home and I have another idea. Maybe I can use the Internet to plot the position of the X in Bandit Woods. I get on the computer and type our street address into a popular mapping site. Sure enough, a map with our street comes up.

I switch to satellite view and zoom in as close as I can. In the satellite picture, I can even see Mom's car parked in the driveway. But this picture is old, there's snow on the ground. It has to be several weeks old. It could even be from last winter. But I don't need a recent picture. What I'm looking for hasn't changed much in over sixty years.

I use the mouse to pan from our house to City Park. It's actually pretty easy to scroll from one part of town to another. I can even make out the Hillbrook Gang Memorial pillar. I then pan directly west and see the pavilion. Further west are the houses. But there's no way to show the distance between the pillar and the edge of Bandit Woods.

I pan further west into the woods. Well this is no good. All I can see are the tops of snow covered pine trees. I can't even see the ground. Just trees and snow. The mapping web site isn't going to help us. Oh well, it was worth a try.

Tom startles me just as I get up from the computer. "What were you doing?"

I explain my idea. He brightens. But then I tell him it didn't work. He decides to give it a try himself and takes my place at the computer. After twenty minutes, he gives up too. We're back to asking girls for help.

Mike Lynch

Saturday

Saturday morning is bright, sunny, and warm. After eating some cereal, Tom and I walk the four blocks to Sally's house. It's only eight-thirty and we're hoping she'll be home. I ring the doorbell and we wait. Tom and I haven't talked about how much we're going to tell Sally and Crystal about our adventure. I assume we're going to tell them everything eventually. But right now I hope we don't need to explain too much to convince them to help with Sally's iPhone.

Sally's mom opens the door. She looks pretty surprised to see us. "Can I help you boys?"

"Yes Mrs. Alton," I answer as politely as I can. "Is Sally home? We'd like to talk to her."

Mrs. Alton gives us a suspicious smile but then asks us to come in. We wait in the entryway as she disappears up the stairs.

Sally floats down the stairs a minute later followed closely by Crystal. I'm used to seeing Sally in school clothes. But now she's wearing old jeans that make her look thinner than usual. Her pink fluffy top has elbow-length sleeves. Long brown hair is down on her shoulders instead of up in its usual pony tail.

By contrast, Crystal is in a blue and white sun dress. Her fiery red hair is cut short. Freckles dot her entire face. She's heavier than Sally, but not fat.

"Hey," Sally says as she reaches the bottom step. She looks at my arm, but doesn't mention it.

Tom is silent. I'm sure he's waiting for me to say something. He barely knows Sally and doesn't know Crystal at all. When I don't say anything, he elbows my left side.

I clear my throat and try to think of something to say, but it's all I can do to repeat her greeting. "Hey."

We stand there awkwardly until Sally speaks again. "I heard about the fight." She looks at my arm again. "You okay?"

"Ah, yeah. It still hurts sometimes, but I feel much better."

At least I'm talking. It's time to bring up our reason for being here. "Do you still have your iPhone?"

Crystal answers before Sally can open her mouth. "She does for the moment. But her mom could take it away any second." Then Crystal laughs out loud. Sally just stares at her.

From our puzzled looks, Crystal knows that Tom and I need an explanation. "Any time Sally does something wrong, her mom takes the iPhone away. I think parents only give kids a cool gadget so they have something to take away when we do something wrong."

Her next laugh includes a brief snort. Her laughing is contagious and I feel myself chucking.

Tom is laughing too. "I know what you mean. My mom used to take away dessert when we were little. Now she's always on the lookout for something we like so she has something to punish us with."

Crystal looks around to make sure Sally's mom is still upstairs. When she turns back to us she's almost whispering. "You should see how Aunt Mary hovers over Sally. She can't wait for Sally to do something wrong so she can get her hands on the iPhone. I think Aunt Mary has used it more than Sally!"

The laughing continues.

Hearing Tom and Crystal kid around makes me feel much better. They've broken the ice so I don't have to. But it's been at Sally's expense and she looks pretty embarrassed. I want to make her feel better. "Don't feel bad Sally. Tom hasn't been allowed to play with his video games in over a month."

I've exaggerated but it's for a good cause. Tom always finds ways around Mom's punishments. But Sally needs cheering up. Now Tom is quiet as the rest of us laugh, including Sally.

We eventually calm down and it's awkwardly quiet again.

"So why do you want to know about my iPhone?" Sally asks.

I'm not comfortable talking about our quest in Sally's house. Someone might be listening. "Can we go for a walk? We'll tell you all about it."

Sally yells up to her mom that we're leaving. Then the girls put their shoes on. Crystal grabs a backpack. Neither waits for a reply from Sally's mom before we leave. I worry that Mrs. Alton will take the iPhone away again if she didn't hear Sally's announcement. But out we go. Tom makes sure we head toward City Park.

"So, what's this all about?" Sally asks as soon as we're on the sidewalk.

"We need a GPS device to do some mapping," I say. It feels good to find my normal voice again.

"What are you trying to map?" she asks.

Tom and I exchange glances. Best to start with the task at hand.

"We need to walk a straight line from one place to another, but there are too many obstacles in the way," I say.

"From where to where?"

I glance at Tom again. He just shrugs. "The starting point is in City Park. It's the pillar for the Hillbrook Gang Memorial."

Sally takes a stutter-step but keeps walking. Tom notices her misstep too but doesn't mention it.

"We think the destination point is directly west of there by 2,250 paces," I continue. "That's equal to 5,625 feet. Just over a mile. We need to stay on a straight line as we walk directly west, but the City Park pavilion is in the way. And after that there's a whole bunch of houses."

Sally and Crystal give each other a brief look. Then they both start talking at the same time. They're so excited that neither of them stops. And they're not making any sense. The only word I think I hear is *geocatch*.

Finally they stop talking. Each is awkwardly waiting for the other. Sally's look tells Crystal to stay quiet.

"Crystal and I have been using my iPhone for geocaching," Sally says. "It's lots of fun."

Tom and I exchange confused looks.

"They're Muggles," Crystal says. "You need to explain geocaching to them."

But Crystal doesn't wait for Sally to explain. "Geocaching is a kind of treasure hunt. Someone hides a 'treasure' and others use GPS devices to find it. There's no value in the treasure. The reward is in the search. When you find a geocache, there's a log to sign. It tells the person that hid the geocache how many people found it. Our goecaching app even lets us keep track of the geocaches we've found."

"But we're not looking for a gcocatch," I say.

"Or a treasure," Tom quickly adds.

"Not geocatch silly. *Geocache*," Sally corrects, emphasizing the *sh* sound. "No, but we can create a *reverse* geocache. We can use the geocaching app on my iPhone to hide a geocache at the pillar. Then we can track our position as we move away from it."

"That sounds like exactly what we need," Tom says.

\* \* \*

We reach the Hillbrook Gang Memorial pillar at Nine-fifteen. Standing next to it, Sally starts tapping away at her iPhone. Meanwhile Crystal reaches into her backpack and pulls out a small plastic box.

"What's that?" Tom asks.

Crystal eyes him. He's asked a stupid question. "It's the geocache. We can't create a geocache without hiding something."

"But what are we going to hide?"

Crystal is digging in her backpack again as she answers. "It could be anything. The bare minimum is a logbook. But Sally and I like to leave a little something extra."

She pulls out a green-colored toy army man that is crouched in a shooting position.

I chuckle. "Where did you get that?"

"From another geocache," she replies.

"So you can keep the treasure you find in a geocache?" Tom asks.

Crystal remains patient with her answer, but it is obvious that she's getting tired of explaining. "Yes. As long as you leave something yourself. It's bad form to remove a geocache treasure if you don't leave something to replace it. Though I think lots of people do."

Crystal places the army man in the box. The box already contains some paper and a little pencil. The logbook, I guess. With the box sealed, she turns her attention to the pillar.

"We have to find a place to hide this," she says. "It can't be too obvious or a Muggle will take it."

That's the second time I've heard this word. "What's a Muggle? Isn't that something to do with Harry Potter?"

"Yeah, that's right," she responds. "But in geocaching terms, a Muggle is someone that doesn't know anything about geocaching. Like you before today.

"Sometimes Muggles make things very difficult for us geocachers. Since we're snooping around when we look for a geocache, they sometimes think we're up to no good. Muggles have even been known to call the police. In this one extreme case I know of, a Muggle saw a geocacher hiding a box in a court house. So the police called in a bomb squad to check it out."

All the while Crystal has been talking she's been studying the pillar. She reaches up and feels behind one of the bronze plaques. Time and weather have hollowed out a small space behind it. She's found a hiding place for the geocache.

Sally looks up from her iPhone. "We're all set."

She holds up her iPhone and sure enough, the screen shows an arrow that's pointing at the pillar. A distance is shown next to it. It's in feet. She walks about ten steps and stands directly west of the pillar. The distance on her iPhone shows twenty-three feet and the arrow points due east. She then takes a few steps to the south. The arrow follows along, and is now pointing northeast. The distance shows twenty-six feet.

"That's so cool!" Tom says.

It looks like we're finally on our way.

As we walk around the pavilion, I think of how easy it was to get Sally and Crystal to help. They didn't even ask why we want to walk directly west for over a mile. Crystal is not from Clear Valley, but Sally's got to know we're heading directly into Bandit Woods. She must be so excited about using her iPhone and the geocaching app that she's not questioning why we need it or where we're going. But that's going to change very soon.

* * *

We walk south around the pavilion. Then west past the houses. We make our way to the edge of Bandit Woods. We walk north until the arrow on Sally's iPhone is pointing directly east. How cool! We're directly west of the pillar! The measurement changed to miles, it now shows 0.27 miles. From the calculations Tom and I did last night, we need to keep walking directly west until the distance shows 1.06 miles. That's equal to 5,625 feet, or 2,250 paces.

Sally and Crystal are carefully watching the arrow and distance, so there's been less chatter between them. Tom and I exchanged a few glances, but I have no idea what he's thinking. I've been worrying about the warnings in Old Man Humphrey's note. I'm concerned that Sally and Crystal may walk into a dangerous situation. With every step we take into the woods, another "challenge" could be waiting.

We enter the woods and walk in about a hundred feet. The pine trees stand all around us; the ground is blanketed in orange pine needles. The going is pretty easy. Even so, I decide to use the woods as an excuse to speak up.

"You know," I say, looking at Sally. "Tom and I can take it from here if you and Crystal are scared. There's no path to follow, and the going could get rougher ahead."

Sally responds as if she's been expecting me to say something like this. "Oh that's okay. We're up for a little adventure, aren't we Crystal?"

"Sure thing. This is lots more fun than normal geocaching."

"Well at least let Tom and I take the lead." I don't wait for an answer. I just push Tom ahead.

"Well aren't they the gentlemen?" Crystal jokes as we brush by.

When we're in the lead, Tom gives me a nod. We're both on high alert as we take cautious steps forward.

We walk for about twenty minutes. Nothing bad has happened. Sally has been calling out distances in one-tenth mile intervals. Right now the arrow is pointing due east and the distance shows 0.98 miles. We're getting close. Bandit Woods has thinned out. We're now standing in a clearing. We can see a fair distance ahead of us. What we see causes me to gasp.

We walk the remaining distance. My fears are confirmed. We've come to a rock face sticking straight up out of the ground. Its massive size consumes our vision from right to left.

Sally holds up her iPhone. "We're here."

We all look at the iPhone. Sure enough, the arrow is pointing due east and the distance shows 1.06 miles.

Sally's next question floors us. "Is this where we're going to dig for the Hillbrook stash?"

* * *

Tom and I are speechless. We both assumed Sally was so focused on using her geocaching app that she hasn't thought about our reasons for coming here. We were wrong. She knows exactly what we're up to.

Tom and I aren't responding so Crystal chimes in. "What's a Hillbrook stash?"

Crystal is from Dayton, Ohio. Maybe she hasn't heard about our little town's most famous event. Or if she has, she must not know the whole story.

"*The* Hillbrook stash," Sally corrects. "It's a ton of money that's hidden in these woods somewhere."

Sally looks me right in the eye. "I think you have some explaining to do."

I look at Tom, but he just shrugs.

"It's really not my story to tell. Tom found the map."

Sally laughs out loud. It's a strange high-pitched laugh. Almost hysterical. "Yeah. I bought one of those maps for fifty cents when I was seven. What do they cost now? I bet with inflation they're up to at least a dollar."

I look at Tom again. "I think you've got to show them, Tom."

"Okay," he replies. "But let's sit down first."

47

We find a few rocks to sit on. Tom reaches into his backpack and pulls out the cigar box. Sally's eyebrows rise when she sees how old it is, but she doesn't say a word. Tom fetches Old Man Humphrey's note and cautiously hands it to Sally.

Sally holds the note so that both she and Crystal can read it at the same time. When she's finished, she pauses, looking from me to Tom.

"So you think this is real?" she asks, looking at Tom.

Tom nods. "I think so. I sure have no reason to doubt it."

Tom tells the story of how he found the cigar box in the library.

Then Sally looks at me. "So is that why you were trying to convince us to go home when we stepped into the woods? And why you and Tom took the lead? Were you worried about us?"

"Yeah," I sheepishly say. "We didn't want you to get hurt if we ran into a booby-trap or something."

Suddenly Sally looks hurt. "Are you sure it wasn't because you didn't want the two of us to come along?"

"No!" I nearly shout. "Tom and I talked about it. We knew you'd never let us use the iPhone by ourselves. You'd insist on *helping* us use it."

"Still, you should have told us what you were up to."

"You're right. I'm sorry."

"Is there anything else we should know?" Sally asks as she looks from me to Tom again.

Tom opens the cigar box and brings out the fuse, the lighter, and the key. He mentions the Derringer, but says it's probably not part of the challenge.

I forgot about the gun. I hope he's right about not needing it.

Sally thinks for a few moments before she brightens. "We're standing exactly..." She glances at the note. "...2,250 paces due west of the pillar. I think now it's pretty obvious what the number fifty means." She looks up the rock face.

I've been concentrating on Sally's reaction. So I haven't thought about our first challenge. Neither has Tom. He looks up where Sally is staring. "You think the Hillbrook stash is fifty paces straight up?"

Crystal chuckles and Tom blushes.

Sally pauses before she speaks. "First of all, I don't think the stash is up there. Old Man Humphrey makes it clear in his note that there are several challenges we need to defeat. This is just the first. Second, I don't think the number fifty means fifty paces. I think it means fifty feet."

We all stand back from the rock face and look up the cliff. I'm no judge of distances, but it doesn't look like the rock face is more than about seventy-five feet high. So Sally must be right that the distance is measured in feet.

Sally moves up close to the rock face to examine it. She walks left and right about twenty feet each way. Then she repeats her motions, but slower this time. At times her nose is almost touching the rock. Finally she stops.

"Look there!" she cries. Her voice is filled with excitement as she points up.

About fifteen feet up is a hole in the rock. It is about four inches square. And it's definitely man-made. Above it and slightly to the left is another hole. Yet another hole is above and slightly to the right. The pattern of holes continues up the rock face.

"I think Old Man Humphrey provided a ladder," Crystal says.

* * *

We decide that Tom will climb Old Man Humphrey's ladder. I can't do it for obvious reasons. Crystal is terrified of heights. And Sally... Well Sally's a *girl*; Tom is too macho to let her climb. Even though Sally figured out most of our first challenge, she doesn't put up much of a fight. She's content to let Tom do the climbing.

First we have to figure out how to get Tom up to the foot-holes. They're nearly fifteen feet up. Old Man Humphrey put the first set of holes up high enough that they wouldn't be noticed by anyone passing by. His ladder is very well hidden even though it's in plain view.

We find what we need just ten feet away. A fallen pine tree. All of its needles are gone so it should make a pretty good ladder. Tom, Sally, and Crystal drag it over and prop it up. I feel worthless since all I can do is watch.

In preparation for his climb, we nearly empty Tom's backpack. He puts it on like a shoulder bag so that the pouch is at his side. This way he'll be able to hang on to the rock face with one hand and reach its contents with the other. At the last minute, Sally adds her iPhone. "Take pictures of whatever you find up there," she orders.

Sally is thinking of things I would never imagine. Suddenly I'm very glad she's with us.

While Sally and Crystal support the tree, Tom climbs up to the first set of holes. Though the holes are spaced for someone taller than Tom, he's able to grip two upper holes with his hands while plugging his feet in two lower holes. To move up, he pulls his body weight upward with his hands. The hole spacing works to his advantage. He's got great upper body strength from playing basketball.

He tentatively takes his first step away from the tree. He reaches up to the next hole with his right hand while his left foot finds the next lower hole. He looks awkward doing this, and his shoe scrapes the rock face in search of the hole, sprinkling sand on our heads. We shield our eyes as we move away from directly beneath him. Tom slowly repeats the process a few times and pretty soon he's nearly twenty-five feet up.

It's hard to watch my brother in this scary position. From down here, he looks like a spider climbing straight up a wall.

"Be careful Tom!" I yell. "And take your time!"

He pauses long enough to call down. "Don't worry Bro. I've got this. It's kind of fun!"

He continues his upward journey. A few minutes later he stops and calls down again. "There aren't any more holes!"

"You must be fifty feet up," Sally yells back. "Do you see anything?"

He pauses before calling down again "Yes! Just to my left is a rock shelf."

He pauses again. "Above it is a wall of stone. It looks man-made. And there's a round hole on my side of the wall."

"Take some pictures and come back down so we all can all see it," Sally calls.

Tom does as he's told and starts to descend. He's unsteady during his first few steps down. I cringe each time I see one of his feet dangle in search of a foot-hole, but with each step closer to the ground his footing is more accurate.

He finally reaches the tree and climbs down while Sally and Crystal hold it steady.

We all huddle around the iPhone as Sally displays the pictures. They are all very clear and in focus. And they show close-ups of the entire structure fifty feet above us.

As we study the pictures, it's obvious that whatever is up there is at least partially man-made. To the left of the foot-holes is a rock shelf. This appears to be natural. It starts about 12" from the foot holes with a 12" ledge that runs horizontal for a near five feet. Above the shelf are stones mortared into place that form a wall, an entombment of some sort. The stone wall runs the length of the rock shelf and is about four feet high. It's unclear whether the rock shelf and cave are natural or man-made, but someone definitely made the wall. It had to be Old Man Humphrey, right?

On the side of the wall closest to the foot holes is a circular pattern of small stones. In its center is a circular recess. And in the middle of the recess is a tiny hole. From what Tom says, this circle is about two feet to the left of foot-holes and a foot above the rock shelf.

While the iPhone is passed around several times, we study the photos in quiet. Tom is the first to speak. "Anyone got any ideas?" He looks right at Sally.

It's clear Sally is now our leader even though she's only known about the cigar box for less than an hour. She figured out three parts of our first challenge: the map points up the rock face, the measurement is in feet and not paces, and she found the foot-holes in the rock face. She and Crystal figured out how to use the Geocache app to guide us here in the first place.

She pauses a moment before she speaks. "Old Man Humphrey intended that the items in the cigar box be used for whatever's up there. So what do we have? A fuse. A lighter. And a key. I think it's obvious what has to be done."

"Right," Tom agrees.

I don't think Tom has a clue about what we're supposed to do. He just keeps looking at Sally for the answer. Just as Crystal and I do.

Sally smiles. She likes being the smart one. "We can tell from the pictures that the little round hole isn't a keyhole. So we can't use the key to open some kind of stone door".

Then she focuses on Tom with a look of worry. "You're not going to like what I'm going to say because it's dangerous." She pauses for effect.

She's still looking Tom right in the eye. "I think you have to push the fuse into the hole and then light it with the lighter. I'm betting that will cause an explosion. The explosion will blow away the mortared stones. Then we'll be able to get to whatever's in the cave."

Tom staggers back a step or two as what Sally said sinks in. "But what will happen to me?"

"I'm not sure," she replies, then quickly adds, "but I think that's what Old Man Humphrey had in mind. What else would we do with the fuse and lighter up there?"

We all try to think of other possibilities. None of us can come up with anything that makes any sense.

With the plan decided, we try to think of ways to protect Tom after he lights the fuse. The fuse is only four inches long. How long will it burn? Probably no more than ten seconds. That's not enough time to climb down. Or even to get down a few steps. What kind of explosives are they? They've been up there for over sixty years. Will they work? We just don't know enough to make any smart decisions.

Sally has an idea. "You said the foot holes are about two feet from the little hole where you'll put the fuse, right?"

Tom nods.

"If you lean as far as you can to the right after you light the fuse, you should be able to avoid the explosion. And maybe you can get even further away if you can somehow position yourself into the right-most set of foot holes."

Tom doesn't look too happy with Sally's suggestion. But in the end, that's what we decide Tom will do. Or try to do.

We again lighten Tom's load as best as we can. This time Sally keeps her iPhone. As she takes it from Tom, I can't help wondering if she's worried that her mom will be mad if it's destroyed in the blast. Tom's backpack now contains only the fuse and lighter. We decide to keep the key on the ground since we have no idea what he'll find once the stone wall is destroyed.

Sally has been very quiet during our preparations. When Tom is ready to climb the tree, she reaches into her own bag and pulls out a package of tissues. "The explosion is going to be really loud. Put these in your ears before you light the fuse."

She tucks the tissues into his backpack.

Tom gives us one more worried look before he starts his assent. "Wish me luck. I think I'll need it."

On his way up we see him practicing his move to the right-most foot holes. If he steps up, he can slide into them. This moves him another two feet to his right. It's a bit awkward and he fumbles around with his left foot a few times. But at least he can do it.

Unfortunately, once he lights the fuse, he'll have to step down one set of holes before he can step back up into the right-most ones. That will take time. When he reaches the top, he practices.

"Hey," he yells down. "Time me to see how long it takes me to get into position."

His first attempt takes nearly twenty seconds. He struggles to find the holes with both his hands and feet. But he gets much better with practice. Once his body memorizes the position of each hole, he's able to move his hands and feet in a brisk motion, without fumbling. His time is down to eight seconds.

I look at Sally and she sees my concern. "That should be enough time, don't you think?" she asks.

"I sure hope so," I respond.

Sally notices that Tom is getting positioned to light the fuse. "Don't forget the ear-plugs."

We can't see exactly what he's doing, but after a few minutes he calls down. "Okay, I think I'm ready. The fuse is pushed all the way into the hole. It bottoms out inside leaving about an inch sticking out. I'm ready to put the tissues in my ears and light the fuse. Is there anything else you can think of before I can't hear you any more?"

Sally, Crystal, and I have moved off to the left and backed into the trees. Each of us is standing behind our own tree.

"No, I think we're ready," I shout. I hope Tom is.

"All right. Here goes," he yells down as he works, "I'm lighting the fuse... NOW!"

I start counting the seconds out loud. "One, one thousand. Two, one thousand…"

Tom has already stepped down one set of holes.

"Three, one thousand. Four, one thousand."

Tom is stepping up and to the right, and he has his left hand in the upper right hole. But he's fumbling with his left foot. He's not practicing any more so he must be pretty nervous.

"Five, one thousand. Six, one thousand."

His fumbling turns frantic. His left foot is moving all over the place trying to find a foot-hole.

"Seven, one, thousand. Eight, one thousand."

Just as he plugs his left foot into position and pulls himself up and to the right, KABOOM!

The ground shakes and a concussion pounds my chest. My ears ring like they did when Larry hit me with that baseball bat. A brief echo comes from some distant reflector. It's got to be ten times worse for Tom up there. How can he possibly hang on? I strain to see him but a cloud of smoke extends out from the rock face, blocking my view. We are hit by a bombardment of rubble spraying out from the blast. We scurry back behind our respective trees like scared little mice. I brush away sand that got in my hair.

When I'm finally able to look up again, the smoke cleared. I'm horrified by what I see.

Tom is dangling by his left arm; he's not moving.

I'm terrified Tom will fall. A fall from that height is like falling from the third floor of a building. It may not kill him, but he'd be badly injured.

There's nothing any of us can do. We just watch in horror as he dangles.

After what seems like forever, Tom slowly drags his right hand up to join his left hand in the tiny depression. He pulls himself upward. Eventually his left foot finds its way to a foot hole. We all breathe a sigh of relief.

He moves back to the left-most holes. He's finally stable.

"Are you okay?" I yell.

He shakes his head. "What?"

"Are you okay?" I call again.

Tom cranes his neck so he can see us on the ground. "I can't hear you. The blast must have killed my hearing."

Sally figures it out right away. She points at her ears with both hands. "You still have the tissue in your ears!"

He nods and takes out the tissues.

"Can you hear me now?" I call.

"Yeah. That's much better. For a minute I thought I lost my hearing."

"Are you okay?" I yell for the third time.

"Yeah. I lost my hold when the rock face shook. It was really scary, but I don't think anything hit me."

"Right," Crystal yells. "It all came down on us."

It hadn't occurred to me that one of us on the ground may be hurt.

"Are you guys okay?" I ask.

"I'm fine," Sally responds.

But Crystal is slow to answer. She's examining her right arm. "Something hit me right here." She points at her bicep muscle.

Sally takes a closer look with Crystal's arm in her hand and gently moves it around. "Nothing seems to be broken."

"The pain is going away now," Crystal says.

We turn our attention to Tom. He cranes his body to the left, but quickly backs away. "Wow! It's hot in there!" he yells down.

"Just give it some time," Sally calls. "The blast must have super-heated the air. It shouldn't take long to cool off."

The stone wall is gone and a small cave has appeared. I can't stop myself from asking. "Can you see what's in there?"

Tom slowly leans to his left again. He pokes his head into the cave. "Yeah. There's a metal box. I think it's a safe. Wait a minute."

He leans his upper body onto the shelf and reaches into the cave. When he pulls back, the box comes into view. From what I can see, it appears about the size of a shoe box.

Tom corrects himself. "It's a tool box. It's locked with a padlock."

I start thinking about how Tom is going to bring the toolbox down to us when Sally beats me to the punch. Again.

"Don't try to carry it down Tom," she yells. "It looks way too bulky to put in your backpack. Just let it drop to the ground."

There's no argument from Tom. We stand back behind the trees again as he lifts the toolbox over the edge and lets go. It scrapes against the rock face and tumbles down. Eventually it crashes to the ground with a thud, but it's still in one piece. After watching the tool box fall, I know Tom would not have survived a fall from up there after all. I say a little prayer of thanks as he comes down for the last time.

So the note was real. So was the map. And now we have defeated the first of Old Man Humphrey's challenges!

\*\*\*

Sally and Crystal hold the tree one more time as Tom climbs down. Suddenly tears well up in my eyes as Tom's feet touch the ground. What's wrong with me? I feel so relieved that he's okay. I can't stop myself from giving him a one-armed hug when he reaches the ground. "I'm glad you're okay," I whisper.

Tom briefly hugs back, but quickly pushes me away. He's embarrassed to be hugging, especially in front of the girls. "I'm fine Steve. Not to worry," he whispers back.

I release the hug and turn back to the girls. Both of them are smiling but neither says a word.

We head over to where the toolbox landed. Crystal flips it right side up and exposes the padlock.

Sally passes the key to Tom. "You did all the hard work, Tom. So you should do the honors."

The key slides perfectly into the lock. Tom turns the key and the padlock clicks open. He removes the padlock and drops it on the ground. He opens the lid. "Here we go!"

It looks a lot like a toolbox my dad had in our garage. There's a top-tray with a round handle that runs its entire length. Nothing is in the top tray, so Tom and pulls it out and drops it on the ground.

We're all crowded around trying to see. We're so close that Sally bumps me out of the way as she leans in to look. From the little I can see, the toolbox is packed to the brim.

Tom pulls out a large coil of rope. Old Man Humphrey carefully wrapped it. Otherwise it wouldn't fit inside the box. Tom sets it aside and reaches into the toolbox again.

This time he removes a hook, it's about six inches long. Opposite the hook end is a snap-ring, it looks like a link that mountain climbers use. Tom puts it on the ground next to the rope.

Now he pulls out a small block and tackle set. I've see one of these before, it was on a car show Dad used to watch. They used it to remove the engine from a car. This he also places on the ground.

Next a leather belt appears. Not a normal belt like you'd use to hold up your pants, it's more like a weight-lifter's belt, about three inches wide. It has a large metal loop near the buckle. He sets it down next to the other items.

Peeking into the toolbox again, Tom frowns. It's empty. He's about to push it aside when Sally stops him.

"Wait!" She points inside the toolbox. "There's something else right there up against the end."

Tom looks where she's pointing. Sure enough there is something there. He carefully removes a stiff piece of cloth about the size of a large note card, but thicker, with a faded gray checkered pattern. It's about the same color as the inside of the toolbox. No wonder Tom missed it. Tom holds it up so we all can see it.

Later, I search the Internet and learn this fabric is called *oil cloth*. It was used to protect its contents from moisture and the elements, much like plastic wrap or a sandwich bag does today.

Sally points to a spot where the oil cloth is peeling apart. Tom gently peels further to reveal something wrapped inside, an envelope. Old Man Humphrey used the oil cloth as a bag to protect the paper it contained. Tom removes the envelope and carefully opens it. It's another note from Old Man Humphrey!

Tom just gets the note out of the envelope when the chorus from a Taylor Swift song booms out of Sally's pocket. *Someday, I'll be livin in a big old city – all you're ever gonna be is mean...*

We all jump except Sally. Her face reddens as she pulls out her iPhone. She checks who's calling and frowns. The speaker is off so we can only hear her side of the conversation.

"Hi Mom. Yeah, we're all right. Really? It's that late already? Yeah, I know. Well, we got to talking and lost track of time. Uh-huh. Yeah. I remember. We'll be there in time. Don't worry. Sure thing. Bye."

Sally looks at the iPhone again and shakes her head in disbelief. "Did you know it's after three o'clock? My grandparents are coming over for dinner at five."

She looks at Crystal. "Mom wants us home. Now."

Sally eyes the note in Tom's hand. "You guys have to promise not to read that until we can get together again."

"That's not fair!" Tom complains.

"But if you do, you'll be tempted to go on without us," Sally argues. "We want to be in on this from now on. Don't we Crystal?"

"You bet your favorite Taylor Swift song we do!"

Sally blushes again but ignores Crystal. "Come on guys. Wait for us. We'll be free tomorrow. It's Sunday. We can get off to a really early start if you want. Please?"

"Just don't expect Sally to bring her iPhone!" Crystal chides, poking Sally in the side. "After today, Aunt Mary will probably take it away again."

Now that I've seen Sally in action, I for one want the girls in on our adventure. "We can wait until tomorrow morning Tom, it's only fair. They've helped a lot. We wouldn't have defeated the first challenge if it wasn't for them."

Tom gives a disappointed nod. "Okay. What time do you guys want to meet?"

"How about seven o'clock at the pillar?" Sally suggests.

"Okay," Tom responds. "But remember. The note gets read at seven-o-one."

"Deal!" Sally snaps a quick picture of all the stuff spread out on the ground.

"Hey!" Tom barks.

"I didn't say not to start thinking about what these things might be used for," Sally says. "It's only fair that we have something to look at too."

Tom grunts in response. He carefully places everything back in the toolbox. This is no easy task since they barely fit.

* * *

Tom is sore from his efforts on the rock face, so the walk home takes longer than normal. Even so, we walk Sally and Crystal all the way to their house, then wait on their sidewalk as they hop up the stairs and go in. I've never been on a date. But today felt like a date. A double-date!

Tom must be thinking the same because as soon as the door closes, he asks, "Do you think Crystal likes me?"

"I wasn't really paying attention Tom. I was pretty focused on our quest."

62

"She smiled at me a lot."

It really wasn't a question but I answer anyway. "Of course she smiled at you. She smiles at everybody. That's what makes her so cute. That and all her freckles."

"You think she's cute? There's a hint of jealousy in his voice.

"Of course I think she's cute, any dummy can see *that*. But she's older than I am, I wouldn't stand a chance with her. Besides…" I cut myself off.

"Besides what?"

When I don't respond Tom raises his eyebrows. "Oh yeah. So Sally *is* your girlfriend."

"I like her a lot, but we haven't spent much time together lately. Up until this year we've always eaten lunch together at school. But now she's found some new friends. Girls she hangs out with and stuff. She eats lunch with them now. And then there's Crystal. If she's not with one of her new friends she's with Crystal. She hardly ever talks to me any more."

I can't believe how much I'm saying. I guess I was missing Sally more than I thought.

Tom gently nudges my arm. "Is that why you went all shy and stuff when we first got to her house?"

"I guess so. Like I said, we really haven't talked much all this year. I didn't know what to say."

I can feel a lump in my throat. Not knowing how to talk to Sally really hurt. I hope Tom doesn't notice the crack in my voice.

"Well she sure is smart," Tom says. "It's almost like she knew what Old Man Humphrey was trying to tell us."

Tom's comment makes me think of something Sally told me a long time ago. She and her Dad used to spend a lot of time walking in Bandit Woods when she was little. But she hasn't said anything about it in the last couple of years. I wonder if she and her dad still take those walks. Were they looking for the Hillbrook stash?

A terrible thought comes into my head. She wouldn't tell her dad about today, would she?

* * *

Mom's in the kitchen when we return home. Saturdays are always short work days for her at the pawnshop. The moment we step through the front door, I smell garlic. She's been cooking? It's been a very long time since Mom cooked a real meal. Boy does it smell good!

"Where have you two been?" she calls out from the kitchen.

"Just around," Tom says. "What's for dinner? It smells great."

Mom is easily distracted by the dinner question, it keeps her from doing any real parenting. Or maybe she's just trying to remember her recipe.

"Spaghetti. You and Steve go get cleaned up. It'll be ready in ten minutes."

We head upstairs. Tom holds the toolbox behind him to prevent mom from seeing it as we pass by the kitchen door. We go to his bedroom and he hides the toolbox in his closet.

"Do you think we should keep this in our special place?" Tom asks.

"I don't think we have to. Mom never comes in here. She wouldn't find it in a million years."

In spite of what I say, Tom throws some dirty clothes over the toolbox and closes the closet door.

We wash up and head down to the kitchen. Mom sets the last of the dishes on the table. The kitchen table hasn't looked this nice since Dad left. Our places are neatly arranged with the good silverware and cloth napkins. We even have the nice water glasses. And, there are serving dishes for the food, not just the pots and pans from the stove.

I'm not the only one who noticed.

"What's the occasion Mom?" Tom asks. "Did you win the lottery?"

Mom smiles but her response is a simple question. "Can't I make a nice dinner once in a while?"

I'm not going to question our good fortune. The table looks great and the food smells delicious. "This is cool Mom," I admit. "Thanks."

I think my enthusiasm surprises her. "Well you're welcome Steve. Now you boys sit down and start before it gets cold "

We sit and dig in. It's difficult with only my left hand, but I fill up my plate with spaghetti and pour sauce all over it. Then I pile on the Parmesan cheese. The spaghetti sauce tastes great even though it's out of a jar. The Italian sausage Mom mixes in gives it a spicy flavor. We also have green beans and garlic bread. And, there's a chocolate cake on the counter. Wow! What a feast!

I look over and see Tom wolfing down his food. It occurs to me that we haven't eaten since our cereal from breakfast.

Mom notices too. "Slow down boys. You'll make yourselves sick."

"I can't help it Mom," I say with a half-mouthful of food. "It's so good!"

With his head bent over his plate, Tom nods and grunts in agreement.

Our plates are clean in minutes.

As we reach for seconds, Mom sits back, lights up a cigarette, and drops the bomb. "I had a visit from Officer Grant at the store today."

Tom and I freeze at the mention of Officer Grant's name. My appetite instantly disappears as I sit back in my chair.

"I think you boys owe me an explanation. And maybe an apology."

"What did he say Mom?" Tom asks as calmly as possible.

Mom's eyes blaze. "Oh no. That's not how this is going to go. *You tell me* the whole story. But you may as well assume that I've already heard it from Officer Grant."

Tom looks at me but I just shrug. I'm not going to tell her!

Tom pauses. I can tell he's trying to figure out how much to say and where to start.

"Well?" Mom prods. "I'm waiting."

Tom decides to start with the fight. "You know how the Hinkle brothers are always picking on us, right? Well they finally went too far and I fought back for once. You're always telling me to stand up for myself, right Mom?"

Tom is playing for some sympathy but it's not working. "Listen buster," Mom says. "You're in major trouble here. Don't even think about throwing this back in my face. Go on."

"Well, the truth is," Tom continues, "they cornered me and I couldn't get away. My only two choices were to fight or get beat up. I didn't even know Steve was there. I sure had no idea that he'd join in."

Tom looks at me and I see a thank-you in his eyes. "After they started punching, I had no choice but to fight back. And I was holding my own pretty well too until Larry Hinkle hit Steve with that baseball bat. When Ed stopped hitting me to look at Steve, well, I did what I had to do. I got the gun out of my backpack and fired. The Hinkle brothers ran away after that."

Tom doesn't mention how carefully he took aim at Larry before he fired. We'll keep that just between us.

"And just where did you get this gun?" Mom asks.

"As I told Officer Grant, the gun was in a cigar box I found in the library. It was a Derringer I think. I didn't even know it was loaded. Heck, I wouldn't know how to load it. Anyway, Officer Grant took it from me."

Tom tells Mom about the book he needed for school. And how he found the cigar box on the strange bookshelf. Then he explains about the old lady, and how she must have called the police after he ran away. But he doesn't mention the note from Old Man Humphrey, or the other items in the cigar box.

Mom looks somewhat satisfied. Officer Grant's version of the story must not be too different from Tom's.

Tom seems to notice Mom's change in attitude too. He adds, "If you ask me, it's those Hinkle brothers that should be in trouble. Not me. Ask anyone. They terrorize the whole school. They have for years."

Mom doesn't take the bait. "Let's just keep talking about you and your brother. You're the only ones I'm responsible for."

The rest of the conversation goes pretty well. Mom asks me to tell my side of the story. I don't have anything to add to Tom's information. She scolds me for lying about Katie's cat and falling out of a tree.

Then she softens. She says, "Officer Grant doesn't think Mrs. Hinkle will press charges. Even for as upset as she was, Mrs. Hinkle knows her boys have caused a lot of trouble over the years. If she presses charges, others in town might press charges against her boys too."

I breathe a sigh of relief though my stomach is still in a knot. I guess maybe I did eat too fast.

Mom's mood lightens, she snuffs out her cigarette, and cuts pieces of chocolate cake for me and Tom. I'm surprised she doesn't punish us for as mad as she was. I think she's satisfied that we opened up to her for the first time since the divorce.

It feels good to know that she might still care about us after all.

* * *

After dessert, Tom and I go up to his room. He sits at his desk, I sit on his bed.

"Should I get the toolbox out?" he asks.

"Leave it Tom. If we get it out, we'll only be tempted to read the note. We know what's in there."

There's the rope, the hook, the block and tackle set, the belt, and of course, the note. At least there wasn't a weapon this time.

"What do you think?" Tom asks.

I take a minute before I speak. "I think we're supposed to devise some kind of winch. And it looks like we'll be lifting something pretty heavy."

"I was thinking the same thing. I sure hope the note explains everything."

I laugh out loud. "Yeah, just like the first note did."

Now it's Tom's turn to laugh.

We talk a few more minutes and decide to go to bed. Seven o'clock will roll around pretty fast. I head to my room. As I dose off, I find myself thinking about Sally.

Sunday

Tom nudges me. "Come on, get up. We're going to be late."

I roll over and look at the clock on my nightstand. Six-thirty.

"Okay," I grumble. But I'm already alert and excited about what we're going to be doing today. My arm doesn't hurt at all. Neither does my head.

We're out of the house in record time. I can even keep up with Tom without my arm throbbing. When we arrive at City Park, the clock on the Hillbrook Gang Memorial pillar says six-fifty. We sit at a picnic table close to the pillar.

Tom vibrates with anticipation. "I wish they'd get here. I can't wait to read the note."

He already has the envelope out of the toolbox. He holds it up to the sunlight trying to see through the paper.

"They said they'd be here at seven." I try to sound calm but I'm excited too.

We wait in agony for five minutes. At six-fifty-five, we see movement at the entrance of City Park.

I didn't notice the chill in the air until I see Sally and Crystal wearing light jackets. Sally's jacket is bright blue and Crystal's is neon yellow. Crystal is wearing a sky blue baseball cap. It's on backwards

71

and makes her look really cute. Sally's brown hair is up in a pony tail. They're both wearing jeans today. The vivid colors are hard to look at in the bright sunlight.

Tom is already opening the envelope when the girls approach the picnic table. He has it out and unfolded as they sit down.

"Wait just a minute more," Sally orders. Sally reaches into her bag and pulls out her iPhone. *So her mom didn't take it away from her after all.* Sally positions the iPhone just above the note and takes a picture. Tom turns the note over and she snaps another.

"Just in case something happens to the note," she says.

This girl thinks of everything!

This note is on the same paper as the first one. Handwriting fills much of it. And yes, there is a map on one side.

Somehow the note ends up facing Crystal and I wonder how Tom let that happen. She picks it up and starts reading out loud.

*All of my life I have been a solitary person. Even as a child I kept to myself. Solitude has been my friend. My trusted companion. My only aspiration has been to be left alone. This is why I lived in a hovel, far from the commune of regular society. I desired none of the repartee that accompanies the assemblage of human beings.*

*Only did one public episode in my life involve the happiness of another's companionship. And that alliance ended badly. The fruit of that union resulted in rot. I will not state the details of this unpleasant period. You will gain the knowledge of it soon enough.*

*On the day of Jeffrey Hillbrook's death, my life became an open book which every person for miles around believed they had the right to consume. I lost my precious solitude in their rush for treasure. Not one of those scavengers considered the torment they were inflicting upon me.*

*When it became obvious that I was at the end of my peaceful existence, I vowed that no vulture would ever find that which they seek. Hence I created these challenges while managing to keep away from prying eyes. Indeed, construction has required very little additional effort on my part. For my hiding places were discovered many years ago, during the days when I lived in peace.*

*It is my sincere hope that as you read this, many years have since passed and those whom pursued me are long since expired. If this be the case then I have no quarrel with you. That you strive to attain the object of my ruin is all that keeps us from being friends. Good friends. You have done well to defeat the first of my challenges. For this I respect you. But alas, our friendship is not to be. In the end, adversaries we must remain.*

*Do not think too harshly of me for challenging you thus. It is your own decision to carry on that propels you forward, possibly to your demise. I only provide you with the means. I genuinely desire that one day you come to understand the wretchedness that became my life. I would wish no such sorrow upon any man.*

*P.S. As relates to your second challenge: You will find that which you seek in a grotto that no other living but me has laid eyes upon. It is indeed a beautiful place, but if you are unprepared, it will be deadly.*

As with the first note, there's a map below the handwriting.

We remain silent for a minute, thinking about what Crystal just read. Sally asks Crystal to read the note again, which she does. Still, no one talks when she's finished.

Old Man Humphrey has given us the reason why he never talked about the Hillbrook stash. He was mad at the people who hounded him. They made his life miserable.

At least now it seems pretty clear that he did find the Hillbrook stash and he hid it somewhere in Bandit Woods. That's good news for us.

Tom is the first to speak. "He sounds really mad."

"Mad enough to kill us," Crystal agrees.

"But there's something else," Sally adds. "Sadness. He must have been miserable after Jeffrey Hillbrook was killed."

"Can we look at the map now?" Tom asks.

Crystal drops the note in front of Tom like it's burning her fingers. She even shakes her hand after releasing it. All of us but Tom are still thinking about Old Man Humphrey's message.

"Why couldn't they just leave him alone?" Crystal asks, almost to herself.

"People are crazy when it comes to money," I state. "Just look what happened during the gold rushes of the eighteen hundreds. People left everything behind, including their loved ones. And for what? The dream of becoming rich? For most of them, that dream turned into a nightmare."

"He should have just let them take what they wanted," Crystal continues. "Once they had the money, people would have left him alone, wouldn't they?"

"I'm not so sure," I respond. "If even a penny of the stash was found, people would have been combing every inch of Bandit Woods for years. At least that's what Old Man Humphrey must have thought."

"That's kind of what happened anyway, isn't it?" Crystal retorts. "One thing's for sure, we need to go to the library and read up on him. We owe him that much."

"You're right," I agree. "But I don't think Tom will want to come."

Crystal gives me a funny look. It takes a moment to remember that she doesn't know about Tom's run-in with the librarian. I tell her the story and she laughs. She is cute when she laughs, especially when she snorts.

There's another reason why I want to learn more about Old Man Humphrey. Something he said in his note has me thinking. He mentioned hiding places created long before the Hillbrook affair. He's using them for his challenges. Maybe we can find some clues in old news clippings.

Crystal and I look over and see that Sally has joined Tom. They're hunched over the note, having a lively conversation.

"That can't be right," Tom is saying. "The starting point is here at the pillar." He points down at the map.

"Look more closely," Sally demands. She places her finger where Tom is pointing. "You're right. This is the pillar. It's where we are right now."

She moves her finger an inch or so. "But *that* is the starting point. It's where the dotted line begins. Where we'll hide the geocache."

"But I don't understand," Tom says. "If that's the starting point, then what are all these little dots between the pillar and the starting point?"

Sally doesn't respond. She looks frustrated, "I don't know yet, but like I've been saying, that's what we need to figure out."

Crystal voices an idea. "Maybe the little dots show how to get from the pillar to the starting point," she says.

Sally points her eyes at Crystal to butt out.

"Just a suggestion," Crystal sheepishly adds.

But then Sally's expression softens. "Crystal may be right. We've been looking at this all wrong. Maybe there are two starting points, one from here at the pillar and the other that will lead us into the woods."

"That's what I've been trying to say," Tom says. But he shuts up as soon as Sally looks at him.

"I still don't understand what the little dots are for," Sally mumbles to herself.

I take another look at the map to see what all the confusion is about. It's clear that the solid dot is in the center of City Park, it has to be the pillar. The little dots lead out from it. Though, whatever is at the other end of the dots is not so clear. It's just a big circle. I look closer. The little dots aren't quite round, they're ovals.

"No wait! I think I've got it!" I nearly scream. "I think the little dots are footsteps. See how they go to the left, then up, then to the left again? I think they represent a person walking from the pillar to the starting point."

"You may be on to something," Sally says while holding the map so the top faces north.

"If you're right…" She looks up from the map, then to her left, and straight ahead. "…then the starting point… should be… over there somewhere." Sally points in a northwesterly direction.

"But how far apart are the footsteps," Tom asks. "And we have no idea how far they go in one direction before they head in another."

He's right. But how do we figure it out? Crystal, Tom, and I give up and turn to Sally. She's our last hope.

After a minute, her eyes light up. She takes one last look northwest. She stands up on her tip-toes to see further. "I think I've got it! Anyone up for some breakfast? I'm starved!"

We're all confused by the sudden change of subject. Food? Who could think of eating now? Sally starts walking toward the City Park exit. Crystal and I follow, questions fly out of our mouths. Sally ignores us. Tom scoops up the map and toolbox in a rush to catch up.

* * *

We stop asking questions when it's clear that Sally isn't going to say another word. She just told us to hold our questions. All will be revealed when we eat breakfast.

Tom and I walk behind the two of them. A serious problem occurs to me. I whisper it to Tom. "Do you have any money?"

Tom shakes his head. "I think I've got a couple of bucks, but that's not enough for even one of us to eat."

Crystal either heard us or read our minds. "Don't worry guys, breakfast is on me today."

I'm relieved to hear this, but I don't feel right letting a girl pay for my breakfast. From the happy look on Tom's face, it doesn't seem to bother him at all.

It takes us only five minutes to walk the four blocks from City Park to town square. There's only one restaurant on the square that serves breakfast, so we all know where we're going: Clear Valley Café.

I can smell bacon the second Tom opens the door and my mouth starts watering. The place is pretty busy. Being Sunday morning, all the church-goers are here after their services. Tom and I haven't been here since Mom and Dad split up but I remember the food tasting pretty good.

A waitress greets us and tells us to sit anywhere there's an open table. Tom and I start to move forward but Sally stops us. "Give us a minute. Okay?" she says to the waitress.

The waitress sighs impatiently.

Sally walks around the restaurant looking closely at every table. She ignores the annoyed looks she gets from morning diners. When she pauses for an especially long time at one of the tables in back, a little boy asks his mom what the strange girl is looking at. Finally, Sally makes her way back to the waitress, who is now tapping her feet. "Would it be okay if we wait for that table?" She points at the table near the back of the restaurant.

"Suit yourself," the waitress replies. She's obviously annoyed by how long it took Sally to choose.

Tom is beside himself as we wait. "Well, we're here. Now are you going to tell us what's going on?"

Sally smiles, "Patience young sir. All will be revealed in its time."

The wait isn't long. Just a few minutes later, the family occupying Sally's chosen table gets up to leave. As we walk by, the little boy gives Sally a suspicious look and keeps his distance. We reach the table just as a busboy cleans it. Sally sits next to the wall. I plop down next to her on the isle side. Tom and Crystal sit opposite of me and Sally. Tom tucks the toolbox under the table.

Tom is still beside himself. "Come on Sally. Are you going to make us eat before you explain?"

Sally doesn't answer right away; she's studying a picture on the wall hung centered with our table. "You guys might want to take a look at this," Sally whispers.

We all turn our attention to the picture Sally is fixed on. It's a black-and-white photograph. An old one. There's a date in the lower-right corner, July 10, 1948. The photograph looks like it's been enlarged because it's pretty grainy.

"See anything of interest?" she goads.

The photograph shows a banner stretched across City Park that reads "Hillbrook Days 1948." It was taken from the southeast side of the Hillbrook Memorial pillar, so the photographer faced northwest. Perhaps he was at the same picnic table we used just a few minutes ago.

In the photograph, the park is crowded, but it is easy to make out the pillar. Several people are gathered around and reading the plaques. But that's not what catches my interest. Further to the northwest is a metal structure. The structure is too large to completely fit in the picture, but it's easy to recognize. It's the Clear Valley water tower that was destroyed by a storm years ago.

Sally gives us a minute to study the photograph. Then she points her thumb at the photograph. "That lady and gentlemen is our starting point."

* * *

The waitress comes to take our order.  I'm hungry, but I don't want to order too much since Crystal is paying.  Sally orders pancakes and sausage and Crystal orders a ham and cheese omelet.  Both order orange juice.

When it's my turn, I order wheat toast.  But as the waitress turns to Tom, Crystal interrupts.  "Wait a minute!  I know you want more than that, Steve Jones.  We don't want hear your stomach growling all day.  Do we Sally?"

Sally smiles and shakes her head no.

"So what do you really want?"  Crystal asks.

I'm too shocked and embarrassed to argue in front of the waitress.  "I'd like a ham and cheese omelet too please, with wheat toast."

Tom knows not to repeat my mistake.  "I'll have the Denver omelet."

"And bring them each a large orange juice," Crystal adds as the waitress turns away to put in our order.

Once the waitress is gone, Sally looks at Crystal.  "Okay, are you going to tell them about your financial situation or am I?"

Crystal's freckles dim into her reddening cheeks.  "It's no big deal."

Sally leans to the middle of the table so she can speak softly.  "Crystal received a large insurance settlement after her parents died.  Most of it has been set aside for her future, college and such.  Let's just say she has more Jackson's than most teenagers – take my word for it.  She won't let anyone pay for anything, I know because I've tried."

I don't know how to respond.  It still doesn't seem right to let a girl pay for my breakfast.  "Thank you Crystal."  It's all I can think to say.  Tom thanks Crystal too.

Crystal looks uncomfortable being the object of our conversation. She changes the subject back to the reason why we're here. "So how are we going to figure out where the old water tower used to be?"

"I know exactly where it was," Sally responds., "Before they stripped the wreckage and built houses over it, it used to be in a big grass field. My dad and I flew kites there when I was little. This one time, I tripped and skinned my knee on one of the cement blocks used as part of its foundation."

"So you knew the water tower would be our starting point?" Tom asks.

"Not exactly. I just remembered this restaurant is filled with old pictures from the Hillbrook Days celebrations. I knew there were many pictures taken at City Park. I was pretty sure at least one of them would be pointing northwest."

I look around the restaurant. Sure enough, black and white photographs are everywhere. It's now obvious why Sally walked the restaurant when we first got here.

Our food comes and we eat in silence. I try to watch my manners. I don't want a repeat of my messy spaghetti dinner performance. I'm getting better at eating with my left hand, but I'm also afraid that the omelet will end up in my lap. I notice that Tom is using his best table manners too.

When we're finished, Sally surprises me with a question. "So why have you been ignoring me this year?"

"Me ignoring you? No, I haven't. You're the one with all the new friends." My voice sounds more bitter than I intended. I try to soften my tone. "Like whenever I see you at lunchtime, you're already sitting with someone."

"So why don't you come and sit with *us*?" she presses. "You're my friend too, you know. I miss talking to you. And, it wouldn't hurt you to meet some new people."

"I thought *you* were ignoring *me*. I never thought to join you guys. It would have felt like I was butting in. I mean really, one guy sitting with a bunch of girls?"

"You wouldn't be butting in," Sally retorts, "I'd introduce you. I think you'd like my friends."

I'm still confused, but something Sally just said makes me feel much better. She misses me! "I promise I'll join you guys from now on."

"See that you do," she orders.

When we get up to leave the restaurant, I'm surprised to see Tom paying the bill. Out on the sidewalk I get him aside. "I thought you didn't have enough money."

Tom smiles but looks embarrassed. "I don't. But after the waitress brought the check, Crystal passed me some money under the table. She asked me to 'be a gentleman' and pay the bill for her."

\* \* \*

It's just after eight-thirty when we return to City Park. Tom pulls out the map to confirm what Sally figured out at the restaurant. When we look at the map again, it's clear that the large circle is the old water tower. Old Man Humphrey couldn't have known it would be destroyed before his map would be used.

Tom clutches the map on our way to where the water tower once stood. We try to follow the path of little dots. We walk a block west, then two blocks north, and finally one block west again. We snake our way between houses and stop in the middle of a subdivision.

Sally holds out her hands as if she's introducing an old friend. "If I'm not mistaken, the old water tower stood right here."

We look for evidence of the water tower. We search for twenty minutes, walking the block several times. Nothing.

We make our way back to where we started.

Crystal points upward, "Maybe that will help." She points at the two street signs on the corner where we're standing.

The east/west street sign says Water Tower Street. The north/south street sign says Water Tower Avenue.

"I think we're as close as we're going to get," Tom says.

"Maybe we can get a little closer," Sally says. Her eyes latch onto a bronze plaque embedded in the asphalt right in the middle of the intersection.

The plaque reads "Clear Valley Water Tower – 1923-1995."

Crystal gives us one of her laughs. "Do you think they buried it here?" she asks between snorts.

The plaque resembles a grave marker.

"Someone in the city council must have really been fond of that water tower," I say, "But at least now we know exactly where it stood."

\* \* \*

From this location our destination appears easy. Well, not easy exactly but familiar. We look at the map again. There's a dotted line that runs directly west from the large circle. At the other end is an X.

There's only one number under the dotted line this time: 3,750. We're in for a longer walk today.

Using the calculator app on Sally's iPhone, I determine the distance to the X is 9,375 feet or 1.77 miles. All that's left is to set up the geocaching app and start walking.

Crystal is digging in her backpack, "We have to do this right. And we can't hide a geocache in the middle of an intersection."

Tom spots a mailbox on the northwest corner of the intersection. "What about there?"

Crystal nods and counts the steps from the plaque to the mailbox. "We just need to remember to count the steps back to the X when we get out there."

Sally sets up the geocache app on the iPhone while Crystal hides the plastic box under the mailbox. This time she uses an elephant-shaped refrigerator magnet for the treasure. Five minutes later we're walking west. The shuffle of our shoes against the road fills the silence between us, no one offers a clue to what we'll do next at the end of our walk.

We walk west out of the subdivision. When we reach Bandit woods, we turn to walk north a bit before the arrow on Sally's iPhone points directly east. The distance display shows 0.22 miles. The over grown vegetation and broken trees slow our search.

Tom and I have taken the lead again. I don't think there are going to be any booby-traps along the way, but why take any chances? After forty minutes we're getting close. The iPhone shows a distance of 1.65 miles and the arrow is still pointing directly east. As usual, Sally calls out our progress every tenth of a mile.

A few minutes later we reach our destination. 1.77 miles from the geocache. And the arrow is pointing due east. Crystal steps back to allow for the distance from the mailbox to the plaque. She should be standing right on the X. "Okay, now what?"

"Let's start looking for a clue," Sally says.

We hear a soft click coming from Crystal's direction. It sounds like the latch when a door closes. Crystal shrieks as the ground swallows her whole.

* * *

"CRYSTAL!," Sally squeals.

We all rush to where Crystal was standing when she vanished. There's nothing to indicate what happened to her.

Sally gets down on her hands and knees and scratches at the ground. "CRYSTAL!," she screams again.

I plop down next to Sally and pound the ground with my left fist. "Wait," I say, "let's calm down. There's got to be some kind of trap door. We all heard the latch click, right? I start pushing dirt around with my left hand but I can't find anything unusual."

"The problem is that we don't know exactly where she was standing when she disappeared." Tom says.

"Yeah," I agree, "that would sure help. You did hear the click just before she disappeared, right?"

"Uh huh," Tom replies. "And I agree. There's got to be a trap door around here somewhere."

Sally's on the verge of tears. "But where?" she wails.

Tom points to the ground. "Look at those stones. Do they look right to you?"

Our digging around exposed four small rocks. They wouldn't be easily visible from a standing position.

"What about them?" Sally asks.

Tom kneels down next to the stones. "They all look exactly the same. And they form a perfect square." Tom reaches for them. "And look, they're stuck to the ground somehow – I can't move them."

I hear a muffled sound coming from below. "Hush!"

"What?" Tom whispers.

I listen but the sound is gone. "I'm sure I heard something."

"There!," Sally shouts. "I hear it too."

We all huddle down in complete silence with our ears to the earth.

"Hey up there! Hello! Can you hear me?" Crystal's muted voice is barely louder than a whisper.

Sally screams back at the ground, "Crystal! We hear you. Are you okay?"

"I'm okay – just a minute."

We're all thrilled to hear Crystal's voice, but waiting for her is agonizing. Two full minutes go by. Then we hear pounding from beneath us.

"I can't get this thing to budge!" Crystal says. Her voice is much louder than before. "I think you guys will need to come down here to help me. Just give me a sec. And, oh yeah. Don't forget the toolbox."

Crystal's last few words fade away. The next time she speaks, we can barely hear her again. "Okay, come on down!"

"She wants us to go down to her," Tom says. "But how do we do that?"

"There's only one way I can think of," Sally says.

Sally gets up and steps into the square formed by the four rocks. There's a worried look on her face. "Well, here goes. Watch and see if you can tell what happens this time."

It takes me a moment to figure out what Sally's got in mind. "Sally! Wait!"

But it's too late. We hear a click and she's gone. An echo of her squeal is all that remains of her.

The trap door opened just long enough for her to fall through, and immediately snapped closed. The entire action couldn't have taken more than a second or two.

Tom instantly drops to the ground and shouts. "Sally!" He puts his head to the ground.

"I'm here!" Sally's voice is louder than Crystal's was before. She knows how hard it is to hear Crystal from above so she must be calling louder. "You've got to see this. Get down here! But whatever you do, don't forget the toolbox."

Tom and I look at each other. I'm worried about my arm. How far down does this go? More importantly, how will I land at the bottom? "You go next Tom. I'm not sure about my arm."

"Okay. If it looks too dangerous for you, I'll yell up and let you know to wait here or get help."

Holding the toolbox in front of him with both hands, Tom steps into the square. It takes a full five seconds before we hear the click. Down he goes.

I listen for Tom's voice, my ear to the ground. "Tom!" I finally yell.

Tom's voice is faint too. "I hear you! You should be fine Steve. It's a slide. I'll be at the bottom to help you stop if you need me."

Here goes. I step into the square. I clutch my right arm in my left hand and wait. My last thought before I hear the click is a question. How are we going to get out of there?

* * *

I'm on by back sliding feet first in a circular path. It feels like a water slide, but there's no water. The circular motion is dizzying. A few seconds later, I'm at the bottom. Tom doesn't even have to help me. I come to rest gently at the bottom of the slide. How far down did I go?

Still on my back I see that the slide forms at least three circles up to the top. We're about twenty-five feet below the surface.

Tom helps me up from the slide.

What I see next takes my breath away. We're in an underground cavern! But it's not like any cavern I've ever seen, not even in picture books. Once when we were on vacation, Mom and Dad stopped at Carlsbad Caverns in New Mexico, so I think I know what caverns look like. But this! This is so much better!

Carlsbad Cavern felt cold and damp. It smelled like a moldy old basement. The air I breathe now is dry, fresh, and even warm. It smells like outside after a fresh rain.

The rock formations in Carlsbad Cavern were brown and gray with water dripping everywhere. Here, all I see are clear and white crystalline rocks. And some of the rock formations look like ice statues. There's no water dripping or condensing from any of them. These crystalline rocks actually shimmer.

It occurs to me that there's enough light to see. It's dim, but as my eyes get used to it, I can see pretty well. Where's the light coming from?

I look at my companions and see Crystal pointing at a clear rock near the end of the slide. On it there is a note. She reads it aloud.

*Hopefully you have the items from your first challenge with you. If you don't, you are going to be here for a very long time.*

I shoot a quick glance at Tom. Sure enough he is standing next to the toolbox. I breathe a sigh of relief.

Sally shivers while looking at the note. "I guess that's what Old Man Humphrey meant about this challenge being deadly if we're not prepared."

"Hopefully that's all he meant," Tom adds.

Crystal points up to the top of the slide. "Well, that's sure not an exit. Getting back up the slide was easy enough. But I couldn't get the trap door to budge. I think it can only be opened by stepping on it from above."

"And you have to stand in that square for at least five seconds," I add. "I guess that explains why nobody ever found it before."

Looking up, a terrible thought occurs to me. What if somebody did find it? If that person was alone, no one would ever know what happened to him. He'd be trapped down here forever. So somewhere in this cavern there could be a dead body. Maybe more than one.

I shake the thought from my head. Better not to think that way. I don't remember hearing any stories about missing people, so I won't mention it. No sense scaring the girls. I shiver and turn back to the cavern.

We walk along a path that leads away from the slide. It's a little rocky but amazingly smooth. There's no problem with the footing. I wonder if Old Man Humphrey put any effort into smoothing it. Soon we come to a slow flowing creek. The water is crystal clear and only a few inches deep. I look to our right and see that the creek disappears into a large hole in the rock. We must be at one end of the cavern.

The ceiling above us is about eight feet high. To our left, the ceiling opens into a huge room. Still, all the rocks are crystalline or white. The path follows the creek to our left but on the other side of the creek is a cavern wall.

We start walking along the path and into the large room. Crystalline rock is everywhere. I look up again. I'm surprised to see that several rocks in the ceiling are actually glowing like huge light bulbs. "Look up there," I say.

Sally's face is full of wonder as she looks up. "The ceiling rocks must be made of whatever these rocks are made of," she says, pointing to all the rock formations around us. "They must be translucent rocks of some kind. They sure are letting a lot of light in."

Tom is looking off to our left. "Look over there!"

The bank slopes upward and away from the creek. There are windows in the rock that expose several rooms. Through one of the windows I can see some wooden furniture.

"Do you guys see that!," I say.

"I think we've found Old Man Humphrey's home," Crystal states. "Though I wouldn't exactly call it a hovel. This place is amazing!"

There's no easy way to get through the rock formations between us and the rooms. The path must lead there somehow.

We continue walking upstream along the path. The rise is barely noticeable. The creek is slowly flowing toward us, so we must be going up hill.

"This place is huge," Tom says.

"I can see why Old Man Humphrey liked his solitude," Sally says. "It's wonderful here."

There's something sticking out of the creek just ahead. It's obviously man-made. A smaller path leads over to it. There's a short wooden bridge and water from the creek is flowing under it.

As we get closer, Crystal is the first to identify it. "Well would you look at that. It's a sink!"

Sure enough a pedestal stands upright out of the creek. A wash basin is on top of the pedestal. A spigot is mounted above the wash basin and a small lever is attached to its left side.

"Try it and see if it works," I say.

Tom pumps the lever a few times. Sure enough, water begins flowing from the spigot. "How cool is that? Anyone thirsty?"

I think of Old Man Humphrey's warnings. "We better not. Remember what Old Man Humphrey said in his note. The water could be bad. Or poisonous even."

Crystal gives me a sour look. It's obvious that she thinks the water is safe. But she doesn't say anything.

Eventually we come to a point where the path divides. One way leads up and to the left. It must go to the dwelling. The other follows the creek around a bend to the right.

Crystal points to the left path. "I bet that one leads to Old Man Humphrey's home."

Tom is at the crossroads, scratching his head. "Which way should we go?"

"Let's see where Old Man Humphrey lived," Crystal suggests.

I'm worried about how we're going to get out of here, but a little exploring sounds fun. "Okay. But let's make it quick. We still have to find a way out of here."

Crystal throws that sour look at me again. This time she doesn't hold her tongue. "Well aren't you the party-pooper."

* * *

We walk a short distance and come to a door-sized opening in the rock. It's the entrance to Old Man Humphrey's home. Crystal starts moving forward but Tom raises his right arm to stop her. "Let me go first. There could be a booby trap or something."

He pokes his head in, then walks forward. A second later he waves us in. We follow, and find ourselves in a small room. Some of the rock in the room has been carved away, so two of the walls are much smoother than the others. Old Man Humphrey must have carved away the rock for more living space; his wood furniture consumes more than half of the space. The room is about eight feet wide by ten feet long, but it feels smaller. There's another door-sized opening on the other side of the room. A large window provides an awesome view down the hill to the creek. Light fills the room from the ceiling.

The room is clean like someone cleaned it earlier today – no dust anywhere. The furniture is old like I've seen in antiques stores. Some of the chairs look home-made while other furniture appears store-bought. It's all very old but there's no odor of decay or rot. This gives the room an eerie feel.

It's easy to tell that this was Old Man Humphrey's kitchen. A table with two chairs is placed along the far wall. Upper and lower cabinets line one of the side walls. There's a counter on top of the lower cabinets.

Along the near wall is a wood-burning stove. A round chimney runs out the stove, up the wall, and disappears through a hole in the ceiling. I wonder where it goes. Next to the stove is a large wooden crate. A door is mounted to its front.

A cup and saucer is on the table. They give the room a lived-in feel. I point them out. "It feels like he's just been here, or that he could come back at any minute."

Sally hugs herself.

We make our way to the next room. It's much larger, at least fifteen feet wide by twenty feet long. For some reason, it's also much brighter. The translucent ceiling rock in this room must be thinner or clearer, or both.

Another doorway is at the far side of the room. And another window that looks out to the creek is in the wall to our left. Bookcases stuffed with books line the three other walls. Two easy chairs are in the middle of the room. Between them is a small round table. Against the wall with the window is a desk and chair. A person sitting at the desk would have a nice view out the window and down to the creek.

We move through the next doorway into Old Man Humphrey's bedroom. It is much dimmer. And smaller. It's about the same size as the kitchen but the ceiling is lower. A bed and nightstand are pushed into the far corner. There is a dresser against the wall on the doorway side of the room.

Thinking we've reached the end of the dwelling, we're about to turn back. But something above the bed catches my eye. It appears to be a window. At least it is framed like a window. But instead of glass within the frames, there are two wooden shutters. How strange.

I walk over and carefully poke open one of the shutters with my left hand. Like Tom, I'm worried about booby traps but when nothing bad happens, I poke my head in. There's another room back there. But unlike the other rooms in Old Man Humphrey's dwelling, it's pitch black. "Sally, does your iPhone have a flashlight app?"

"Sure does." She pulls it out of her pocket and selects the app. She turns on the flashlight and hands me the iPhone.

I awkwardly shine light into the room with my right hand while holding one of the shutter doors open with my left. My right arm hurts a bit at the effort, but it's good to be using it again. The room behind the window is small, and the ceiling is much lower. It's about five feet high. And the room itself is about six feet square. It's empty.

"I wonder what this room was used for," I say.

Upon hearing that the room is empty, no one seems very interested. I turn off the light and close the doors.

Sally takes a step toward the door. "There's a lot here to investigate. I'd like to take a look in that desk or at the books in the library. They may give a clue as to what kind of person he was."

Tom grunts. "I think we already know that. Angry and bitter."

"I'm not so sure," Crystal says. "I think he just wanted to be left alone."

I point at the toolbox in Tom's right hand. "I think it's time we get back to the task at hand. We've got a clue to find. Then we've got to find a way out of here."

\* \* \*

Though everyone wants to spend more time exploring, we decide to look for the clue and exit first. We make our way out of the rooms and back down the path that runs along the creek. We then turn left and continue along the bend in the creek. Here the cavern opens up to an even bigger room. It's about thirty feet wide and forty feet long. The ceiling is at least twenty-five feet high.

There's an odd looking platform in the middle of the room. It's made of wood. It looks sort of like a stage. A wooden cabinet resembling an electrical box is mounted on one side. Two ropes run from the cabinet to the ceiling. One more rope runs back from the ceiling to the middle of the platform and hangs down to roughly four feet of the floor where a ring is attached.

In the middle of the platform is a toolbox. It's identical to the one Tom is carrying.

"Do you think that's the clue for the second challenge?" Crystal asks as she points at the toolbox.

We hurry over to investigate. On top of the toolbox, there's a note like the one on the rock at the end of the slide. *Do not open until you have defeated the second challenge.* "

Tom picks it up. "Yup. I think this is it. Well, that part was pretty easy.

* * *

Sally points at the ropes going up to the ceiling. "I think that's the way out of here."

I study the two ropes that go into the cabinet. They hang from a pulley mounted to the ceiling. I see a ledge up there.

Crystal looks worried as she points at the rope hanging down to just above the floor. "Are we supposed to climb that rope up to the top?"

Sally shakes her head. "I don't think so. Remember. Old Man Humphrey used this exit until he was pretty old. I don't think someone his age could climb a rope to that height every day."

Sally's right, I think. He was at least fifty-seven when he stopped coming down here.

Tom opens the first toolbox and pulls out the belt and hook. "I think this hooks on right here." He clips the hook onto the belt loop. Then he grabs the hanging rope by the ring. He clips the other end of the hook to the ring.

Crystal is still looking worried. "Now what? Are we supposed to ride up in that belt?"

Tom puts the belt on. He reaches over and grabs one of the two other ropes coming down from the ceiling. He pulls each one in turn. Nothing happens.

Sally's reaching back into the toolbox. "Wait up, Tom. There's one more item. She takes out the block and tackle set. "This must go somewhere too."

She opens the cabinet door to reveal a contraption filled with mechanical gears. Sure enough, something appears to be missing. Sally places the block and tackle set into the empty space. It's held in place by a latch and she snaps it in. Then she threads the two ropes coming from the ceiling through the pulleys in the block and tackle set.

Sally looks back to Tom. "Now try it."

Tom pulls on one of the ropes but nothing happens. Then he tries the other rope. As he pulls, his feet lift off the ground. He pulls again and he moves up higher.

He pulls a few more times. "Wow! This is cool!"

Before anyone can say a word, he's at least ten feet up. "This is easy! I don't have to pull hard at all."

Sally points to the upper landing. "Go up and see what's there."

Crystal shivers and hugs herself. "But be careful."

Tom goes the rest of the way up. He steps onto a ledge at the top. The rope attached to his belt gives him enough slack so that he can remove the belt. As he steps away from the rope, he releases the belt. Surprisingly, the belt starts descending on its own. Startled, he quickly grabs the rope. When he pulls it again, the belt rises. And when he lets go, the belt descends.

"This is so cool!" he says.

"What is up there?" Sally asks.

Tom moves away from the rope and out of our site for a few seconds. Eventually we see him back at the ledge. "The exit is up here all right. It leads out to Bandit Woods. What do you want to do? Should I come back down or are we leaving now?"

Sally pulls out the iPhone. "It's only three-thirty. I think we have time for a little more exploring if you guys are up for it."

I feel much better exploring now that we have a way out. "Come back down Tom. Lets' look around some more."

Tom doesn't have to be asked twice. He puts the belt back on. Thirty seconds later he is back on the wooden platform with the rest of us.

"It sure is a good thing we brought the toolbox with us," Sally says. "We wouldn't be able to get out of here without it."

I nod. Crystal shivers again. I remember what I was thinking at the slide. At least we didn't find a dead body.

* * *

We look around the exit room some more. But we don't find much more of interest. The creek begins flowing into the cavern from this room. It oozes through a small hole the size of a silver dollar at the wall facing the entrance to the room. The water creates a nice little fountain, spurting out and down into the creek on the floor of the cavern. Other than that, there's nothing more worth exploring.

Crystal points toward the paths. "I want to get back to the library. Maybe Old Man Humphrey left us more clues without even knowing it."

We all agree. We take the path along the creek and then the one up to the dwelling. As we near the entry this time, I'm struck by the feeling that this could be the entrance to just about any home. I almost expect to see a welcome mat in front of the doorway and a mailbox out in front.

In the kitchen, Sally starts opening cabinets. She doesn't appear to be looking for anything in particular. She's just exploring. We all file in behind her to see what's in each cabinet. The first cabinet is filled with boxes of food. Sally pulls out a few boxes. Sugar Pops, Shredded Wheat, and Minute Rice. I'm surprised. We can still get all of these foods today.

The next cabinet contains canned goods. Several cans of Campbell's soup are immediately visible. Again, they're just like the soups found in the grocery store in town. But the labels are totally different from any I've seen before. Sally does some rearranging to expose five cans of Spam and a few cans of Stokely's sugar peas.

I walk over to the wooden crate next to the stove. I open its door to reveal several brown paper covered items. They look like butcher's meats and have a fowl odor. I quickly close the door. "This must have been his refrigerator."

"Ice box," Sally corrects. "Back then refrigeration was just getting off the ground. And it required electricity then just like it does today. Before refrigeration, people used an insulated box like this one. They put a large block of ice in it to keep things cool."

Sally opens another cabinet door. This cabinet is filled with candles and matches. It hadn't occurred to me, but this cavern must get pretty dark at night. I scan the room. Three candle-stick holders are in plain view. Two of them are mounted on the walls and there's one on the table.

Another cabinet contains pots and pans. In another are eating utensils. And there's another one holding knives. The last cabinet is filled with dishes, cups, glasses, and bowls.

Tom frowns. "Well, we sure didn't learn anything about Old Man Humphrey from this."

Sally shakes her head. "On the contrary. We now know he went to town regularly to get supplies. And he bought foods that just about everyone else was eating back then. Lots of pre-packaged stuff. And he prepared his own meals."

With the kitchen explored, we make our way to the library.

"I think this is where he spent most of his time," Sally says. "Look how worn out those chairs are."

Crystal looks puzzled. "If he lived alone, why would he need two chairs?"

"Maybe he just wanted some variety," Tom suggests. "I don't always sit in the same chair at home."

Crystal doesn't look satisfied, but remains quiet.

We turn our attention to the desk. The top center drawer contains paper and writing utensils. I instantly recognize the paper. It's the same as Old Man Humphrey used for his notes. He was probably sitting right at this desk when he wrote them. The thought sends a chill up my spine.

There is more paper and some envelopes in the top right drawer. The top left drawer contains tape, string, glue, a magnifying glass, and some other work-related items. In the lower right drawer we see a stack of letters. The lower left drawer is filled with a neatly organized set of files.

The letter drawer seems the logical choice for learning more about Old Man Humphrey. Sally pulls out the stack of letters and places them on the desk. They are tied together with a string, which Sally carefully unties and removes. She thumbs through them and then points at the top letter. "Look at that. These letters are all addressed to *Jeremy* Humphrey. He's 'Old Man Humphrey' to us. And all of them were sent to a box at the Clear Valley Post Office."

Crystal nods. "That makes sense. He sure couldn't have them delivered here."

"And look at the stamp," Tom says. "Postage was only two cents back then."

I look at the postmark. April twenty-ninth, nineteen-ten. "Wow. These letters are really old."

We can tell from the handwriting that all of the letters came from one person. And that person was a woman. The letters are in order, starting from the oldest. Sally picks out the first one and starts reading aloud.

It's a letter of introduction from a woman named Annabelle. Her return address is in Seattle, Washington. Most of her sentences are short and to-the-point. The letter itself is pretty short.

We don't have the letter that Old Man Humphrey wrote back to her, but he must have responded. Her next letter is much warmer. And she's explaining more personal stuff about herself.

Her third letter contained her photograph. She refers to it in the letter, but it's missing.

Her warmth continues to grow. By the tenth letter, Annabelle is speaking like a woman in love.

It's obvious that Old Man Humphrey is responding in the same manner. He must have been falling in love too. It's hard to think of him as a young man. We've always referred to him as *Old* Man Humphrey. But Old Man Humphrey was once Jeremy Humphrey. And he was once twenty-one. And in love. Jeremy was in love with Annabelle.

Crystal interrupts Sally mid-sentence. "It's amazing to think that they never met, yet they fell in love."

"And it sure was a long distance love affair," Tom adds. "Seattle to Clear Valley."

Sally smiles. She's been reading ahead. "It doesn't stay long distance much longer."

We all look where Sally is pointing and read the next sentence to ourselves.

*I Annabelle Alton, on this third day of May in the year of Our Lord Nineteen-hundred-eleven do accept your proposal of marriage, Jeremy Humphrey, and commit to become your wife.*

A moment passes before it occurs to me. Annabelle has the same last name as Sally. "Sally. Did you notice Annabelle's last name?"

Sally hesitates before she answers. "Yes. It's the same as mine." She's still looking down at the letter.

We wait for an explanation, but it doesn't come.

"Are you related?" Tom asks.

"Yes," Sally reluctantly answers. "Annabelle Alton is my great, great, great, grandmother."

Our mouths all drop at the same time. What? Sally is related to Annabelle?

"And yes," Sally continues. "That means Old Man Humphrey is my great, great, great grandfather."

* * *

We sit in silence for a few seconds, considering the implications of what Sally has just admitted. I immediately think of our conversations about Sally's father. This makes him Old Man Humphrey's great, great, grandson. "Is that why you and your dad went for so many walks in Bandit Woods?"

Sally shrugs. "I guess so. When we started going for those walks I was only five or six. I was way too young to understand about Old Man Humphrey. Or the Hillbrook stash. But as I grew older, I could tell that Dad was acting pretty strange. He would stop for no reason and stare off into space. Or, he'd put his ear to just about anything. A rock. A tree. You name it. He even stuck his head in a creek once. God only knows what he was listening for. He'd even climb high up into a tree and just look around.

"This one time, we spent the whole afternoon on our hands and knees combing a small area. He said he was looking for acorns and that I should help. Of course I didn't find any acorns. Acorns don't grow on pine trees. But I didn't know that until I got older."

Sally pauses at the memory. "Now I think he knew about this cavern and he was trying to find it. Anyway, once I was old enough I started asking questions. He didn't want to answer at first so I threatened not to go for walks with him anymore unless he explained.

"Eventually Dad told me the story about Old Man Humphrey. Actually, he told two stories. First he told me the one everyone knows. You know, about how Old Man Humphrey was supposed to have helped Jeffrey Hillbrook. And how everyone pestered him to tell where the stash was hidden. Everyone knows that story.

"Later, Dad told me another story. Our family story. He said Old Man Humphrey is my great, great, great grandfather. That in itself was enough to make me cry. Imagine finding out that you're related to someone so infamous.

"Then Dad told me about my great, great, great grandmother. Annabelle. She had seen an article in the Seattle newspaper about long distance love affairs. It explained how people could exchange letters to get to know one another."

"Kind of like an early version of an Internet dating service," Crystal chimes in.

Sally smiles, but it's a sad smile. "The newspaper provided an address where people could write to learn more about the process. And that's just what Grandma Annabelle did. She submitted her name and address. That's when she started corresponding with Grandpa Jeremy.

"No one but Gramma Annabelle ever saw his letters. She must have destroyed them. She said that Grandpa Jeremy was untruthful in his letters. And that was the reason why she left him just a few weeks after their wedding.

"Dad taught me the family blood line and made sure I memorized it. Old Man Humphrey – Jeremy, married Annabelle Alton. Annabelle left him and took her maiden name back. She became Annabelle Alton again. No one is sure if she knew she was pregnant when they split up, but  when her son was born, she gave him her last name. She named him Edmond Alton.

"When he grew up, Edmond married Theresa Simmons. They had a son named Terrence. Terrence Alton. When Terrence grew up, he married Susan Stevens. They had a son named Timothy. And Timothy married Jennifer Jennings when he grew up. Their only son is my dad. James Alton. Though everyone calls him Jim.

"And now, here I am. A direct descendant of Old Man Humphrey. Fortunately, people in town seem to forget the Alton family connection to Old Man Humphrey. So no one ever bugs me about being related to him."

Sally looks up for the first time since she started her story. She gives us a serious look. "I expect it to remain that way."

We all nod.

Sally looks tired. Tired and sad. And there's something else in her eyes that I can't quite put my finger on.

"It's getting late. I think we should be getting back," she says.

No one disagrees.

I take Sally's hand as we walk out of the dwelling and make our way back to the exit room. She gives my hand a gentle squeeze.

\*\*\*

Once we're on the lower platform, Tom puts on the belt and attaches the hook. He grabs one of the tool boxes and pulls himself up to the upper platform. "Come on up. Just don't forget the other toolbox."

He takes off the belt and latches it back on to the hook. When he releases them, they descend on their own.

Tom wants me to go next because he's worried about my arm. But when I look at Crystal, I see a look of sheer terror in her eyes. "What's wrong Crystal?"

"I don't like heights. Not since I fell out of a tree when I was eight."

I find myself wondering if she was trying to rescue a cat when she fell. I quickly shake it off. "It'll be all right. Sally and I will be here below and Tom will be above you. We'll make sure the belt is extra tight so there's no way it can slip. And Tom will pull you up from above. All you have to do is hang on."

Sally isn't waiting for a response. She's is in no mood to comfort Crystal. Or anyone for that matter. While I have been talking, she's removed the belt from the hook and has wrapped it around Crystal's waist. She tightens it. Really tight. Then she nudges Crystal closer to the hook and latches her in. She's done all this without saying a word.

Crystal has a deer-in-the-headlights expression as she grabs hold of the rope with both hands. Her knuckles instantly turn white. She whimpers as Tom starts pulling her up.

"Close your eyes if you're afraid," I say, watching her as she goes up. "Tom will unhook you when you get up there."

Crystal sobs for the whole ride. At the top, Tom pulls her to the ledge and unhooks her. When she's safely on her feet, she immediately hugs him as if her life depends on it.

Eventually she releases her embrace. She moves away from the ledge and out of sight. Tom sends the belt back down. Again he says I should go next because of my arm. As soon as I'm latched in, Tom starts pulling and I start to rise. Like Crystal, all I need to do is hang on.

Last comes Sally. She has the other toolbox in one hand as Tom pulls her up. Finally all four of us and the two toolboxes are on the upper platform.

Tom leads the way along a short path and through a little cave. The cave opens up at another rock face. I wonder if this is part of the same rock face where we found the first toolbox. We're standing on a ledge that is about fifteen feet above the ground. There is a pipe driven into the rock floor about two feet from the edge. It sticks up about six inches.

Tom gets the rope out of the first toolbox. One end already has a loop, which he slips over the pipe. "This is our way down."

I worry that my arm won't support my trip to the ground.

As usual Tom goes first. He drops both tool boxes to the ground. The knots tied in the rope transform it into an escape ladder. Tom descends to the ground without effort.

They want me to go next. I'm no expert like Tom, but I find that if I'm careful, I really don't need my right arm. Slowly but surely, I make my way down.

"Great job Steve!" Tom pats me on the back when I step away from the rope.

Crystal and Sally descend and soon the four of us are all safe on the ground.

I look up at the ledge and I see where the rope disappears. But from our position on the ground, I can't see the cave. I walk away from the rock face and I still can't see it. Old Man Humphrey had a well hidden exit from his home.

Tom tosses the rope up onto the ledge to hide it. It takes him three tries, but eventually he gets the rope to stay up there and out of sight.

* * *

We're not sure where we are in Bandit Woods, so Sally checks her iPhone to get our bearings. From what we can tell from her geocaching app, this rock face is an extension of the one with the cave. We begin our walk home.

Tom takes the lead but quickly looks back. "When do you guys want to open the second toolbox?" He's carrying both of them.

Sally looks at her iPhone. "It's four-thirty. By the time we get home it'll be after five. Crystal and I have homework so we can't get together again tonight. How about tomorrow after school?"

Tom nods. "Sounds like a plan. Four o'clock at the pillar?"

"Okay," Sally quietly agrees.

Tom doesn't seem nearly as anxious to open the second toolbox or read the note it's sure to contain. He seems content to wait until tomorrow at City Park with the girls.

We walk for about ten minutes when Sally stops. Crystal is walking with her so she stops too. But Tom and I are in the lead so we don't even notice.

"Hey guys," Crystal calls out. "Wait up a minute."

Tom and I turn back to see Crystal giving Sally a worried look. Sally is staring at the ground.

"I've been thinking," Sally says. "I want to ask you guys something but I'm afraid of what your answer will be."

We all just stare at her so she continues. "I told you about my dad. He's been searching these woods for as long as I can remember. The more I think about it, the more convinced I am that he's been looking for Grandpa Jeremy's home. I'm sure he'd do anything to see what we found today." Tears are forming in Sally's eyes.

"When you guys first asked me to help with my iPhone," she continues, "I knew you were on the trail of the Hillbrook stash, but I thought we were going off on a wild goose chase like so many others before us. It sounded like fun so I agreed. I never in a million years thought we'd actually be on the right track.

"Then, when we defeated the first challenge, I started thinking about Daddy. And today in the dwelling, I felt really guilty. It will just kill him when he finds out that I've been on the hunt for the Hillbrook stash without him."

Sally pauses as she looks from Tom to me. "I want to tell Daddy what we're up to and ask him to join us. But I won't do it if you don't want me to. *But,* if I can't tell him, then I really can't be in on this any more either."

Tom puts on an outraged expression. He's about to say something but Sally stops him with a wave of her hand. "Don't answer right now, just think about it okay?"

Tom nods with me, but I can tell he is itching to say something.

We walk the rest of the way home in silence. Somewhere along the way, Sally takes my hand.

* * *

When we're in front of Sally's house, Tom and I wait for the girls to go in. After they hop up the steps Crystal turns around to face us. "Now listen here you two." She shakes her finger at Tom. "Don't you open that toolbox until we're together."

Tom smiles and nods. "Don't worry, we won't."

Once the door is closed, Tom and I turn and head toward home.

"What do you think of telling Sally's dad?" I ask. "She really wants him in on this."

"I don't know. But I don't like it. Parents have a way of ruining everything."

I shake my head. "But Sally and her dad are really close. Maybe he'd be able to help us. We didn't want the girls to help us at first but look how far we've come in just two days. We've defeated two of the challenges. Without them, we'd probably still be working on the first one. Maybe having an adult's help will make things even easier."

Tom doesn't look convinced. "I'm tired. Let's talk about it later."

We get home at five thirty. Mom's in the kitchen pouring herself a glass of wine. I don't smell dinner. "It's about time you boys got home. I was starting to worry."

"We've been out playing," Tom says as we sit down in the family room.

Mom walks into the family room. "I was about to order a pizza. How's that sound?"

"That sounds great!" Tom says. "I'm starved."

She looks at the two toolboxes on the floor next to Tom's chair. "What are those?"

I can't believe Tom left the toolboxes out in plain sight. He must really be tired.

"Uh, just some stuff we found," Tom replies. He's telling the truth, but he sounds a bit too casual.

Mom wrinkles her nose. "Well they look dirty. So get them off the carpet. Now!" She looks from Tom to me. "And look at your clothes! They're filthy. Get off the furniture!"

We are pretty dirty from the day's adventure.

Mom angrily shakes her head and goes back to the kitchen to order the pizza.

I follow Tom to his room and he puts the toolboxes into the closet.

The pizza comes a half hour later and we eat in front of the television.

After dinner I join Tom back in his room. He's on his bed staring at the second toolbox. I sit in his desk chair.

"You're driving yourself crazy with all of this, Tom. Look at you. You can't think of anything but the Hillbrook stash."

"You're one to talk. You're as excited about all of this as I am."

I have to admit he's right. "Wouldn't it be cool if we find it? We'd be famous."

Tom gives me a serious look. "What I think would be cool is being able to bring Dad home."

Tom starts fiddling with the latch for the toolbox. I notice for the first time that this toolbox doesn't have a padlock.

Tom's mind is elsewhere. He's not thinking about the Hillbrook stash after all. "I think we should ask Sally's dad to join us," he eventually says. "I just hope you're right about how close he is to Sally."

"Oh, they're close all right. She used to talk about him all the time. And Tom, he's not like Dad."

Tom expression reddens and he nearly shouts, "What's that supposed to mean?"

Tom's hot response surprises me. "I just meant he'll stick by us. Not like Dad. I mean Dad abandoned us and moved to Texas."

"He didn't abandon us!" Tears are forming in his eyes. "He had to find work."

"Okay, okay. I didn't mean anything."

We sit in silence. Now I'm the one who's thinking about Dad. I miss him. I can't understand why he had to move away. Sure, he had to find work. I understand that. But he never talks about coming home. And he's only been back to see us once – for two days. Mainly for a funeral. One of his high school friends was killed by a drunk driver. It's not like he came back to see us. Now I feel tears forming in *my* eyes.

Tom shakes me out of my sad thoughts. His voice is calm again. "What I started to say is it came as a real surprise that Sally and her dad are related to Old Man Humphrey. That changes everything. Maybe Mr. Alton knows some things about Old Man Humphrey that no one else knows."

I see where Tom is going with this. Mr. Alton's father may have passed something down to him that he hasn't passed along to Sally. Yet.

"One thing's for sure," Tom continues. "He's got to know more about Old Man Humphrey than either of us. Or anyone for that matter."

I nod in agreement. "He may even know more than Sally thinks he knows. Remember that walk she told us about? The one where he was on his hands and knees when he told her to look for acorns? Then later Sally said she thought he must have been looking for Old Man Humphrey's underground home. How could he know it was underground? That's not in any of the stories I've ever heard."

"Yeah," Tom agrees. "And he made her memorize their family tree like his dad must have done with him. It makes you wonder what else got passed down, generation to generation.

It's decided. We want Mr. Alton to join us.

Monday

School now seems strange to me. So much has happened in the last four days. I'm finding it hard to get back into the swing of things. I'm looking forward to opening the toolbox this afternoon, but even that seems strange. I'm in a fog as I walk to my first class.

I'm lost in thought so I don't see Larry Hinkle coming. I look up just in time to see the sneer on his face. He roughly bumps the right side of my body. The blow nearly knocks me down.

"'Scuse me," he says without stopping.

My arm hasn't hurt this bad in two days. A sharp pain rushes down my right arm. It quickly subsides. I turn to see Larry disappear around a corner.

When I turn back to continue walking to class, I see Perry Hinkle standing at his locker. He's looking right at me, but I can't judge his expression. Is he smiling?

I guess a gun fired in their direction isn't enough to scare off the Hinkle brothers.

The first subject of the morning is math. I come in late and Sally is already in the classroom. She's in a blue dress and her hair is up in a pony tail. She's sitting off to my right and a few rows ahead of me. She glances back at me and smiles as I take my seat. I can't wait to tell her about our decision.

The morning drags on. During recess Sally is with her new friends. I catch her eye a few times. But I can't seem to make it clear that I want to talk to her *alone*. When she waves me over I actually look behind me to see if she's motioning to someone else.

"Hey Steve," she starts. "These are my friends. Lisa, Laura, and Ashley." She points at each of them in turn. I know them all, of course, but I can't remember ever talking to them.

"Hi," I nervously say.

"We heard about your arm," Laura says. "Does it hurt?"

"It didn't until this morning when someone bumped into me," I respond. I don't name my attacker.

Ashley looks at my cast and wrinkles her nose. It's gotten pretty dirty from our activity over the weekend. And I haven't thought to wash it. I do my best to hide the dirtiest spot with my left hand.

"Those Hinkle brothers should be expelled," Lisa says.

"They weren't on school property when they started the fight," Ashley comments, "so there's nothing the school can do."

Then Ashley moves in closer to me and whispers, "Did Tom really shoot a gun at them?"

I'm not surprised that Ashley knows about the shooting. We live in a small town. Everyone in school probably knows the whole story.

I shrug. "I was unconscious."

"I'd have given anything to see the Hinkle brothers running away," Lisa says. Then she chuckles. "I bet they wet their pants!"

The bell rings and we begin walking back into school. I nudge Sally and she stops.

"Tom and I decided."

She looks at me expectantly.

"We want your dad to join us."

Sally's face lights up. "Great!" I think for a moment that she's going to hug me, or kiss me on the cheek or something. But the moment passes. "Today's his day off. Would you mind if he joins us at City Park today?"

I'm surprised by her question. She's obviously been planning for a positive response. "I don't see why not."

We start moving toward the school again. Once inside, we go our separate ways. I have gym. She has geography.

At lunch I tell Tom that I talked with Sally.

Tom swallows a bite of food. "Crystal said she'd probably want her dad to come today."

"You told Crystal?" Talking to Crystal hasn't occurred to me.

"Sure. Why not?"

I just shrug. Tom is closer to Crystal than I thought.

* * *

I get to City Park before anyone else and sit alone at "our" picnic table. It's a quarter to four. I came straight from school but Tom ran home to get the second toolbox. I'm hoping he'll bring the other stuff we've found to show Mr. Alton.

Tom returns out of breath a few minutes later. "The Hinkle brothers were waiting for me just outside the school grounds. I saw them first and went another way. They're probably still waiting there. The jerks."

I rub my cast. "I wasn't so alert this morning." I tell Tom about Larry Hinkle bumping into me.

"We've got to do something about them."

"Yeah. Like there's anything we can do. How about getting them transferred to another school?"

"No I'm serious," Tom persists. "We're smart. We ought be able to come up with something that'll get them off our backs."

I wonder what Tom has in mind. Whatever it is, it'll have to wait. Sally and Crystal are entering City Park. Like us, they're still wearing school clothes. But they look a lot nicer than we do. Crystal is in a green top and jeans. Sally is still wearing her blue dress. Tom and I are both in tee shirts and blue jeans. At least our clothes are clean. Well, they were this morning.

It's just a couple of minutes to four when they join us at the picnic table.

Sally gently taps my arm. "Thanks again for letting my dad in on this. He's going to freak out."

I can't hide my surprise. "You didn't tell him?"

Sally shakes her head. "Nope. This is your picnic. I thought you guys should tell him. I told him to meet us here at four o'clock and he'd be in for a big surprise."

Mr. Alton runs the grocery store in town. This one time he caught Tom trying to steal a package of Reese's Peanut Butter Cups. Tom was only eight at the time and I had just turned seven. I still remember that angry look in Mr. Alton's eyes when he lectured Tom. He let Tom go, but he said he'd call the police if he ever caught Tom stealing again. I believed him. So did Tom. I don't think Tom has stolen another thing since. Unless you count the cigar box, of course. I shiver at the memory. I wonder if Mr. Alton remembers it too. I hope not.

Tom is pacing around the picnic table. "When will he be here?"

It is now one minute after four.

Any minute," Sally answers. Please be patient. He's never very late."

Sure enough, we see a tall, thin man walking through the entry gate to City Park. As he approaches, I can't help but notice family resemblances. He has Sally's nose and his face is thin like Sally's. His brown hair matches hers in every way but length. He's wearing light brown work pants and a blue short sleeve shirt that has a name tag just above the left pocket.

He looks surprised to see the four of us and takes a seat next to Sally. He eyeballs the toolbox in the center of the table. "What's this all about?"

"Well Daddy," Sally starts as she points to Tom and me. "This is Steve Jones and this is his brother Tom. I think you know them. You've probably seen me hanging out with Steve. Steve is in my class and Tom is a year ahead of me like Crystal. I'm pretty sure you know their mom and dad too. Well, his dad moved to Texas last year."

Sally must be nervous because she's rambling on. Finally she gets to the point. "They have something they want to tell you. You should find it very interesting."

Mr. Alton volley's looks from Tom to me and then back to Tom. Neither of us says a word. Tom kicks me under the table. I guess he wants me to do the talking.

I clear my throat, trying to think of how to start. "Well Mr. Alton… You see, ah… Tom and I have, ah… Well, the thing is…"

"Just tell him!" Tom commands.

"Tom found a map from Old Man Humphrey."

Mr. Alton's reaction is the same as Sally's when we told her. He laughs, but his laugh is much more bitter. "Right. You and just about every other poor sucker in this town."

He stands, ready to leave. He turns back and looks down at Sally, anger building in his eyes. "This is why you brought me here?"

Sally meets her dad's angry gaze. "I think you should sit down and listen, Dad. We found Grandpa Jeremy's underground home."

That stops Mr. Alton cold. He slumps down on the picnic table bench. His eyes gloss over and I'm worried that he's about to pass out.

Sally sees it too. She pulls on his left arm. "Daddy! Are you all right?"

Mr. Alton's eyes refocus. He clears his throat, "Yes, I'm fine." His voice is almost a whisper.

The anger in his eyes transforms to amazement. He draws Sally close. They're almost nose to nose. "Is it true, Sweetheart? This isn't a joke, is it? You… You found the cavern?" He sounds like a little boy.

"*We* found the cavern Daddy." Sally motions to all of us. "We did it together. And there's more. We're on the trail of the Hillbrook stash – it's real."

\* \* \*

It takes us a half hour to explain it all. Sally does most of the talking. I'm glad because it sounds a lot better coming from her. Tom brings out the cigar box and the first note, which Mr. Alton reads twice.

Tom explains how he found the cigar box in the library. And how Officer Grant took the gun away.

Sally explains how we've been using her iPhone and setting up Geocaches to navigate the maps into Bandit Woods. She describes Saturday's adventure at the rock face and how we defeated the first challenge. She tells her dad about getting the first toolbox out of the cave.

Tom brings out the second note which Mr. Alton also reads twice. Sally then explains how Crystal found the trap door and entered Grandpa Jeremy's underground home. Mr. Alton is quite interested in the letters from Annabelle. Sally describes how we explored the cavern and defeated the second challenge. Finally, she says we're about to open the second toolbox.

When Sally finishes, Mr. Alton sits in silence absorbing our news.

Tom tugs on Mr. Alton's arm with one hand and points at the second toolbox with his other. "Can we open this now?"

I think Mr. Alton is still considering all he's heard, but gives a weak nod. I'm not even sure he heard Tom's question.

Sally, obviously concerned about her dad, shakes her head. "No. Wait Tom. Give Daddy a chance to digest all of this first."

"This feels like a dream," Mr. Alton finally says. "Everybody knew about the log cabin where Jeremy was supposed to have lived. But in our family, we've always believed he had a second home. An underground home. I've searched for it all my life just like my father did before me, and his father before him."

He studies Sally with pride in his eyes. "And now my little girl has found it in just two days."

119

His eyes swell on the verge of tears again, but they're happy tears. He hugs Sally.

Sally hugs him back and holds the embrace. "I keep telling you Daddy. I didn't find it by myself. I wouldn't have known about any of this if Steve hadn't asked for my iPhone. Thank goodness Mom didn't have it."

Mr. Alton smiles at all of us. "Well then I guess I better tell your mother not to take it away from you again. No matter what you do wrong."

"That would be just so awesome!" Crystal says.

We have a good laugh. Crystal snorts.

* * *

Tom points at the clock on top of the pillar and it's four-forty-eight. "It's getting late. We have to get home for dinner soon. Can we open the second toolbox now?"

Now that Sally's dad is all-in, I'm excited to see what's in the toolbox too. "So open it!"

Sally doesn't stop him this time.

Tom immediately opens the toolbox. This time the oil cloth containing Old Man Humphrey's note is in the top tray. Tom removes it and places it unopened on the picnic table. Then he pulls out the top tray to expose what's below.

It's empty.

"What's this?" Tom asks.

My first thought is that somebody found the toolbox before us! But that can't be right. They'd have taken the note too.

"I guess we won't be needing anything special to defeat the third challenge," Crystal says, though she sounds unsure of herself.

Tom puts the tray back in the toolbox and closes it. "I thought it felt too light. It was the same weight as the other toolbox after we emptied it. But I sure didn't think it would be empty."

Sally picks up the note and removes the oil cloth wrapping. "Well, not quite empty." A paper envelope is within. And inside the envelope is the note.

This time it is Sally's turn to read the note aloud.

*Now that you have been in my residence, you probably imagine that you comprehend me. I would caution you not to be overly confident in this regard. Not until you complete your next challenge. Then you will know me. Absolutely and without reserve, you will know me. I only hope you will remain alive long enough to reflect upon your new acquaintance.*

*I must assume that you have been clever. I must believe you brought the contents of your first challenge into my domicile. In this case you are no doubt reading this correspondence while in the comfort of some other abode. But if this be not the case and you still reside in my home, I fear you will be there for as long as you draw breath, for there is only one exit. So reading further will be pointless.*

*Before his death, Jeffrey Hillbrook and I spent three days together in the wondrous place you have visited. I regret for his sake to say that he grew to know me as you soon will. It will be his revelation that you will use to discover my reason for desiring solitude.*

*You have been in my library. You have looked in my desk and may have perused a few books. But alas, you only begun your quest to discover my true nature. It is in this repository that you will begin your next challenge. Defeating this challenge will require your cunning, not your brawn.*

At this point I interrupt. "I don't understand. What does he mean by this challenge requiring our cunning and not our brawn?"

Sally looks at her dad, but he seems lost in thought so she answers. "It means we'll have to think more than work. Cunning implies using your brain – brawn means using your muscles."

Tom nods his understanding with me so Sally continues with the note.

*Twelve volumes there must ye seek. Depending upon your literary expertise, you may easily recon some of their titles. Others will surely trouble you. But only when you have all twelve books in your possession will you have the means to solve my puzzle. These volumes will show you the way. The order is quite important.*

*\* The best tale of revenge ever conceived*

*\* One for all and all for one*

*\* Nineteen years a prisoner*

*\* Invaders from another planet*

*\* A bleak future indeed*

*\* In the end it is Eloi versus Morlocks*

*\* Underwater adventure with a mad captain*

*\* Hideous creatures combining man and beast*

*\* Some animals are created more equal than others*

*\* An African tale of adventure*

*\* A search for diamonds*

*\* Life from death*

*With these volumes in your possession, use the moon of 1949 to guide you.*

This time it's Crystal who asks Sally to read the note again, which she does. We all sit quietly thinking.

During the silence, Sally pulls out her iPhone and takes a picture of the note.

Tom is the first to speak. "This is getting scary. It sounds like Old Man Humphrey had some pretty nasty secrets. I'm not sure I want to 'discover his true nature'."

Sally lays the note on the picnic table. "At first I thought he was just lonely and sad, but now I'm not so sure. Maybe he really was an angry and bitter old man."

Crystal shrugs, "And dangerous. He sure wants us to uncover his secrets though.

"Yeah," Tom agrees. "Explaining himself seems as important to him as giving us clues."

* * *

Mr. Alton hasn't said a word since before Sally started reading the note. "Before we go any further with this little adventure kids, you should know a few things. My father told me a story about Jeremy Humphrey that no one else has ever heard. At least no one alive. He said the story began with Edmond, Jeremy's son. Edmond passed the story along to Terrence, my grandfather, who passed it on to my father, Timothy. And of course my father passed it on to me."

Mr. Alton faces Sally when he continues. "Before he died, Grandpa Timothy told me to make sure that only you hear this story, sweetheart, since you are my only child. But considering the circumstances, I think it's only fair that Cousin Crystal and your friends hear it too."

Mr. Alton seems to be waiting for Sally's approval. Sally nods.

Now Mr. Alton looks at Tom and me. "Now, much of what I'm about to tell you is very private. So you can't tell anyone, okay?"

Tom and I both nod. "We won't," Tom says.

Crystal must feel left out. "I won't tell anyone either."

Mr. Alton smiles as he hugs Crystal at the shoulders.

"This is the story my father told me," Mr. Alton starts. "Grandma Annabelle came from Seattle to marry Jeremy. They were only married for a month or so, but Annabelle became pregnant. After she left him, she took back her maiden name, Alton. Though Edmond was Jeremy's son, Annabelle raised Edmond completely on her own. So Edmond was born Edmond Alton, not Edmond Humphrey."

"I told them about our family tree, Daddy," Sally interrupts, "when they realized that Annabelle's last name was Alton."

"Oh," Mr. Alton replies, nodding at Sally. "Then I'll tell you what happened after. It's a story I haven't told anyone. Not even you, sweetheart.

"Edmond figured out who his father was when he was about ten. He was curious, so whenever he saw Jeremy, he'd run up and try to talk to him. But Jeremy despised Edmond and tried to ignore him. Jeremy never said a word except this one time. One day Jeremy slapped

Edmond across the face in the general store, many people witnessed it. Jeremy was fed up with Edmond's pestering. He said, 'Stay away from me boy, if you know what's good for you.'"

Crystal shudders.

"Edmond stopped approaching Jeremy after that," Mr. Alton continues, "but followed him instead."

"My father's story gets a little strange at this point, and I never really knew how much to believe. But, from what you four have told me, I now think at least part of it is true.

"Edmond claimed there were times when he saw Jeremy vanish into thin air. One second Jeremy was standing right there in the woods – the next he was gone."

Crystal interrupts. "That must have been when Jeremy was using the trap door. You know, entering his home."

Mr. Alton nods. "Now I think so too, Crystal. But until today I didn't know quite what to make of it. Like my father and his father before him, I suspected that Jeremy had an underground sanctuary, but no one could ever prove it. At least not until yesterday."

I think of the day Mr. Alton told Sally to look for acorns. Now I'm sure he was searching for an entrance into Old Man Humphrey's home.

Mr. Alton continues, "There were several accounts of Jeremy's vanishing act even after Jeffrey Hillbrook was killed. People started following Jeremy, hoping he'd lead them to the Hillbrook stash. They'd come back telling stories of how Jeremy could disappear. One such account told of how several people had Jeremy surrounded from all sides. But when they closed in on the middle, Jeremy was gone. It led some people to think he was bewitched. There was even talk in town of his being a warlock. Or something worse. Something supernatural."

Mr. Alton chuckles, but no one else is even smiling, not even Crystal.

"And there's another story I've never been able to make any sense of. One time Edmond followed Jeremy and hid behind a tree. Jeremy stopped as if to listen, so Edmond sat still and waited for Jeremy to move on. Jeremy was only about fifteen feet away, so Edmond was extra quiet and breathed shallow breaths. Jeremy turned to face Edmond's direction. A few seconds later, Jeremy started walking toward Edmond.

"Edmond thought Jeremy spotted him. He panicked. He stood and turned to run away. He had only gone a couple of steps when he came face to face with a witch. At least that's what Edmond called her. A witch! She was dressed all in black and had long, stringy, black hair. Her face was dirty and her dress was torn. Edmond froze in fear as her hollow dark eyes blazed right into him. Then she grabbed him. Her bony fingers clenched his shoulders like a hawk to a rodent. He kicked her in the shin and she let go. He ran away without looking back, and didn't stop until he arrived in town."

Mr. Alton pauses, giving us time to think about the witch story. All of us are speechless so he eventually continues. "After that, Edmond stopped following Jeremy. It was just too scary. Instead, he struck up a friendship with Jeremy's younger brother, Gerald.

"You kids probably know Gerald's descendants. Gerald's only daughter married into the Hinkle family. And since Annabelle took back her maiden name, the Humphrey name died out three generations ago with Jeremy."

I shudder and ask, "You mean Larry, Perry, and Ed are related to Old Man Humphrey?"

"Yes," Mr. Alton answers. "Jeremy is their great, great, great uncle. And of course Gerald is their great, great, great grandfather."

"They *sure* got their uncle's mean streak," Tom says.

Tom doesn't realize that he just insulted the entire Alton family. They're much more closely related to Old Man Humphrey than the Hinkle's.

Mr. Alton ignores Tom's unintended insult. "Uncle Gerald cautioned Edmond to stay away from Jeremy. He said Jeremy was a 'bad apple' and no good ever came from being around him. Gerald didn't go into any detail, or if he did, that part of the story was lost somewhere. So I don't know what Gerald said exactly, but whatever it was it made an impression on Edmond, because the next time he went to see his father, it was for his funeral.

"Edmond did, however, keep tabs on Jeremy. Especially after the Hillbrook affair. And he stayed in close contact with Uncle Gerald, who seemed to know more about Jeremy than most people. Gerald told Edmond that there was more to Jeffrey Hillbrook's death than met the eye. He was sure Jeremy had something to do with it though he could never prove it."

Mr. Alton rubs his forehead, his eyes peer at us under the ledge of his brows. You kids have committed yourselves to a dangerous little adventure here. I want to help, but we need to be a lot more careful from now on. You've been really lucky so far."

He's right. Tom could have died falling off the rock face. Luckily we had the first toolbox or we could all be dead in the cavern now.

Mr. Alton frowns, and without a blink he says, "Promise me that you won't do anything more to defeat Old Man Humphrey's challenges without me."

We all nod our promise in return.

"Great," he says with relief. He hugs Sally, "Thank you for letting me in on this, sweetheart."

It is after five-thirty and Tom and I have to get home. We agree to meet back here tomorrow at four o'clock. In the meantime, we'll all work on the list of books needed to solve our next puzzle.

Mr. Alton will take off work tomorrow . With the help of Sally's iPhone, he's going to the cavern to look around. We argue that we want to be there too, but he promises not to work on our next challenge without us. After so many years of searching, he just wants to see the dwelling for himself. No one can blame him for that.

* * *

Tom and I don't walk the girls home since Sally's dad is there to escort them. I miss our walk together, it makes the afternoon feel different somehow. It doesn't feel like we've been on a double date anymore.

We head straight home. My stomach is growling and I hope Mom has dinner ready.

Mom's in the family room watching T.V. The only thing I smell are her cigarettes, my hopes for dinner sink. Nothing is cooking in the kitchen.

"Hey guys," Mom greets us. "I've got some great news, so I thought we'd go out to dinner to celebrate."

My heart races. And I almost blurt out what I'm thinking. *Dad's coming home!* But I hold my tongue. Mom's idea of "great news" isn't the same as mine.

I see Tom's eyes light up for a second too. We're thinking alike.

But food is food, and I'm hungry. We haven't been out for dinner since Dad left. Unless you count McDonalds.

"Sounds good mom," Tom says. "Where're we going?"

"How about something special? I was thinking of D'Angelo's."

Wow. That *is* special. D'Angelo's is the best restaurant in Clear Valley. I've never been there but I know it's fancy. Tom and I exchange a look. He shrugs.

"You boys go get cleaned up and put on some nice clothes. We'll make a date of it."

Tom and I rush up the stairs to do as Mom says. Five minutes later we're back downstairs and waiting for Mom. It takes her a little longer to get ready.

When she comes down the stairs, Mom's wearing an elegant blue dress. Her golden hair is out of its bun and flowing for the first time since I was in the hospital. She looks great. I guess we are going out on a date.

Mom grabs her purse. "You boys sure do clean up nice." We head out the front door.

D'Angelo's is on the other side of town, but everything in Clear Valley is less than five minutes from everything else. The parking lot is pretty full for a Monday night, but Mom finds a parking spot near the entrance.

We walk in, but instead of going to the hostess stand, Mom turns right and heads into the bar area. We follow. Maybe she wants a glass of wine before dinner.

But it's not wine she's after. She walks over to her boss, who's sitting at the bar. At first I don't recognize him because he is facing away from us. But when Mom taps him on the shoulder, he turns around and smiles at her. It's Marvin all right.

Tom and I groan together as Mom calls us over. "Come over here guys. You know Marvin from the pawn shop, don't you? I know you've seen him in the store. But I thought it would be nice for you to meet him in person."

Marvin stands up from his bar stool and turns to face us. "Hey kiddos. Nice to meet you," He grabs my right hand and gives it a hearty shake. This causes a jolt of pain in my arm.

I can't help but wince. "Ouch!" I pull my hand away as fast as I can.

My reaction surprises Marvin. "Oh, sorry. I didn't mean to hurt you."

He looks at Mom. "I barely touched him Annie. It couldn't have hurt that bad."

Mom ignores the both of us. She puts her right hand on my shoulder. "This is Steve."

She pulls Tom over with her left hand. "And this is Tom."

Mom squeezes my shoulder. "Boys, say hello to Marvin Matthews."

"Hello Mr. Matthews," Tom and I say together.

Marvin learned his lesson. He holds out his hand and waits for Tom to take it. Tom considers, but doesn't reach out.

Marvin ignores the snub. "Call me Marvin. Mr. Matthews is my father." Marvin laughs at his joke.

"Okay, ah, Marvin," Tom says.

"Can I get you all something to drink?" Marvin asks. Then he looks at me. "How 'bout a beer? Or a gin and tonic?" He laughs again.

"Well, I would like a glass or red wine," Mom says. "Do you guys want a coke or something?"

Tom and I are in pout mode.

"Water would be fine," I say.

"Water for me too please," Tom says.

We get our drinks and Marvin pays. Then he turns to us. "You guys look hungry. Why don't we take our drinks to the table?"

We walk over to the hostess and she seats us at a round table. She places menus in our hands. I'm hungry, but I don't want to show it. I'd rather be home eating pizza.

Marvin points at Tom's menu. "Go ahead and order whatever you want, guys. 'Cause I'm buying."

I don't recognize most of the items on the menu. When the waitress gets to me, I order the only thing I'm sure of. "Spaghetti and meatballs, please."

Tom orders chicken parmesan. We both sit fidgeting while we wait for our meals. Mom and Marvin start talking about the pawn shop.

While they're talking, Tom looks over to me. "I'm glad Mr. Alton is helping us. The next challenge sounds like it's going to be really hard. And scary."

Mike Lynch

I'm not sure I want to be talking about our adventure in front of
Marvin. I glance over at him before I answer. He's still engaged in a
lively conversation with Mom, ignoring us. "Me too. And it sure makes
Sally happy."

"Have you thought about what books we'll need?"

I nod. "Uh huh. But the only one that I'm sure of is The Three
Musketeers. One for all and all for one. That's pretty obvious."

Tom nods back. "I thought so too. For the one about revenge, I
was thinking about the movie *Payback*. Do you think it's a book too?"

I shake my head. "It may be. But remember, all of the books had to
be published before Nineteen-fifty or so. I don't think *Payback*
qualifies."

Tom taps his forehead. "Yeah, you're right. Anything after that and
Old Man Humphrey wouldn't have been alive to read it."

Mom and Marvin are in their own world until the food comes. The
waitress puts our plates in front of us. Things quiet down as we begin
eating.

When we finish, Marvin tells us to go ahead and order dessert. I
order chocolate cake and ice cream. Tom orders apple pie ala mode.
Mom and Marvin will split a Crème Brule.

We're waiting for dessert when Mom looks away from Marvin for
the first time since we sat down. "Well guys, time for the good news.
What do you think about my new boyfriend?" She leans over and grabs
Marvin's arm at the elbow and pulls him in close.

So this is Mom's good news. Good news for Mom maybe. Not for
us. I had hoped Mom and Dad would eventually work things out. It's

now pretty obvious that's not going to happen. Neither Tom nor I say a word.

When we don't respond, Mom tries to explain. "Marvin and I have decided to see each other socially. I told him I wanted you both to know all about it before we started. So what do you think?"

Tom hasn't so much as looked at Mom since he saw Marvin in the bar. I haven't thought much about it, but now I'm pretty sure he's been fuming inside. "I think it stinks."

The waitress is putting the dessert dishes down as Tom gets up and walks away from the table. At first I think he's going to the bathroom. But instead he heads for the front door. He's going to walk home.

I choke down my cake and ice cream. I feel guilty for not joining him.

* * *

When Mom and I get home, Tom has locked himself in his room. Mom is really angry and wants him to open his door "right this minute". But Tom doesn't respond at all. Mom gives up after five minutes of ranting.

After Mom goes downstairs, I knock softly. "Tom, it's me. You okay?"

"Go away," he responds. Then he adds. "We'll talk tomorrow."

I'm relieved to hear his voice.

Mike Lynch

## Tuesday

When I wake up Tuesday morning, Tom is gone. He's not in his room and he's not downstairs. His backpack is gone too. He must have left for school.

Mom is getting ready for work in silence. If she knows Tom isn't home, she's not showing it. I go through my normal morning routine, except I skip breakfast. Then I head out for school without saying goodbye.

About a block from school, I see flashing lights. They're coming from an ambulance and police car near the school's main entrance. I cringe, thinking of Tom's mood last night. Somehow I know he's involved.

As I get closer, I see Tom sitting on the top step. I breathe a sigh of relief. But relief turns to worry again when I see who's bent down and talking to him. Officer Grant.

Behind Tom and Officer Grant, two paramedics bring someone out on a stretcher. I make my way through to the front of the crowd just in time to see who's on the stretcher. It's Ed Hinkle! They carry him right past me. He looks terrible. Bruises and scratches cover his face. Blood is flowing from both nostrils. He's conscious and moaning loudly. The paramedics put him in the ambulance and close the door from the inside.

Tom stands and walks down the steps with Officer Grant to the police car. Officer Grant holds the driver's side back seat door open and Tom gets in. Officer gets in the front seat. They drive off, leaving me to wonder the heck just happened.

Kids are already talking.

"He finally got what he deserves," Mike Spaulding says.

"That should teach him a lesson," says Terry Scott, a fellow seventh grader.

"Maybe now he'll think twice before he picks on us," John Graves says. John is on the basketball team with Tom.

The ambulance is pulling away when I see Sally's friend Ashley rushing toward me. She smiles. "At least now you guys will know who to call when Ed Hinkle picks on you."

"What do you mean?" I ask.

"You haven't heard?" Ashley doesn't wait for an answer. "Well let me fill you in."

Ashley seems quite pleased to be the one telling me. Several kids have gathered around to listen in. "I don't know all the details. But from what I've heard, Tom was in the boys' locker room when Ed Hinkle came in. Ed did his usual bully thing, but before he could get close enough to hurt Tom, Tom launched himself. Ed must not have seen it coming. Tom's first blow broke Ed's nose and knocked him down hard. And it didn't stop there. Tom jumped on Ed and just started punching away. Somebody yelled 'fight' and that's when three other boys joined in. They were all punching and kicking Ed when Mr. Potter came in."

Mister Potter is our principle.

"Nobody stopped even when Mr. Potter started yelling. He had to pull all of them off of Ed," Ashley finishes.

But Officer Grant just took one boy away.

* * *

I'm not sure what to do. Should I go to school or go to the police station? Should I tell Mom? She'd have left for work by now. I decide to walk to the police station since it is only five blocks away.

I see Tom as soon as I walk through the door. He's sitting by himself in the waiting area. He looks up as I approach and quickly rubs his face on his sleeve. I can see by his red eyes and puffy cheeks that he's been crying.

"What happened?" I ask. "The whole school is talking about you."

"I was sick and tired of being picked on. And after what Mom did last night, I just didn't care any more. I had to do something.

"You know how the Hinkle brothers always get to school early, right? They shoot hoops in the gym. Well, I went there this morning to face them. I didn't care if they pummeled me. I just wanted to go right up and start punching the first jerk that got close enough. If I got enough punches in, maybe then they'd leave us alone. But whatever happened, I wanted them to know that I'm never going to back down from them again. Never."

Tom waits for a my reaction, but I don't say anything. So he continues. "When I got to school, I was surprised to see Ed shooting hoops by himself. He was all sweaty so I knew he had to go to the locker room to clean up before school started. So I went there and waited for him. I was hoping to surprise him, but I got distracted by

Mark Roach who wanted to talk about basketball. When Ed came in, I was on the other side of the locker room.

"You should have seen the look in his eyes, Steve. He thought he had me cornered and he was going to pound the crap out of me. But his expression changed as soon as I rushed him. He was too fat and slow to react. I lunged and rammed the top of my head right into his nose. I heard it crunch so I'm sure I broke it.

"He went back hard against the lockers and fell to the floor. He was on his side holding his nose, sobbing like a baby. But I didn't care. I just kept hitting and kicking him. Then I jumped on him and hit him some more. Two other guys came in right about then. I thought they were going to pull me away, but they didn't. Everyone including Mark started pounding on that bastard with me."

Tom's body is trembling and his arms are throwing imaginary punches.

"I saw red, Steve. It's like I blacked out. I don't remember anything after that until Mr. Potter yanked me away. A few minutes later I heard the sirens."

I'm amazed. No one has ever beaten up Ed Hinkle before. He's huge. And since he's been held back twice, he should be a sophomore in high school, not an eighth grader.

I nod toward one of the police desks. "What are they going to do?"

"They already did it. They called Mom. I'm sure she's on her way here right now. She's probably all pissed off at me for making her to take time off from her precious job."

I sit with Tom not really knowing what to do. The cop at the greeting desk gives me a nod, so I guess it's okay if I just sit here with my brother.

Mom makes her entrance a minute later. She barely glances at Tom and me as she blows by the cop at the greeting desk.

He tries to stop her. "Hey lady, you can't go back there."

Mom ignores him. She's got a purpose to her step but at first I can't tell where she's going. Then I see Officer Grant standing next to a coffee machine. He's got a donut in his hand. Mom heads right for him.

"What the hell gives you the right to haul my kid off to jail?" She's almost screaming.

Everyone in the room stops what they're doing to stare at Mom.

Officer Grant didn't see her coming. He's definitely shaken. He scrambles to keep from dropping his donut. "Calm down Mrs. Jones. Your son is not in jail. He's waiting right over there."

He points at Tom.

Mom doesn't even look. She takes two more steps and gets right in his face. "I want him released. Now!"

Officer Grant is backing up. He points to a door that is close by. "Please Mrs. Jones. Can we all go in here and just talk about this for a few minutes please?"

Mom doesn't respond but enters the room.

The cop at the greeting desk nods back toward the room. "Go on back now, boys."

The room we enter is a small conference room. A large grey oval-shaped table nearly fills the room. Metal chairs are crammed in around it. Officer Grant closes the door behind us. No one sits down.

Officer Grant keeps his distance from Mom. "Your son assaulted and badly injured another boy this morning, Mrs. Jones. That boy is now in the hospital."

He's about to say more but Mom cuts him off. "Kind of like my son Steve, who was in the hospital last week? And who put him there? Ed Hinkle and the Hinkle brothers, that's who. But did you arrest them? No. Did you allow me to file a complaint? No. 'These things always have a way of working themselves out.' you said.

"Now Ed Hinkle is in the hospital. A bully who's feared by every kid in that school. And my son, who's half his size, put him there. Half the kids in that school will want to give Tom a medal for what he did. Principal Potter told me as much when he called this morning.

"And by the way, Potter said there were three other kids involved in that fight. I don't see any of them here. Where are they? I only see my boys."

Mom finally stops talking to take a breath. This gives Officer Grant a chance to respond. "Please try to understand, Mrs. Jones. I'm trying to help here. I'm not going to arrest Tom. He'll be free to go in just a few minutes. I just wanted to talk to you about what's going to happen next. That's all."

I'm relieved to hear Tom will be released soon. This seems to calm Mom down a bit too. She remains quiet, waiting for Officer Grant to continue.

When he doesn't, she questions, "Well?"

Officer Grant hesitates. It's obvious that he doesn't know quite how to continue. "Mrs. Hinkle has already called," he finally says. "She's very upset."

Mom cuts him off again. "Oh, you mean more upset than I was last week?"

Officer Grant ignores the question. "What I'm trying to say is that I don't want this to go any further."

"That's commendable Officer," Mom says with as much sarcasm as she can muster. "Then you should have let me file a complaint last week. Maybe then Mrs. Hinkle would have put a leash on her rottweillers."

Officer Grant rubs his forehead. "I can't undue what's already been done, Mrs. Jones. I can only try to keep things from getting out of hand."

Mom gets her nose right in his face again. "What are you saying?"

Officer Grant looks almost afraid to answer. "I don't want Tom going after any more of the Hinkle brothers."

For the first time since she entered the building, Mom looks at Tom. "Then you better keep those little bastards away from him. Because he has my permission to protect himself, and his brother."

Officer Grant shakes his head. "You know I can't promise that Mrs Jones. But I must caution you..."

Mom cuts him off again. "Now you're going to caution *me*? That's a laugh. You tell Mrs. Hinkle that if her boys come anywhere near my kids again, her boys will be the least of her worries. I will personally kick her fat ass."

She grabs Tom by the arm and pulls him toward the door. Tom winces. "Come on Tom, we're leaving."

She looks back at Officer Grant. "Either arrest him or we're out'a here."

Mom doesn't wait for a reply. She's dragging Tom out of the room and heading for the exit.

I look up at Officer Grant. He's shaking his head and looks exhausted. Then I hurry to catch up with my family. *My family.* I realize that for the first time, I've pictured "my family" without Dad.

* * *

Tom and I remain quiet on the way home. But Mom is ranting. "Marsha Hinkle was a bitch in high school and she's still a bitch today. Well her delinquent son finally got what's coming to him. Now she knows how it feels to have a kid wind up in the hospital. Do you know how many mothers in this town have spent hours worrying about their kids because of Ed Hinkle and his brothers? Well I'll tell you how many. Lots. That's how many. Now it's her turn. I don't feel a bit sorry for her, or for him. She and her sons can rot in hell for all I care."

Mom stops ranting and looks at Tom. "I'm proud of you Tom. I don't care what Officer Grant says. It was about time someone stood up to that bully. It took a lot of courage to do what you did. And like I told that cop, you have my permission to stand up to any Hinkle that bothers you and Steve. And get lots of your friends to help. Maybe as a group you can put the fear of God into them."

I've never heard Mom talk like this. I look at Tom, but he just shrugs. He looks as surprised as I am.

"Okay, Mom," he weakly replies.

* * *

It's after noon, so it looks like we won't be going back to school today. Mom fixes sandwiches and we all sit at the kitchen table to eat them.

142

When we're finished, Tom and I start to get up from the table but Mom stops us. "I need to apologize for last night. It wasn't right to spring Marvin on you guys like that."

I'm amazed. I can't remember Mom ever apologizing to us. Or to anyone for that matter.

Tom looks as shocked as I am. "It's okay, Mom."

Mom shakes her head. "No. It's not okay. It's the reason you went after Ed Hinkle this morning, isn't it?"

Tom blinks back his surprise. "What do you mean?"

"You were mad at me. And you wanted to take it out on somebody. Since you couldn't take it out on me, you went after Ed, right?"

Tom doesn't respond.

"But you can't go around reacting like that Tom. It will get you hurt some day."

"Uh huh," Tom replies.

Mom looks at the clock and starts fidgeting with her rings. She's getting anxious about work.

Tom notices. "You can go on back to work now, Mom. We'll be okay, won't we Steve?"

I nod.

There's a sincerity in Tom's voice that I haven't heard when he's talking to Mom since Dad left. I think Mom hears it too.

"Thank you, Tom. If you're sure, I will get back to work. But if you want, I'll stay here with you guys this afternoon."

"There's no need for that. We'll be okay."

Mom taps her forehead. "Oh I forgot. I have to cover for the evening shift manager tonight. I won't be home until after nine o'clock. There's leftover pizza in the fridge. Will you guys be okay with that?"

"Sure Mom. We'll manage,"—Tom says.

She stands up to leave. "Okay then. You guys take care of yourselves."

"We will," Tom responds.

Then Tom does something that would have been unthinkable just a few hours ago. He gets up from the table and gives Mom a hug. Even though Mom doesn't like hugging, she affectionately hugs Tom back.

* * *

Tom and I spend the afternoon working on the third challenge. I go on-line and start typing the phrases that Old Man Humphrey used for his clues.

I type *The best tale of revenge ever conceived*, but nothing helpful comes up. There is a book called *Tales of Revenge*, but it was published in 1983.

I type 'books about revenge'. The results are all related to how you can get even with somebody. I try a few other phrases but nothing comes up that makes any sense.

Next I type *One for all and all for one*. Sure enough, several links point to the book *The Three Musketeers*, written by Alexandre Dumas in 1844.

Tom starts a list of the books we find.

The next clue I type is *Nineteen years a prisoner*. This phrase renders several links to someone named *Jean Valjean*. Further attempts lead to a book entitled *Les Miserables*, written by Victor Hugo in 1862. This must be the book we need. Tom adds it to the list.

We continue using the search engine to help us find books. I do the typing and Tom updates the list. We eventually discover five books that we're pretty sure of. Tom hands me the list.

*The best tale of revenge ever conceived :* Unknown

*One for all and all for one* : The Three Musketeers, Alexandre Dumas, 1844

*Nineteen years a prisoner* : Les Miserables, Victor Hugo, 1862

*Invaders from another planet* : Unknown

*A bleak future indeed* : Unknown

*In the end it is Eloi versus Morlocks* : The Time Machine, H.G. Wells, 1895

*Underwater adventure with a mad captain :* Twenty Thousand Leagues Under the, Sea Jules Verne, 1874

*Hideous creatures combining man and beast* : Unknown

*Some animals are created more equal than others* : Animal Farm, George Orwell, 1945

*An African tale of adventure* : Unknown

*A search for diamonds* : Unknown

*Life from death* : Unknown

Tom is looking over my shoulder as I look through the list. "Sally is pretty smart. I bet she figured out a lot more than we did."

I nod. "And Mr. Alton is older. He'll probably come up with more too."

"What do you think Old Man Humphrey meant by *'use the moon of 1949 to guide you'*."

I'm not sure. So I type "moon of 1949" and do a search. At the very top of the results page, there's a link to a web site called "Full moon calendar for 1949". I click the link to get to the web site and print the list.

### *Full moons in 1949:*

*Friday, 14 January 1949*

*Sunday, 13 February 1949*

*Monday, 14 March 1949*

*Wednesday, 13 April 1949*

*Thursday, 12 May 1949*

*Friday, 10 June 1949*

*Sunday, 10 July 1949*

*Monday, 8 August 1949*

*Wednesday, 7 September 1949*

*Friday, 7 October 1949*

*Saturday, 5 November 1949*

*Monday, 5 December 1949*

"Notice anything special?" I ask.

Tom looks up from the computer screen. "What?"

"There are twelve full moons in 1949 and we need to find twelve books. I think we're on the right track.

\* \* \*

Tom and I get to City Park at three-forty-five. We're early, but we couldn't stand being in the house any more. Tom has the note from the third challenge in his backpack, along with our book list and the full-moons list.

Sally and Crystal also arrive early. It's three-fifty when they stroll in. We all sit at our picnic table.

"We weren't sure you guys were going to make it," Crystal says as she takes a seat next to Tom. "You wouldn't believe what's been going on at school!"

"What?" Tom asks.

"Well, first of all, everyone is talking about *you*," Crystal says as she leans in and looks Tom square in the eye. "Tom, my boy, you're famous. Although by one account you're in jail and charged with attempted murder. But of course, you've been charged as a minor."

Tom and I laugh together.

"You may think it's funny," Sally says. "But there are kids that believe it. Parents too I think."

"Then there are the kids who want to take up a collection to pay for your defense," Crystal adds. "Everyone ever bullied by the Hinkle brothers wants to contribute."

Crystal grabs Tom's leg at the knee with one hand covers her mouth with the other. "Oh, and then there's the 'other' Hinkle brothers...

She laughs until she snorts. "...both of them were beat up pretty good at lunch time. Just about every boy in the school was in on it. So Perry and Larry ended up going home with their mom. When they walked out of the school, kids were throwing stuff at them through the second floor windows."

Sally picks up the story. "Yeah, and the whole school was chanting, 'Don't come back! Don't come back! Don't come back!'"

Crystal finally stops laughing. "I think you're going to be revered for many years to come, Tom. The boy who beat up Ed Hinkle."

Tom is speechless. I don't know what to say either.

"Well. What do you have to say for yourself, champ?" Crystal asks.

Tom shrugs. "I just hope we've seen the last of the Hinkle brothers."

For as much as I hope Tom is right, I doubt it.

\* \* \*

Mr. Alton arrives at four-ten. We've been so engaged in our conversation that we didn't even notice that he was late. He's in jeans and a sweat shirt. And he's pretty dirty. He must have heard us talking while he approached. "What's all the excitement about?"

He obviously hasn't heard about Tom's newly acquired fame.

"Well Daddy," Sally says as she points at Tom. "You're looking at the most famous person in Clear Valley Middle School."

We describe the day's events but Mr. Alton isn't really listening. His mind is elsewhere. I think he wants to get on back to the reason why we're here.

"Wow," he says without much enthusiasm. "It sounds like you've had a really big day."

Then he changes the subject. "I've had a big day too. I visited a place that my father and grandfather tried to find all their lives, but only dreamed of seeing. It was fantastic."

He hugs Sally. "I can't thank you enough for letting me in on this, Sweetheart."

Then Mr. Alton faces us all. "As I promised, I didn't go looking for any clues or anything. I just went through the dwelling like you did. And I read Annabelle's letters. But I did come up with some things that should be useful."

Mr. Alton pulls out his list. It looks a lot like Tom's. "I think I know all but one of the books we need. And after giving it some more thought, I'm pretty sure I know how to determine that one too."

He shows us the list. Sure enough, eleven books are listed.

Tom looks astonished. "How did you come up with so many? We only figured out five of them."

"I read a lot of books in the public domain," Mr. Alton explains. "Copyrights on books run out after a certain number of years. After that they can be freely distributed. Many public domain books are among the best books ever written. There's a website I use called gutenberg.org. You can download public domain books there for free. Most of the books on Jeremy's list are in the public domain. And they're classics, so I've read them."

He puts his list in front of us.

*The best tale of revenge ever conceived* : The Count of Monte Cristo, Alexandre Dumas, 1844

*One for all and all for one* : The Three Musketeers, Alexandre Dumas, 1844

*Nineteen years a prisoner* : Les Miserables, Victor Hugo, 1862

*Invaders from another planet* : War of the Worlds, H.G Wells, 1898

*A bleak future indeed* : Nineteen Eighty-Four, George Orwell, 1949

*In the end it is Eloi versus Morlocks* : The Time Machine, H.G. Wells, 1895

*Underwater adventure with a mad captain :* Twenty Thousand Leagues Under the, Sea Jules Verne, 1874

*Hideous creatures combining man and beast* : The Island of Doctor Moreau, H.G. Wells, 1896

*Some animals are created more equal than others* : Animal Farm, George Orwell, 1945

*An African tale of adventure* : Unsure

*A search for diamonds* : King Solomon's Mines, H. Rider Haggard, 1885

*Life from death* : Frankenstein, Mary Shelly, 1818

Mr. Alton looks back to us and smiles. It's obvious that he's proud of his list. "The only book I don't know is *An African tale of adventure.* But after thinking about it and noticing that some of the books on the list have the same author, I think it was written by H. Rider Haggard. He wrote lots of adventure books set in Africa. We just have to figure out which one is the book we need. And whichever book it is, it will be in Grandpa Jeremy's library."

Tom pulls out the list of full moons. "Steve and I think this is important too."

Mr. Alton anxiously takes the list from Tom. "Great! I was thinking along these lines too, but I hadn't started looking for a list yet."

"So what are we waiting for?" Sally asks. Let's go get the books!"

The clock on top of the pillar says four-forty. Mom won't be home until at least nine o'clock. So she won't miss us if we're out late on a school night.

We head out of City Park and into Bandit Woods. Sally already has her iPhone in hand and is calling up the Geocache App that will get us to the entrance of Old Man Humphrey's home.

* * *

We have no trouble navigating Bandit Woods. Soon we're standing by the four stones that frame the trap door.

Tom goes first. He takes his backpack off and holds it in front of him. He steps into the square and we wait for the familiar 'click'. Down he goes. I go next. Tom is at the end of the slide waiting for me. Then come the two girls and finally Mr. Alton. He's holding his backpack just like Tom was.

For some reason, it seems darker. The sun must be lower in the sky or something. Mr. Alton reaches into his backpack and pulls out a flashlight. He checks to make sure it works, then puts it away.

We make our way to the library.

Mr. Alton heads for the bookshelves on the far wall. "Though I didn't look for any books on the list, I did check out how Grandpa Jeremy organized his library. He did everything alphabetically by authors' last names and titles. It's a little unorthodox since there are no major categories, but it should be easy to find the books on the list."

Mr. Alton finds the first book located under D, for Dumas. *The Count of Monte Cristo.* It's an old hardcover book and very thick. He brings it to the desk.

He thumbs through it a few times but finds nothing out of the ordinary. Tom reaches into his backpack and pulls out the list of full moons in nineteen forty-nine.

"This is the first book," Tom says. "Old Man Humphrey said the order is important. Whatever we're looking for must correspond to the first full moon, right? The one in January."

Mr. Alton nods. "That makes perfect sense, Tom. When was the first full moon in nineteen forty-nine?"

Tom references the list. "Friday, January fourteenth. So maybe you have to turn to page fourteen?"

Mr. Alton does just that. We all hover around as he places the opened book flat on the desk.

At first we don't see anything special on page fourteen. But then Sally shrieks. "There!" She points about a third the way down the page.

Mr. Alton turns on the flashlight and shines it where Sally is pointing. Sure enough, there is something there. Tiny, faint writing between two lines of print. It's too small and faint to read with the naked eye.

Remembering that there is a magnifying glass in one of the desk drawers, I fetch it and hand it to Mr. Alton.

"Ah. That's much better," he says. "But it doesn't make a lot of sense."

"What does it say Uncle Jim?" Crystal asks.

"Get a pen and write this down."

Sally gets a pen and paper of her backpack.

"Ready?" Mr. Alton says. *"One more be required for your treasure to greet"*

"Well, it's definitely from Old Man Humphrey," Tom says.

We all think for a minute but soon realize there is much more to do. Mr. Alton finds the second book. *The Three Musketeers.* Also on the Dumas shelf. He brings it back to the desk. "When was the second full moon?"

Tom has already found it. "Sunday, February thirteenth."

Mr. Alton turns to page thirteen and scans the page. This time he is already using the flashlight and magnifying glass. After two minutes, he gives up. "There's nothing here."

"Then there's got to be more to this," Sally says. "Maybe it's not day of the month but day of the year. That would mean only the date for the first full moon would directly correspond to a page number. January fourteenth. It's the fourteenth day of January and the fourteenth day of nineteen forty-nine."

Sally thinks for a minute, then adds, "Since there are thirty-one days in January, February thirteenth is the forty-fourth day of nineteen forty-nine.

Mr. Alton turns to page forty-four. "That's it!"

The tiny writing appears between two lines about one third the way down the page.

"Write this down," Mr. Alton says. *"Secrets to you that may not appeal"*

We find the third book, *Les Miserables* by Victor Hugo, right where it should be and bring it to the desk.

"This will be the March full moon. But what if 1949 was a leap-year?" Sally asks.

"That will screw up the numbering," Tom answers

"Let's go on the assumption that it wasn't a leap-year," says Mr. Alton. "If nothing is on the expected page, we'll just turn to the next page."

The March full moon was on the fourteenth. Adding thirty-one plus twenty-eight plus fourteen, we get seventy-three. Mr. Alton turns to page seventy-three.

"It must not have been a leap-year," he says. "Here it is so write this down. *It was never my intention for them to die.*"

We continue doing this for the rest of our known books. When we get to the one Mr. Alton doesn't know, *An African tale of adventure,* he looks at the other books that were written by H. Rider Haggard.

"I think this is it!" he excitedly says.

He shows it to us. *People of the Mist*

We take it to the desk and confirm that, sure enough, writing appears on the appropriate page.

We repeat the process for the last two books. We're all pretty confused even before we study the writings. We already know they don't make much sense.

*One more be required for your treasure to greet*

*Secrets to you that may not appeal*

*It was never my intention for them to die*

*When you are finished you won't be the same*

*Of telling you all the things that I ask*

*You may agree it's not hidden the best*

*Be sure to rest there just take a seat*

*On which side of my dwelling you consider the end*

*It resides in a room that is more like a hole*
*In order to find the treasure you seek*
*Off with you now go on your pursuit*
*Be alert and be ready at your final turn*

"This just doesn't look right," Sally says.

"Yeah," Crystal agrees. "It's like the sentences are all jumbled up."

Mr. Alton smiles. "They're not jumbled up Crystal. We just don't have them all. Can I use your iPhone, Sally?"

"Sure Daddy. I'm amazed it gets any signal down here."

We all look over Mr. Alton' shoulder as he taps away for a few minutes.

He finally looks up. "Got it!"

He holds up the iPhone to expose a web page entitled *Phases of the Moon for 1949*. "We just didn't find all the sentences. There are four moon phases every thirty days or so. Only one of them is a full moon So we only have one quarter of the clues!"

We start over, using the phases-of-the moon list. The first listing is for a first quarter moon on January seventh. We look at page seven in *The Count of Monte Cristo*. The handwriting is near the top of the page.

Mr. Alton uses the flashlight and magnifying glass to read it.

*Four items you need for this challenge to beat*

"I think we've got it!" Crystal says.

It takes a while, but by seven fifteen we have the whole message written down. It's actually a poem. It contains twelve verses, one for each month or book. Each verse contains four lines.

Sally reads it out loud.

*Four items you need for this challenge to beat*

*One more be required for your treasure to greet*

*I have hidden them all in my abode with care*

*Find them you must to proceed out of there*

*Along the way I will also reveal*

*Secrets to you that may not appeal*

*But this is all to be part of my game*

*Play it you must to achieve your fame*

*Those others may never know where they lie*

*It was never my intention for them to die*

*Their fate was sealed when they entered below*

*Now you can free them now they can go*

*On with my riddle on with my game*

*When you are finished you will not be the same*

*Humans are capable of such hideous deeds*

*You may think me evil matching my needs*

*Digress no more must I from my task*

*Of telling you all the things that I ask*

*Start searching in earnest find what you can*

*Here are my clues here is my plan*

*The first item lies where I take my rest*

*You may agree it is not hidden the best*

*Discover a secret and try not to faint*

*My reputation be poor but you must further taint*

*Next you must wander to where I eat*

## The Hillbrook Stash

*Be sure to rest there just take a seat*

*If you look around I am sure you will find*

*The next item you'll need though you won't think it kind*

*Where you go next will surely depend*

*On which side of my dwelling you consider its end*

*Look for a hole that does not belong*

*Rest assured that it's there I won't lead you wrong*

*One more item is needed to reach your goal*

*It resides in a room that is more like a hole*

*Look closely don't worry and never fear*

*Be patient don't hurry it will surely appear*

*At last you have the means to succeed*

*But I'm sorry to say there is one final need*

*In order to find the treasure you seek*

*A map be required you must have a peek*

*So now you know what things you must do*

*Or at least you've been given a substantial clue*

*Off with you now go on your pursuit*

*Work hard and you'll surely come up with the loot*

*One final challenge you may not expect*

*Awaits out of sight so please don't neglect*

*Be alert and be ready at your final turn*

*Ignore my warning and surely you'll burn*

We all remain silent while Sally reads the poem again. Still no one says a word when she finally finishes.

Crystal speaks first. "Well isn't this a happy challenge." She laughs but it's a nervous laugh. No snort this time.

Mr. Alton organizes the things on the desk and puts away the magnifying glass. "It's getting late."

Tom senses that we're about to leave. "Can't we just take a quick look in his bedroom? That's where the first clue is hidden, right?"

Mr. Alton shakes his head. "It will be dark soon and I think we should be out of the woods by then. And I don't like all the warnings. We mustn't rush anything. Let's all take some time to consider the poem. Then we'll figure out what to do next."

Before he can pick up the hand-written poem, Sally snaps a few pictures. "You guys take the hard copy. We'll keep the pictures. Then we'll all have something to study."

Mr. Alton leaves the twelve books stacked neatly on the desk in two columns of six, though I don't think we'll need them again. We then exit the dwelling and make our way home. Along the way we agree to meet again tomorrow in City Park at four o'clock.

* * *

We get home at eight forty-five. Mom isn't home yet.

I go into the house after Tom. Once in, he points at the floor behind me. "What's that?"

I turn around and see an envelope on the floor. Someone must have slid it under the door. I pick it up and I'm surprised to see that it's addressed to me.

*Steve Jones, Please open in private. M.*

I open it on the way to the kitchen table. Tom sits next to me after turning on the kitchen light.

*Dear Steve,*

*I am aware of what you and your brother are up to and I want in. You need me. I have information that will save your lives. Please meet me at the Starbucks in town tomorrow as soon as you get out of school. Your brother can come too if it makes you feel better. You shouldn't have any trouble recognizing me, but if you do, I will definitely recognize you.*

*Michael*

Tom gives me a suspicious look. "What do you make of that? And who is this Michael guy? He sounds like he knows you."

I have no answer to either question but two things are certain. Michael knows us and he knows about our adventure.

"I don't know, Tom. I don't know anyone named Michael. Do you?"

Tom thinks for a few seconds. "Well, there's Michael Thompson, the mayor. And Michael Mantle who works in the post office. But I don't think either of them knows us."

Neither of us can come up with an answer. We'll just have to wait until tomorrow.

Mike Lynch

## Wednesday

I wake up at seven o'clock. Mom got home late last night. It was after ten when Tom and I heard her car pull into the driveway. We were still up, but to keep from getting in trouble for staying up too late on a school night, we rushed to our bedrooms and pretended to be asleep.

I can't stop thinking about Michael. Who is he and how does he know about our quest? Did one of the girls tell him? Or Mr. Alton? I can't picture any of them talking about the Hillbrook stash to anyone outside our little group. I guess we'll know soon enough.

Mom is in the kitchen when I go downstairs. She's eating a bowl of cereal at the kitchen table. There's a cup of coffee in front of her. A cigarette is burning in a nearby ashtray. "Were you guys okay yesterday?"

I nod. "We were bored so we went out and played for a while. We had the pizza for dinner."

"No more of the Hinkle brothers?"

I pour myself a bowl of Fruit Loops. "We didn't see them. But they must have been pretty shook up after what happened at lunch time."

It dawns on me that I should have no way of knowing what happened at lunch time. Tom and I were supposed to be home. Oops.

From her change of expression, I can tell Mom noticed my slip. But she simply asks, "What happened?"

I explain about how all the boys in school beat them up. And how Mrs. Hinkle had to take them home. And how kids were all chanting and throwing stuff when they left the school.

"Well good," Mom responds. "Maybe they'll leave you guys alone from now on. Now that they know they'll have a fight on their hands whenever they start something."

"I hope you're right Mom," I say as I take my first bite of the cereal. "But that Larry Hinkle is just plain crazy. I wouldn't put anything past him."

Tom walks into the kitchen and takes a seat next to Mom. He fixes himself a bowl of cereal too.

Mom nudges his shoulder. "I meant what I said yesterday Tom. I'm very proud of you."

Tom seems surprised by her touch. "I know Mom. Thanks."

"Steve was just telling me what happened to Larry and Perry. How did you guys hear about it?"

Uh oh. There it is.

"Some friends came by and told us all about it," I lie.

Mom smiles like she knows a secret. "Would these friends have been girls? As in *girlfriends*?"

Tom and I exchange an astonished look. How much does Mom know?

"Well… Yeah…" Tom stutters. Then he reconsiders. "Though they're not girlfriends exactly. How'd you know?"

Mom chuckles at Tom's discomfort. "Mrs. Latimer over on Shooter Street came into the store yesterday. She said she saw you boys walking with two pretty girls the other day."

I try to hide my relief. "Yeah, that's Sally and her cousin Crystal. You know Sally Mom. I've known her since kindergarten. Crystal is living with her. We were just hanging out."

Mom smiles.

* * *

Tom is the most popular kid in school. Since I'm his brother, I'm second most popular. We spend every free minute telling and retelling the story of Ed Hinkle's downfall. The kids at school can't get enough of it. Finally Tom and I get tired of telling the story and Ashley takes over. The change in story tellers doesn't seem to matter. Everyone is captivated by the Jones-Hinkle affair.

Larry and Perry Hinkle aren't in school. Rumors are flying about why. Some say Mrs. Hinkle pulled them out of Clear Valley Middle School. They'll be going a school in Dalton from now on, twenty miles away.

Others say Perry Hinkle committed suicide. That gives me an unsettling feeling. Knowing Perry's two-sided personality, this rumor sounds all too possible. I put it out of my mind.

Another rumor even has Larry Hinkle getting a gun and shooting the rest of his family. Then he goes to the hospital and shoots Ed before turning the gun on himself.

With all the excitement, Tom and I forget about the mysterious note from last night. At lunchtime, we finally remember and tell the girls. They insist on going with us to meet Michael.

"I'll call my dad and tell him we'll be late," Sally says.

I'm worried about the girls meeting Michael since I don't know who he is or what he wants. Starbucks is a very public place but having an adult with us sure wouldn't hurt. "Why don't you ask your dad to meet us at Starbucks?"

Tom nods enthusiastically. "Great idea!"

"Okay." Sally responds.

* * *

After school, the four of us take the short walk from school into town. Mr. Alton has agreed to be at Starbucks at three forty-five. He's waiting at one of the tables up front when we come in.

As we walk over to Mr. Alton, I look past him to a table in the back of the room. An older man is looking right at me. He's in a wheel chair and facing a young woman. She's looking at him so I can't see her face. Both of the man's legs and one of his arms are in casts. His has grey hair and he looks like he hasn't shaved for a couple of days. His shirt and pants look well-worn and have been cut to accommodate his casts. He watches Tom and me as we approach Mr. Alton.

Though I've never seen his face, I recognize him immediately as the man who shared my hospital room. So this is Michael.

Tom sees where I'm looking. "Do you know him, Steve?"

"Not really. But I do know who he is. He was in the bed next to me in the hospital."

I can't remember if Tom ever saw him. Tom may not even have known I had a roommate. His expression changes to one of suspicion. "Did you tell him about the cigar box?"

164

"No!" I'm shocked that Tom would think such a thing. "He wasn't even conscious the whole time I was there."

"Well he must have been awake for part of it," Tom retorts. "He sure seems to know you. And what we're doing."

Michael keeps watching us. He seems content to wait until we come to him.

The young woman turns around to see what he's looking at. She's got brown hair that's up in a pony-tail. She's in jeans and a pale yellow sweatshirt. She looks at me and smiles. Then she turns back and says something to Michael. He nods.

The girls and Mr. Alton have been listening to Tom and me bickering. All the while we've both been looking at Michael. Now Crystal puts in her two cents worth. "It's not polite to stare gentlemen. I think you guys should go over there and say hello."

Tom and I walk over to Michael followed closely by the girls and Mr. Alton. Sally pushes a table up close to Michael's and pulls up a few chairs. We all take seats near Michael.

"Hello Steve." Michael has a southern accent. "Before I forget, thank you for the get-well card."

I forgot about the home-made card I made for him. This raises Tom's suspicion again. "So you did talk to him!"

Michael responds for me. "No he didn't Tom. I just happened to be awake when Steve left the card on the table next to my bed. It was very thoughtful of him."

Neither Tom nor I want to be the first to speak. We wait for Michael.

Crystal surprises us both. "So you're the mysterious Michael. I'm Crystal Gent." She points at Sally and Sally's dad. "This is my cousin Sally Alton and her dad, Jim. I guess you already know Steve and Tom Jones."

"That I do," Michael replies. "My full name is Michael Maxwell. And this is my granddaughter, Judy Maxwell. We're from Lubbock in the great state of Texas. And we are very happy to make your acquaintance."

We all nod at one another. For me it's a nervous nod since I'm still worried about our situation.

Michael looks at Tom and me. "Well I guess you figured out by now that I overheard you boys in the hospital."

Tom's expression darkens.

"Don't worry, Tom," Michael continues. "I haven't told any one., except Judy here. Nor do I intend to. I'm not here for the…"

Michael hesitates and then continues, "Let's just say that Judy and I are not here for the reason you may think. But you know what? I really don't want to talk about this in public. And I don't suppose you do either. We're staying at the hotel next door. Would you mind if we go to my room so we can talk in private?"

The hotel next door is The Hideout Hotel. I've never been in it.

Mr. Alton answers, "Not until you explain what this is all about."

Michael reaches into his pocket and pulls out a yellowed sheet of paper. It looks like one of our notes from Old Man Humphrey. He unfolds it and puts it on the table in front of us. "This should do the trick."

Everyone gasps except Mr. Alton. In front of us is a sketch that must have been drawn by Old Man Humphrey himself. We recognize it immediately. It shows the small cave in the rock face. But in this picture the cave is not walled up with stone and mortar.

The sketch includes a young man, presumably Old Man Humphrey himself, eating a picnic lunch in the cave. He's sitting on the ledge with his feet dangling over the side. Even the small foot holes leading up to the cave are depicted in his sketch.

We all stare. Mr. Alton is the only one that doesn't recognize the scene. "So what does this prove?"

"It's the site of the first challenge Daddy," Sally answers. "Where Tom found the first toolbox."

Michael raises an eyebrow but doesn't comment on Sally's admission. "Can we go to my room now? I can assure you that we mean you no harm  And in my condition, I don't think I could hurt anyone much at this point anyway."

He raises his arms to display himself.

Judy chuckles as she nods at his wheelchair. "I don't know, Grandpa. You've run over my toe a few times in that thing."

We laugh and it breaks the tension. It's good to hear Crystal snort again.

* * *

Due to his condition, The Hideout Hotel has given Michael and his granddaughter two adjacent rooms on the first floor. But unfortunately, the hotel is pretty old and the only entrance with a wheelchair ramp is in back of the building. We have to walk to the end of the block and then up an alley to get to it. Judy pushes her grandfather the whole way.

I can't help but feel a twinge of fear as I realize that we're alone in an alley with the Maxwells. We're hidden from view of everyone in town. But my fear quickly passes as we make the way up the ramp and into the lobby's rear entrance. Judy wheels her grandfather down a hallway to our right and stops at the first door on the left. Michael already has a key out and ready.

Michael's room is surprisingly large. There's a queen size bed facing a television. A large picture window looks out to the street in front of the hotel. A square table and four chairs is in one corner of the room. A fifth chair is at a desk next to the window, so only one of us has to sit on the bed. It's Judy.

Michael wheels up to the table as close as he can. "Now that we have some privacy, we can tell you our story. It's pretty long, so please be patient."

He pauses. He seems to be waiting for a response. Tom and I just nod.

"As I said, we're from Lubbock," Michael begins, looking at Tom and me. "And my family has a seventy-five year old mystery that Judy and I are trying to solve. In nineteen thirty-five, my grandmother Meredith's sister disappeared."

Michael shakes his head. "I'm sorry. I don't know what to call her. What do you call your grandmother's sister? Would she be my grand aunt? Or my great aunt? I'm not sure."

Tom and I shrug. Mr. Alton shakes his head.

Michael sees our impatience and quickly continues. "Anyway, Aunt Judith, I'll call her, was twenty-three when she vanished without a trace. She had never married, and in those days an unmarried twenty-three year old woman was considered an old maid. It sounds strange today, but back then very few women found husbands after the age of about twenty.

"My Grandma Meredith, rest her soul, told me the story of Aunt Judith's disappearance when I was a boy." Michael nods at me. "I was about your age Steve. She said that Aunt Judith was a very private person. She lived with my Grandma Meredith and Grandpa Laurence, along with some other family members in our family home.

"Aunt Judith was a real loner. She only came out of her room for her meals. She did go into town once a week to get what Grandma Meredith called 'her personal items'. But Aunt Judith rarely talked to anyone outside the family. And she only talked to family members when she had a good reason to.

"According to Grandma Meredith, Aunt Judith loved to read. So there were only two times when Aunt Judith talked with anyone. One was when she had just finished a particularly good book and she just had to talk about it. The other was when she'd ask for the evening newspaper which she read religiously every day.

"The house has been in our family since eighteen ninety-four. And it's huge. Seven bedrooms. It is so big that when Aunt Judith went missing, believe it or not, no one even noticed. So they couldn't be sure exactly what day it was. According to Grandma Meredith, it had to be sometime between May third and May sixth of nineteen thirty-five.

"Grandma Meredith was planning on going into town and she thought Aunt Judith might want some books from the library. When she went to Aunt Judith's room to ask, there was no answer to her knock. She went into Aunt Judith's room, but found it empty. Nothing seemed to be missing or out of place so no one was too worried at first. They all thought that Aunt Judith went into town on her weekly trip. But when she didn't come home that night, Grandma Meredith called the police.

"No trace of Aunt Judith was ever found. And as far as anyone could tell, nothing was taken from her room. But since no one really knew her all that well, no one was absolutely sure that nothing was missing."

Michael must have forgotten to breathe. He gasps, catching his breath. "Fast forward some seventy-one odd years to November of last year. I was the last person living in the family home. It was just me since my wife Lucy passed away four years ago. I was still working but about to retire. That big old house was just getting to be too much for me. Well maybe I was a bit lazy too. But since no one in the family wanted the house and I was the only one living there, I decided to sell it and move into a condo.

"I had an estate sale and sold off most of the furniture in the house. Family members took the rest. When I was going through the house one last time on the day before the closing, I found the first clue to Aunt Judith's disappearance in over seventy years.

"Several family members had lived in Aunt Judith's room over the years, but nobody moved the furniture around much. With all the furniture out of the room when I did my final walk through, I noticed a couple of floorboards under where the bed used to be had popped up. I reached down to put them back in place. That's when I noticed something beneath them. A shoebox was lodged between the floor joists."

Michael reaches into his suitcase and pulls out the shoebox from Aunt Judith's room. He pulls off the lid and shows that it's filled with letters. He takes one out and shows it to us. "Do you recognize anything?"

The return address on the envelope is for Jeremy Humphrey.

* * *

My head is spinning. How can this be? By his own admission, Old Man Humphrey was a loner. Sure, he struck up a relationship with Annabelle, but that was his only attempt at seeking companionship, right? He said as much his first note.

Tom, Crystal, Sally, and Mr. Alton look as confused as I am.

Michael senses our confusion. "I can tell this comes as a shock to you. I guess that's a good thing."

I'm not sure why Michael thinks our confusion is a good thing, but I don't comment. I want to hear his explanation.

But instead of talking, Michael reaches into the shoebox again. He pulls a newspaper clipping and puts it in front of us.

It doesn't take us long to figure out what it is. There's no date, but based on how yellow it is, it's old. The headline for the article reads *Find True Love Via Post Office*. I don't have to read it to know it's an article much like the one Annabelle responded to. Judith Maxwell must have responded to it as well.

Michael gives us a few minutes to consider the clipping. He turns to face Mr. Alton. "I think you're familiar with what this is, Jim."

Mr. Alton's voice cracks when he answers. "I never saw the actual article, but from what I've heard, this looks like one my great, great grandmother responded to in nineteen ten."

Mr. Alton hesitates a moment and then asks, "But how did you know about Annabelle?"

171

Michael nods toward his granddaughter. "Judy uncovered your story during our research. We learned about Annabelle's marriage to Jeremy. And how she took her back her maiden name after they divorced. Alton. I assume you're related."

Mr. Alton considers Michael's explanation for a moment and appears to accept it. "So you're saying there is a connection between Annabelle and your Aunt Judith?"

Michael nods. "Only that they both responded to newspaper articles and hooked up with Jeremy Humphrey. But the article Annabelle responded to was published in nineteen ten. The one my Aunt Judith answered was from nineteen thirty-four." Michael points to the postmark on the first letter. Sure enough, it's from nineteen thirty-four.

He gives us a minute let us consider what he's just said. If Old Man Humphrey corresponded with two women, one in nineteen ten and one in nineteen thirty-four, could there have been others?

\* \* \*

Judy is the next person to talk. "Tell them the rest of the story, Grandpa. Maybe then they'll help us."

There's more? Wasn't that enough? Old Man Humphrey, Sally's great, great, great grandfather, has misled one woman into marriage and kidnapped at least one other. What more is there to tell?

Tom doesn't appear to be as shook up as I am. "Go ahead Michael. Tell us the rest of the story."

Michael leans forward in his wheelchair. "The shoebox letters tell the whole story of why Aunt Judith disappeared. All except why she didn't tell anyone that she was leaving. Jeremy eventually convinced Aunt Judith to leave home and come to him here in Clear Valley, but he never gave any specific instructions not to tell her family. I've thought about that a lot. But in the end I guess she just didn't much care for her family. Or maybe she was too embarrassed or ashamed to tell anyone that she was going away to live with a man.

"The letters from Jeremy Humphrey tell the story of her seduction. He skillfully played upon her weaknesses. She was a loner, so he could easily seduce her with fantasies of living alone in the woods with no one to bother them.

"That sketch I showed you in Starbucks was included in one such letter. The letter painted a beautiful picture of love and bliss in the woods that Aunt Judith must have found impossible to resist. And it didn't hurt that the sketch pictured a good-looking young man. When I first read the letters, I thought that Aunt Judith may have found exactly what she was looking for. Love and privacy with someone who would care for her.

"Later, after we started researching, we learned that Jeremy was in his fifties when he wrote that letter. This deception gives him a much more sinister appearance.

"And there were more sketches included in his letters. We'll show them all to you later. One shows him reading a book in an immense library. Considering Aunt Judith's love for reading, that too would have been irresistible.

"Early on I couldn't figure out how Aunt Judith got so many letters without Grandma Meredith knowing about them. But then I remembered Aunt Judith went in to town every week. She obviously had a post office box. So she was going to the post office get letters from Jeremy and mail letters to him."

Michael points at the address on one of the letters. "See here? The address shows a post office box, not the street address for the family home."

He pauses as we look.

"After reading the letters I made myself a promise," he continues. "As soon as I retired, I'd go to Clear Valley and solve the mystery of what became of Aunt Judith. I retired a month ago. I spent two weeks getting ready and well… here I am.

"While I was waiting to retire, I did lots of research. Wait… that's not quite true."

Michael looks at Judy. "Actually Judy did all the research. I have always hated computers, so I needed her computer skills. It now seems appropriate that Judy was named after Aunt Judith. Without Judy's help, we wouldn't be here.

"I was surprised at how it was to get just about any information she wanted on-line. Do you want to know all about the town that Jeremy Humphrey is from? Just type Clear Valley and you'll learn all about the town and its biggest story. The Hillbrook stash.

"Imagine our surprise when we learned that Jeremy Humphrey was right in the middle of the infamous affair, yet there was no mention anywhere about Aunt Judith. There wasn't much information about him directly, but we were able to piece together his story. He was a hermit happily living alone in the woods until a gangster came to town and forever changed his life."

Mr. Alton's expression changes to one of astonishment.

Michael meets Mr. Alton's gaze. "Don't look so surprised Jim. I may not know quite as much as you do about the Hillbrook stash, but I do know a lot. I know that everyone believes that Old Man Humphrey somehow got hold of the stash and hid it somewhere in Bandit Woods. And that people have been searching for it for years. Actually, that's what I was doing when I had my little fall."

Judy groans. "It wasn't a *little* fall Grandpa. You almost killed yourself. Tell then about the rock face."

Crystal gasps. Michael notices. "That's right Crystal. I fell while climbing the rock face that's shown in Jeremy's sketch. The one where, in the Starbucks, Sally said something about Tom finding the first toolbox."

Now I gasp. Michael does have good ears.

Michael smiles at my reaction. "I was walking in the woods just like everyone else who looks for the Hillbrook stash when I came to the rock face. But unlike everyone else, I had the sketch that Jeremy drew. It was only a matter of time until I found the foot holes. I couldn't see the cave but I knew it was there.

"I was stupid to climb up, especially at my age. But I was so excited I just had to try it. I pulled a dead pine tree over and used it to get up to the foot holes. But I immediately had a problem. I must be quite a bit taller than Jeremy was. I'm six-foot-three and the foot holes were way too close together for my hands and feet. That made climbing all the more awkward. I should have stopped right away. But instead, I ended up on the ground.

"Thank God I had my cell phone so I could dial nine-one-one before I passed out. And thank God it had signal."

Crystal looks confused. "Wasn't Judy here to help you?"

Michael shakes his head. "No. We never planned on her coming. She only came because I ended up in the hospital."

Judy picks up the story. "The paramedics said that Grandpa must have passed out right after dialing nine-one-one because there was no voice message during the nine-one-one call. They had to use the GPS signal from his cell phone to track his location in the woods."

Now it's Michael's turn again. "Later, they told me that a tree had fallen on me. I must have hit the pine tree on my way down so it ended up on top of me. Since I didn't want anyone to know what I was really doing, I didn't correct them."

Judy interrupts again. "They called me right after he was admitted to the hospital, but I had work commitments and couldn't get away for six days. So I got here two days ago, on Monday. It was the day grandpa was released from the hospital. I wanted to take him back home to Lubbock, but he refused."

Judy looks from Tom to me. "He told me about your conversations in the hospital. So I agreed to stay too."

That explains why no one came to visit Michael in the hospital while I was there. Judy couldn't get away from her work. This makes me think of Mom.

Then I think of Michael's letter to me. Judy must have slid it under our door. "In your letter you said you have information that will save our lives. What is it?"

For the first time, Michael puts on a dubious expression. "Before I answer. I need you to promise that you'll tell us everything you've learned during your adventure so far. And that you'll allow Judy and me to help from this point on."

No one in our little group responds so Michael continues his plea. "It would be only fair. Judy and I have told you almost everything we know."

"And we promise," Judy continues for him, "that we don't want any part of the Hillbrook stash. We only want to find out what became of Aunt Judith."

Tom doesn't even look at anyone else before he answers. "Okay. So what is this information that will save our lives?"

While I agree with him, I think Tom should have at least asked our opinions. From the sour look on Crystal's face, she thinks so too.

Michael's expression turns serious. "I'm sure Jeremy rigged a terrible booby trap where the Hillbrook stash is hidden. I know what it is and how to disable it."

* * *

Tom, Sally, and Crystal start bringing Michael and Judy up to date with our efforts so far. Michael's phone has a camera so he takes pictures of Old Man Humphrey's three notes along with his poem.

Tom starts to explain how he found the cigar box in the library, but Michael stops him. He heard this part in the hospital and he's already relayed it to Judy. So Crystal picks up at the point when we started on the first challenges.

As she explains the geocache app we used for navigating Bandit woods, Mr. Alton picks up the shoebox full of letters. He holds it up and gets Michael's attention. He gives Michael a questioning shrug. Michael nods while still listening to Crystal.

Mr. Alton brings the letters to the bed and turns on the nightstand lamp. I'm not interested in hearing our story again, so I join Mr. Alton at the head of the bed.

Mr. Alton holds up the shoe box again. "Think of it Steve. I hold in my hands more information about Jeremy Humphrey than anyone in my family could ever hope to learn. And it's all written in his own words."

I sit watching Mr. Alton while listening to Crystal and Tom. Each provides its own moments of excitement.

"Listen to this, Steve," Mr. Alton says after only three minutes of reading. "This is in the first letter he sent Aunt Judith."

*My Dearest Judith. It fills me with joy that you want to continue corresponding with me. After your first letter, I felt a strong connection with you, but I was unsure of our future as you seemed hesitant to continue.*

*I too am alone and feel unsure of the people around me. No one seems to have my best interest at heart. They all want me to conform to their methods, and ignore my own. I have found ways of dealing with my disappointments and if we pursue our relationship further, I would be happy to share them with you. Indeed, I eagerly anticipate the opportunity to get to know you better.*

*Even though I am but a young man, I have the experience of many years when it comes to providing for myself. I have created a unique and hidden dwelling in the woods. It is a beautiful place and provides me with the solitude I so much desire. I would be honored to show it to you some day.*

Mr. Alton then shows me the letter. At this point in the letter there is a sketch in the same style as the sketch showing the rock face. This sketch shows a young man in the cavern. He's bent over and taking a drink from the stream. Beautiful crystalline rock formations are all around him.

"This is what Michael was talking about," Mr. Alton says. "It sure sounds like Jeremy was seducing Aunt Judith. It would definitely attract her to him. And did you catch his lie about being a *young* man? This letter was written in nineteen thirty-five. He'd have been what, fifty-five years old then?"

Mr. Alton doesn't wait for me to respond. He goes back to his reading. I look over to the others. Sally is at the part when Tom lit the fuse at the rock face. She mimics my counting. "One, one-thousand, two, one-thousand..." Her voice sounds surprisingly similar to mine.

When she gets to eight, one-thousand, Crystal shouts. "Ka-boom!"

Everyone jumps, including Mr. Alton.

Michael looks at Tom. "That was pretty foolish. You could have been blown right off the rock face along with the stone wall."

Tom looks sheepishly down. "I almost was."

Mr. Alton is motioning me over again. He has a different letter in his hand. "This is interesting. Look. In this letter, Jeremy talks about another cavern."

I look at the paragraph in question.

*I know what you mean about feeling pursued, Judith. I often feel the pursuit of others. Sometimes it is imagined, but I'm afraid that all too often it is real. I'm fortunate to have found a second hidden home where I can take refuge when I feel prying eyes upon me.*

I'm not convinced. "But he doesn't say it is a cavern. It could have been that old cabin that burnt down."

"The log cabin wasn't hidden," Mr. Alton retorts. "Besides, the cabin was Grandpa Jeremy's official home. Everyone knew about it. It was where he and Annabelle lived. You're right though, he doesn't explicitly say that his second home is a cavern. Whatever it is, it could be a hiding place for one of his challenges."

I nod in agreement. "Is there a sketch?"

The letter is three pages long. Mr. Alton quickly scans them before looking up again. "No. No picture."

I look back to Tom. He's been watching and listening to us. He gives me a nod.

Crystal is explaining how she "dropped in" to Jeremy's home. She laughs and snorts during her story.

Michael and Judy look confused, so Sally explains about the trap door and slide. "I was terrified when Crystal disappeared. Thank goodness Tom found those four small stones."

Mr. Alton looks up from another letter. He wants me to look again. "Read this." There is a serious expression on his face.

*You are right when you say that solitude demands defense Judith. My solitude is most precious to me, and I have taken measures to protect it. Woe be he who tries to take that which I possess.*

Mr. Alton waits until I look up. "What do you make of that Steve? Doesn't it sound like he's booby-trapped the cavern in some way?"

I have to admit it does. But we've come and gone several times without any problems. "I don't know. Wouldn't we have run into a booby-trap by now?"

Jeremy's words sound hauntingly familiar to me. "Wait! I'm pretty sure those are the exact words he used in his first note. The one in the cigar box."

I dig through Tom's backpack and find the note. I point at the passage.

*If you persist in finding the treasure which you know I have possessed, then you must be able to meet and defeat the challenges I have created – and even the least of these can place you in your grave.*

Now I'm not so sure. "*…the treasure which you know I have possessed.* Well they're not exactly the same words. But pretty close."

"You're right about the wording," Mr. Alton admits. "But Grandpa Jeremy wrote this letter in nineteen thirty-five. Long before the Hillbrook stash. And even longer before he put that note he put in the cigar box."

He's right. But the wording in the two documents sounds too similar to be a coincidence.

Mr. Alton shrugs. He goes back to reading.

Turning my attention back to the others, I hear Tom explaining our exploration of the cavern. He's describing the rooms in Grandpa Jeremy's home.

Something he says makes Judy stop him. "Wait! You just said there are two chairs at the kitchen table. And two easy chairs in the library. Yet, you've believed all along that Jeremy lived there alone. If he did, why would he need more than one chair in each room?"

"I said the same thing when we first saw them," Crystal says. "But I didn't know what to make of it."

Everything we've just learned about Aunt Judith will require rethinking what we already know. Did Aunt Judith live in the cavern with Jeremy? If so, did she do so willingly?

This time Mr. Alton actually jumps as he gets my attention. "Wow!"

"What is it?" I ask.

Instead of answering, Mr. Alton just starts reading out loud.

*The explosives were remarkably easy to acquire. I have purchased enough to blow even the most numerous of pursuers to kingdom come.*

"We know one place where he used them," I state. "The rock face. Does he mention others?"

Mr. Alton skims ahead. "No. Nothing more about the explosives."

Michael was obviously listening to Mr. Alton. "Keep reading Jim."

Crystal looks annoyed with the interruption. She's in the middle of explaining about discovering Annabelle's letters. "Hello. Anyone listening?"

Michael looks back and she continues. "That's when we learned that Old Man Humphrey is Sally's great, great, great Grandfather. We were all pretty stunned."

Sally then explains how we beat the second challenge. She leaves out the part about Crystal being afraid of heights.

Mr. Alton pulls me over again. "I think this the sketch that Michael was talking about."

He hands me a letter. The sketch shows a young man in a large library. He's peacefully reading a book in solitude. A candle is burning on a table next to him. It looks appealing even to me. It must have been unbelievably so to Aunt Judith.

"This is his most seductive letter so far, Steve," Mr. Alton says before he starts reading aloud again.

*So you devour books, as do I. With solitude comes time. Time to think. Time to plan. Time to rest. Just time, to do with as you please. My favorite way to pass the time is to read. No person alive today can reach me like my masters. Dumas, Hugo, Verne, Wells, along with many others. They each had a great voice. And they understood the true nature of Human Beings. Some days I forget to eat, even when I'm reading a book for the tenth time. You may have different masters, but we share the same passion. Imagine! Whiling away the hours together doing the thing we love the most.*

There is much truth in what Jeremy is saying. Mr. Alton calls it seductive, but Grandpa Jeremy is actually being pretty truthful. We found his library to prove it. He must have loved to read.

Now Sally is describing how we brought her dad in on the quest. She explains opening the second toolbox and how surprised we were to find it empty. She reads the third note, including the clues for the twelve books. And she explains how her dad solved them all.

Mr. Alton holds up another letter. "Listen."

*I have come to treasure your letters more than you can know. You are acquainted with my love for reading, but reading your letters provides me with a pleasure that I find in no manuscript. I feel it too long between our correspondences. The wait for your next words is torturous. From the tone of your recent letters, it seems that you feel as I do.*

*Imagine not having to wait for our postal system. Imagine being able to talk together whenever we desire. Imagine waking up and knowing that the person closest to you will cherish your company. I do not presume to ask anything of you yet. But if you feel as I do, please provide me with an indication of such.*

Mr. Alton looks up from the letter. "Grandpa Jeremy is getting ready to ask Aunt Judith to come to Clear Valley."

Crystal is telling Michael and Judith about the twelve books and the moon-phases puzzle they contained. She gives Tom credit for coming up with the solution and finding the pages, but Tom shares the credit with Mr. Alton.

Mr. Alton is nearing the bottom of the stack. He doesn't make any indication to me this time. He just assumes I'm listening as he begins reading aloud.

*Yes, my love, I am certain that I can ensure your security. As I have previously stated, my dwellings are well hidden. And seldom do people venture out into these woods after dusk. So indeed we will be alone. But if you wish, I can take further measures. I can place hindrances that will deter even the most persistent of unwanted guests.*

"I think Jeremy may be talking about the booby-trap," Mr. Alton says.

Michael has been listening again. "You're almost there, Jim."

Sally reads the twelve-verse poem aloud for Michael and Judy. Judy shivers when he finishes.

Michael now looks at Mr. Alton. "Jim. Read the beginning of the last letter aloud for everyone. It describes the deadly challenge that Jeremy talks about in the last verse of his poem.

Mr. Alton picks up the last letter.

*I am overwhelmed with happiness. My love has agreed to come to me. I look forward to greeting you at the train station in Dalton at the time you have provided. My heart pounds in anticipation of our meeting.*

*As you requested, I have prepared my second dwelling for you. We can live separately but share our days together. But my love, you must fully appreciate the danger of what you are requesting. Any misstep could mean your death, so you must always remain alert. I will, of course, show you the trapping when you arrive, but I would feel more secure if you were to memorize its placement before your departure.*

*Here is the manner by which you must enter your abode. Again, any deviation from this procedure will be deadly.*

Below these words is another sketch. It shows the entrance procedure to Jeremy's second hidden dwelling, though it doesn't show where the entrance is located in the woods. It depicts the mechanism that will trigger an explosion if the procedure is not flawlessly followed.

It's after five thirty when we finish exchanging information. Michael and Judy have been brought up to date on our efforts. And we know what they know about Aunt Judith and Jeremy Humphrey.

Tom and I need to be getting home soon, so we make a plan to meet in Michael's room tomorrow right after school.

Michael won't be joining our expeditions for obvious reasons. But Judy wants to come with us and we see no reason to deny her.

* * *

Mom is waiting in the kitchen when Tom and I get home at six o'clock. She calls to us as soon as she hears the door close, so we head right for the kitchen. She's sitting at the kitchen table with a glass of wine in on hand and a cigarette in the other. There is no evidence of a prepared meal.

Tom and I take seats at the table next to her, Tom on one side and me on the other. Her hair is still up and she's in her work dress. There's a serious look in her eyes. "Officer Grant came into the store today. He said Ed Hinkle is in a coma."

I'm not exactly sure what a coma is, but I know it's not good. Neither Tom nor I say a word.

Mom must not be expecting a response because she quickly continues. "According to Officer Grant, it may have been related to a prior injury, but it was probably made worse by the beating he took from you and your friends, Tom.

"He said Mrs. Hinkle may want to press charges. I think he was just trying to scare me though. He probably wants to get even for me yelling at him yesterday. But you should know that this could get serious. No matter what happens, we'll get through this together. Okay?"

"Okay, Mom," Tom answers. "I didn't think I could hurt him that bad. Even with all the help I had. I thought I'd be the one who'd be beaten up when the fight was over."

Mom puts her hand on his shoulder. "That's what makes you so brave. I can't imagine how much courage it took to stand up to him."

Mom's expression changes, becoming more severe. "There's something else I want to talk to you guys about. I know neither of you like Marvin. But I do. I don't expect him replace your father, but that doesn't mean you can't be nice to him. Or at least tolerate him. So from now on, try not to be so rude. Okay?"

I haven't thought about Marvin since Tom was taken to the police station. But apparently Tom has. "I'm sorry about how I acted Mom. But like you said before, you shouldn't have sprung him on us like that. You said we were going out on a date. You didn't say the date was with Marvin."

Mom softens. "You're right. I could have handled it a lot better. But I wasn't sure how to. And maybe a part of me just didn't care. You two have been giving me hell since your father left, you know."

She's right, of course.

"I know you miss your dad," she continues. "But that's no excuse to blame me for everything that went wrong in our marriage. There was plenty of blame to go around. And you've got to understand that there is absolutely no way that we're ever getting back together. And whether you believe it or not, your dad feels as strongly on that point as I do. If you don't believe me, ask him the next time you talk to him.

"Now I just want to get on with my life. I don't know if Marvin is the right person for me, but I'd like to find out. And I'd like my two boys to support me regardless of how badly it goes."

She snickers. "He is a bit eccentric, isn't he?"

"More than a bit," Tom adds.

Mom playfully hits Tom on the arm. "Well he was nervous, you know. Meeting two angry kids of a divorced woman took a lot of guts. So cut him some slack for acting a bit odd. If you give him a chance, you may find that he's actually a pretty nice guy."

"He did pay for dinner," I say.

Mom taps the table. "That's right. He's very generous."

Mom brightens. She's said what she wanted to say. More importantly, we've responded like she wanted us to respond. "Well I'm hungry. What do you guys want for dinner, pizza or McDonalds?"

We opt for McDonalds.

* * *

Later, in his bedroom, Tom and I discuss our meeting with Michael and Judy. We both agree that it's good to have them with us. But for some reason Tom is still suspicious of Michael. "I can't believe he could hear us in the hospital room. We were being really quiet."

"He does have good hearing," I point out. "He caught right on to Sally's comment about the toolbox for first challenge."

"That's just good listening, Steve, not good hearing. Let's just be careful when he and Judy are around, okay?"

I don't know quite what Tom means, but I agree.

We have school tomorrow, but we'll be off Friday because of a teachers' conference. We'll have a three-day weekend to work on Old Man Humphrey's puzzles.

## Thursday

Larry and Perry Hinkle return to school on Thursday. As we pass the gymnasium, the doors are open and Tom and I see them shooting hoops. We stop and watch them.

Tom's eyes are burning with anger. "So much for the rumors about Mrs. Hinkle moving them to another school. And it's pretty obvious that Perry didn't kill himself."

I nod. "Nobody is bothering them either. Maybe no one knows they're here yet."

"Since Ed's not here to protect them, it could be another rough day for them," Tom says.

I hate to admit it, but I'm relieved to see Perry. I halfway believed the rumor about his committing suicide.

Perry sees us before Larry does. He stops to stare us down. Larry notices and looks our way too.

I want to move on to our classrooms, but Tom stands firm. His face is filled with defiance. I think he's silently challenging them to approach. I want to get him away from here. "Come on Tom. Let's go."

Tom doesn't budge. Sure enough, Larry starts walking our way, followed closely by Perry.

"You're going to catch yours now," Larry says, pointing his index finger at Tom. "My mom is pressing charges against you for what you did to Ed. You'll be in jail before the weekend is over. And when you're gone, we'll have lots of fun with your little brother here. Won't we Perry?"

Perry stares at me but doesn't respond.

This isn't what I expected. Normally the Hinkle brothers don't talk. They just fight.

Tom remains quiet, though his whole body is quivering. I drag him away before he can explode again.

"Yeah, you guys just run along now," Larry calls after us. "We'll catch you later."

As we walk away, I see Principal Potter in the hall and looking our way. It's a good thing Tom didn't explode or he'd probably be on his way to the police station again.

School drags on for the rest of the day. Larry and Perry lay low and don't come outside during recess or lunch. No knows where they are, so no one can bother them. Perry disappears from my classroom about ten minutes before three thirty. When school lets out Larry and Perry are nowhere to be seen.

* * *

Crystal, Sally, Tom, and I leave school together. When we're on the sidewalk in front of the school, Ashley rushes up to talk to Sally and Crystal. She wants them to come to a party tonight. Sally says no for both of them, saying she and Crystal have to do something with their family tonight.

We arrive at the hotel at three forty and knock on Michael's door. We hear male voices coming from inside the room.

Judy opens the door for us and we hear Mr. Alton and Michael arguing.

"Things are going to get very dangerous from this point on Michael," Mr. Alton is saying. "We've got to do things in the same order specified by the poem."

"I understand that, Jim," Michael responds. "And I don't disagree on that point at all. But you've got to understand that I'm not the least bit interested in the Hillbrook stash. All I want… That is, all Judy and I want is to find out what became of Aunt Judith. I don't want her getting ignored while you're off in search of treasure. And I sure don't want any of her possessions lost or damaged during the process."

"Don't worry. We won't ignore Aunt Judith," Mr. Alton says. "If we find something that causes us to slow down, we will. I promise."

Michael doesn't respond causing Mr. Alton to add, "So we're agreed?"

"Agreed," Judy says for both of them.

Michael doesn't look satisfied.

Our plan for this afternoon will be what we all figured it would be. We'll search Jeremy's bedroom looking for the first item discussed in his poem. Sally retrieves the poem and reads the appropriate verse.

*The first item lies where I take my rest*

*You may agree it is not hidden the best*

*Discover a secret and try not to faint*

*My reputation be poor but you must further taint*

Sally puts away the poem and six of us exit Michael's room.

Michael stays behind. He nudges Judy as she's going out the door. "Be sure to stay in close contact. I want to know what's happening at all times." Michael holds up his cell phone. Judy quickly checks her phone's battery status and nods.

Tom calls Mom at the pawn shop to tell her that we are going to have dinner with Sally and Crystal. Well, it isn't a lie exactly. We'll probably eat with them when we get back.

The walk into Bandit Woods is uneventful. Sally checks her iPhone when we reach the entry to Jeremy's underground dwelling. It's four thirty. We should have at least three hours to work in the cavern before it starts getting dark.

We go down the chute one by one. Judy is amazed at how efficiently the trap door works. She goes just before me. There's a worried look on her face when she hears her click. Then it's my turn. Mr. Alton goes last.

Mr. Alton, Tom, Sally, and I make a bee line for the dwelling. But Crystal and Judy lag behind. Judy is in awe of the crystalline formations. And Crystal is happy to walk slowly with her. Crystal is repeating much of the story from last night. Judy is so captivated by her surroundings, she doesn't seem to mind.

Once in the dwelling, we all head right for the bedroom. We begin with the dresser, removing all the drawers and carefully searching their contents. We find nothing but clothes. Then we inspect the drawers themselves. And their bottoms. We find nothing.

Tom and Mr. Alton pull the dresser away from the wall and we look behind and underneath. Again, nothing. So they push the dresser back into place and Sally replaces the drawers.

We turn our attention to Jeremy's bed. The sides are very low. They're almost touching the floor so we can't see under the bed without removing the mattress. So Mr. Alton carefully removes the bed coverings. First he removes the blanket and hands it to Sally. She folds it and sets it on top of Jeremy's dresser. Then come the two sheets, one of which covers the mattress. Sally folds both and places them on top of the blanket.

Mr. Alton lifts up the mattress by its side, exposing its bottom. There's nothing there. He sets the mattress back down and Tom helps him pull the bed away from the wall. He pushes the mattress back toward the wall and lifts again. This time the mattress stands upright against the wall on the other side of the bed.

Now we can see through the box springs all the way to the floor. There's something there!

Mr. Alton sees it too. "Help me lift the bed up Tom."

As the bed goes up on its side, we can see that there's something tied to the bottom of the bed. It's a shovel. And between the shovel and the bed is a cloth bag. Another note?

Mr. Alton shakes his head. "That seemed a bit too easy."

Sally shrugs. "Well, Grandpa Jeremy did say it wasn't hidden very well."

Crystal and Judy are just entering the bedroom as we remove the shovel and cloth bag from the bed. Crystal is still talking. Judy sees the shovel and waves Crystal off. She immediately calls Michael to give him an update on our good fortune.

Sally looks at her dad. "I think Grandpa Jeremy wanted his secrets known Daddy. He doesn't seem to be making it too difficult for us so far."

I hope Sally's right.

Mr. Alton and Tom replace the bed on the floor and the mattress on the bed. Then they slide the bed back up against the wall. We leave the bed clothes on the dresser and head for the library where there is more light.

We all gather around the desk. Sally carefully removes the envelope from the oil cloth bag and the note from the envelope. She begins reading aloud.

*You are probably disappointed in my choice of hiding places. Forgive me, but it is difficult to conceal a shovel in my dwelling. I promise to make the next challenge a bit more difficult.*

*In this challenge you must dig. How deep you dig depends upon the strength of your heart. But dig you must if you have any hope of finding my treasure. Oh! Do not set your hopes so high! This be not your final challenge. It is but one more step along the way.*

Beneath Jeremy's writing is a map.

We study the map for less than thirty seconds when Sally speaks. "This looks pretty simple. It's only twenty-five paces from the trap door to the X. Due East."

Crystal gives a worried sigh. "We shouldn't even need the geocache app for that. Maybe I'll just wait here."

I bet Crystal is worried about using the exit mechanism again. She sobbed the whole way every time and ended up in Tom's arms.

Tom gives her a reassuring look. "I think we all better stay together."

I think Tom just wants another hug.

But Mr. Alton agrees with Tom. "We don't know what we're going to find out there or what we'll do once we find it. So Tom's right. We should stay together."

We make our way to the exit room and Crystal insists upon going right after Tom. She seems to be getting use to the ride up, but she still whimpers along the way. And yes, she latches on to Tom at the top.

The rest of us make our ascents. Mr. Alton carries up the shovel.

In just a few minutes, we're all standing out in front of the rock face. Since we're not sure we'll be back tonight, Tom throws the rope ladder up to the ledge, hiding it.

Sally pulls out her iPhone so we can locate the trap door from our present position. We quickly make our way back there. She uses the iPhone's compass to keep us walking due East as we count off twenty-five paces. I'm concerned that our steps aren't exactly thirty inches long, but no one thinks we need the geocaching app.

Mr. Alton kneels down. He brushes pine needles and loose dirt from where the X should be. After he clears away only a half inch of top soil, he nearly shouts. "I've got something!"

We all bend over for a closer look. Mr. Alton points out a stone that looks just like the ones framing the trap door.

"Dis must be da place," Crystal says.

Tom starts digging. After five shovels full, the hole is about a foot deep. On his next downward thrust, we hear the tell-tale thud of a shovel hitting something other than dirt.

Tom digs faster. Eventually, he exposes the outline of another toolbox. It's wrapped in the same oil cloth that covers Old Man Humphrey's notes.

Mr. Aton waves his arm. "Hold up, Tom."

Tom is so excited that he's been frantically digging and Mr. Alton wants to slow down. He opens his backpack and removes a small hand shovel. It's like one used for gardening. "I'll take it from here."

Mr. Alton carefully digs around each corner of the toolbox. He eventually grabs the handle through the oil cloth and pulls the toolbox up and out of the ground. He then removes the protective oil cloth. Although the wrapping has protected the toolbox pretty well, it still shows signs of being in the ground for sixty years. All four corners are corroded, and part of the handle pulled apart when Mr. Alton removed it from the ground.

"Well," Crystal says. "Grandpa Jeremy was right about this not being the Hillbrook stash. It looks way too small."

Judy is on her cell phone again, updating Michael.

* * *

We decide to take the toolbox back to Michael's room before we open it. We're all very excited so the trip seems to take forever. In reality it takes thirty-five minutes of brisk walking.

Michael has prepared for our return. Newspapers cover the table.

"Who's going to do the honors?" Michael asks as Tom sets the toolbox down on the newspapers.

Crystal points at Tom. "I think Tom should. He's opened every one so far."

Tom has trouble opening the latch. It's rusted shut. Mr. Alton gets a screwdriver from his backpack and pries the latch completely off the toolbox.

With the latch broken, Tom has no problem opening the lid.

In the top tray there is a wooden Christian cross. It appears to be homemade and nearly fills the top tray. It's about twelve inches long and five inches wide. Tom carefully picks it out from beneath the tray's round handle. When he turns it over, we see the characters carved in its long side.

*RIP   PENELOPE   PETERS   1893 – 1919*

Crystal and Sally gasp together. Instantly, I feel sick to my stomach. This is a grave marker.

Beneath the cross there is an oil cloth covered envelope. Tom opens the envelope and we discover two pieces of yellowing paper. Neither is a note from Old Man Humphrey. One is a letter. The other is a newspaper clipping.

We've seen the newspaper clipping before, or one just like it. It's entitled *Find Love Via The Post Office*. We don't have to read the article to know what it contains. It's an appeal to lonely people to submit their names and addresses in hopes of finding their true love.

The letter is something new. The letter-head is from the Chicago Tribune. It's dated March twenty-first, nineteen thirteen and is addressed to Jeremy Humphrey. Tom reads it out loud.

*Dear Mr. Humphrey,*

*Thank you for your recent submission concerning your esteemed organization. Your article will be published in this coming Sunday's morning edition, as well as any other editions we elect to publish on that day. We find the work your organization is doing to be admirable, and wish you success in your endeavor to help lonely people find each other by whatever means is at their disposal.*

*Best regards,*

*Jason Meyers*

*Editor, Human Interests and Life Styles*

Michael gasps the loudest. "My god! Jeremy Humphrey wrote the article for attracting lonely women himself!"

Mr. Alton agrees. "He sure fooled that newspaper editor. And others like him. That couldn't have been easy."

Tom doesn't give anyone time to consider the implications of what he just read. He removes the top tray to expose two more items below. Both are wrapped in oil cloth.

The first package contains a stack of letters. They're all addressed to Jeremy Humphrey and come from a woman named Penelope Peters. The return address is 6304 Melvina Street in Chicago, Illinois. We don't need to read the letters to know what they contain. We've seen a stack of letters just like these from Annabelle. No doubt they will tell the story of a young woman who falls in love with Jeremy and comes to Clear Valley to be with her soul mate.

Mr. Alton takes the stack of letters from Tom and examines the top one. It's postmarked April second, nineteen thirteen. He then pulls out the bottom one. It's dated September twelfth, nineteen thirteen. Assuming the letters are stacked in order, Penelope corresponded with Jeremy for about five months, and must have come to Clear Valley shortly after September twelfth. And according to her grave marker, she died six years later.

Michael points at the letter from the Chicago Tribune. "I guess this answers the question of whether Old Man Humphrey lured other women to Clear Valley. Now the only question seems to be 'How many others were there?'"

Tom seems reluctant to remove the last package in the toolbox so Mr. Alton does it for him. He removes the oil cloth to reveal two more items. First, there is another thin oil cloth covered bag containing what must be another note. And second, there is a small metal pry-bar. It's about eight inches long.

Mr. Alton then opens the thin oil cloth bag. There's an envelope containing two more sheets of yellowed paper.

One of the sheets has two straight edges and two torn edges. It is obviously a corner of a full sheet of paper that has been ripped in half twice. From its orientation, we can tell that this is the upper-left corner of the page.

"Look at that!" Tom yells as he points at the page.

*THE HILLB*

A vertical tear cuts the page off just after the letter B.

"That's got to mean the Hillbrook stash!" Tom claims.

The rest of the page shows a portion of a map. But since it is only the upper left corner of the map, we can't tell much from it. There's neither a starting point nor an X.

"The rest of the map pieces must be hidden with the other items mentioned in the poem," Sally says.

Mr. Alton nods in agreement.

Judy picks up the other piece of paper that was in the envelope. It's another note from Old Man Humphrey. She reads it out loud.

*Now you know my true reason for desiring solitude. Do you not think me evil? Indeed, I enticed women to my home. This I cannot deny. But how well do you know my true nature, you judge of another's evil tendencies? And to what ends will you go to attain that which you yourself desire? Oh, judge me if you will, but beware of your own sinful tendencies. Others may lie in wait to judge you as you judge me.*

*Judge me harshly if you desire to do so, but concede to do me a service as well.*

*This woman, Penelope Peters of Chicago, Illinois, now rests mere feet beneath where you have dug. She is certainly missed by someone, though of this I cannot be certain. During her years with me she mentioned not a one of them. Maybe she is not missed so much as one would think. She was a solitary soul, but surely someone wonders what has become of her.*

*If you be a gentleman, you will seek out those that may miss her and put their minds to rest. With what you find at the end of this road, you will surely have the means. And when you find Penelope's people, please pass along an utterance from me: She was loved.*

*And now the end of your journey has finally begun. You have in your possession one of four items you will need to defeat my final challenge. You also have one quarter of the map that will direct you there. There is still time to surrender your pursuit. But not much.*

Again we're speechless. At Michael's request, Judy reads the note again.

Mr. Alton is the first to speak. "Well at least he didn't admit to killing her. But he does admit to luring her here."

Michael doesn't sound so sure. "But then what? Did she just stay here of her own free will? Or did Jeremy hold her captive?"

Judy shakes her head in confusion. "We don't know enough to come to any kind of conclusion about that. He did say she was loved. It's implied that he loved her. But he doesn't actually come out and say it."

"And he wants her family notified," Crystal adds. "That's got to mean something."

Tom picks up the note. "But there's another warning. He seems to enjoy tormenting us. So maybe he also enjoyed tormenting his captives."

"We should find more answers tomorrow," Michael says. "With school being out, you guys will have all day to work on it."

Then Michael changes the subject. "It's six thirty. Shall I call room service or do you want me to order a pizza? Either way, It's my treat."

Crystal looks like she's about to say something but thinks better of it.

Our choice is pizza.

\* \* \*

After eating, we agree to meet at Michael's room tomorrow morning at seven o'clock. That will give us the whole day to work on Old Man Humphrey's challenges.

Tom and I walk part of the way home with Crystal, Sally, and Mr. Alton. Just after we separate and about a block from Seventh Street, a police car pulls up from behind and stops at the curb right next to us. Officer Grant gets out and leans over the roof. "You'll be happy to know, Tom, that Ed Hinkle is out of his coma and is doing better. And Mrs. Hinkle has decided not to press any charges."

What a relief!

"Thank you, Officer Grant," Tom replies.

Officer Grant starts to get back into his squad car, but reconsiders. He looks at Tom again. "I'm not sure whether I should say any more. But I think you should know that your mother had a lot to do with Mrs. Hinkle's decision."

"What did she do?" Tom asks.

Officer Grant is already getting back into the car as he answers. "I can't tell you any more. But let's just say I don't approve of her methods."

Officer Grant drives off leaving us wondering what Mom did.

\* \* \*

Mom is in the living room watching a *CSI Miami* re-run when we get home. "Hey boys. Did you have a good time with your girlfriends?"

I chuckle at Mom's assumption. "I don't think they're girlfriends exactly." Then I think of the hugs that Crystal has given Tom.

"Well at least for me," I add. "Though Sally is a good friend. Tom on the other hand… I think he's found true love."

Tom jabs me, making me pull away. The awkward motion causes the first real pain in my right arm in over a day.

"Is that so?" Mom says, and then asks, "When do I get to meet these girls?"

The thought of Mom meeting Sally turns my stomach. "Uh… I don't know Mom. Maybe sometime over the summer?"

Mom ignores my suggestion. "How about tomorrow night? I'll make dinner." She's not really asking. "You've been spending a lot of time with these girls lately and I want to meet them. I can call Mrs. Alton if you don't want to ask them yourselves."

"No!" Tom and I shout together.

Tom and I exchange horrified looks. I shrug.

"We can ask them but they may have other plans," Tom says.

Mom nods. "Well if they have other plans, that's okay. But I don't want you seeing them again until I get a chance to meet them."

Now we're between a rock and a hard place. "Okay Mom," I say.

Tom gives me a dirty look, like he thinks this is all somehow my fault.

Tom changes the subject. "Officer Grant stopped us on our way home tonight."

Mom taps her forehead. "Oh yeah. Did he tell you that Ed Hinkle is out of his coma?"

Tom nods. "Yeah, he told us Mom. He also said Mrs. Hinkle isn't going press charges. And that you had something to do with that."

"Why that little bastard!" Mom raises her voice but she doesn't sound very angry. "He wasn't supposed to say anything about that."

"What did you do, Mom?" I ask.

"Actually *I* didn't do anything. It was Marvin."

I'm astonished. "Marvin from the pawn shop?"

"Yes, Marvin from the pawn shop," Mom replies in a sing-song voice.

"What did he do?" Tom asks.

"Well he didn't really do all that much either. But his *associates*. Now that's another story." Mom is almost laughing now.

"Come on, Mom!" Tom sounds exasperated. "What happened?"

Mom finally spills the beans. "Principal Potter called me at the pawn shop this morning after your little run-in with Larry and Perry near the gym. I couldn't believe that those little jerks were still harassing you after all that's happened. I must have been talking pretty loud. Marvin overheard my side of the conversation.

"When I got off the phone, he asked me if you guys were still having problems with the Hinkle brothers. When I said yes, he disappeared into his office and didn't come out for half an hour.

"When he finally emerged, he just said we shouldn't have any more problems with the Hinkles. I had to really press him to find out what he did.

"What did he do?" Tom asks.

Mom lights a cigarette before she continues. "In the pawn business Marvin has to deal with some pretty unsavory characters. For the most part, he stays away from stolen goods. He's not a fence. But he does buy and sell with some guys you wouldn't want to meet in a dark alley, if you catch my drift."

We do.

"Well," Mom continues. "Three of these guys have owed Marvin money for a long time. Marvin was pretty sure he'd never see his money. So he had called one of them and told him that in lieu of paying him back, the three of them could do him a favor. The favor was to take care of your little problem."

Mom chuckles as she looks at Tom. "That's what he called it Tom. Your little problem. And they did. And I think they enjoyed it. The Hinkle brothers won't be bothering you again."

Mom stops, but sees we're anxiously waiting for more. "Oh, you want the details?"

"Yes! What did they do?" Tom pleads.

"They went to the Hinkles' house and had a little chat with them. All the Hinkles were there, except for Ed of course. Even Mr. Hinkle. They made it clear in no uncertain terms that none of the Hinkles were ever to bother you boys again. Nor were they to bother any other kids for that matter.

"While they were there, they broke a Play Station and a flat screen television in the living room. They said that they'd love to come back and finish the conversation some day. But it was entirely up to the Hinkles to invite them back."

Tom and I sit in awe as Mom casually walks out of the room. Mom has connections! No wonder Officer Grant didn't approve. I wonder how much of the story he really knows.

Mike Lynch

Friday

On Friday morning we're out of the house by six forty-five and at Michael's hotel room door at five to seven. This time we're the first to arrive.

Michael responds to our knock. "Come on in guys. The door isn't locked.

We enter and see Michael shaving in the bathroom. Or trying to shave. He's in his wheelchair, which doesn't make it any easier. He's cursing every few seconds. Having just one hand to work with only compounds his problem.

"Judy just called," he says between curses. "She'll be here any minute. Go on in and turn on the television if you want."

We go in and sit at the table but neither of us turns on the T V Looking out the front window, we see the girls and Mr. Alton coming up the walk to the hotel's front door.

Michael wheels himself into the bedroom a minute later. He's using his broken arm to help turn the wheel of the wheelchair. This makes me jealous since I haven't been using my right arm very much yet. His face is shaved but there's still part of his beard showing. And there are five little white pieces of tissue paper clinging to his cheeks and chin. Each has a tiny spot of red in the middle. "This has been quite an adventure for you two, hasn't it?"

I nod. "Yes. It seems like it's been going on forever. Hard to believe it's been just over a week."

Michael scoots himself in toward the table. "Well you sure are nice kids. Sally and Crystal too. And you look good together."

It seems someone else thinks we have girlfriends. I guess I'm getting used to the idea. I wonder what Sally or Crystal would say about Michael's comment.

Michael picks up a letter and holds it out to us. "Judy and I read all of Penelope's letters last night after you left. They're all pretty much what we expected. But I think you should hear this one."

We left the door unlocked and Crystal, Sally, and Mr. Alton enter the room as Michael starts reading.

*Dearest Jeremy,*

*Like you, I long for more frequent correspondences. When I receive a letter from you, my heart races with such exhilaration that I fear it will surely burst. I read every sentence many times in a feeble attempt to prolong my connection with you. And woe is the moment when I finish. For I know it will be many days before I will receive your words again.*

*We will soon eliminate this cumbersome burden, my love. For I have found your accommodation to be acceptable. And so will I make the necessary travel arrangements to join you in your paradise. Details will be sent in my next letter.*

*Though I have no concern for what others may think of me, I cannot in my own heart agree to share your bed. While love you I do, we can never be properly joined in matrimony. This be the only concession to our agreed arrangement. But alas, it is a cruel one.*

*So the separate sleeping quarters you are arranging will be acceptable and necessary. I will take rest in the bedroom, you in the library.*

The letter continues, but Michael has finished reading the part he wants us to hear. He looks up to all of us. "So Jeremy had his underground dwelling in nineteen thirteen. I think that's significant. Before that, and when he married Annabelle, he was still living in the cabin. So sometime after Annabelle and before Penelope, he must have found the cavern.

"I was thinking that Jeremy went to great lengths to lure Penelope here. If his intentions were evil, he could have told her just about anything. He could have told her that his dwelling had two bedrooms. Or that it contained several private chambers. He could have said there were two separate dwellings even before he found the second one. But instead of any of those, he told Penelope the truth. He did not deceive her in that regard. And she came anyway."

Judy enters the room and we're a complete team. "So, what's the plan for today?"

* * *

Sally finds Old Man Humphrey's poem. She reads the verse that applies to our next challenge.

*Next you must wander to where I eat*
*Be sure to rest there just take a seat*
*If you look around I am sure you will find*
*The next item you'll need though you won't think it kind*

"This one sounds pretty simple too," Tom says. "The clue is hidden in the kitchen."

We're off to Jeremy's dwelling, leaving Michael behind again. Before we leave, he tells Judy to check her cell phone's battery status, which she does.

On the way, I want to ask Sally if she and Crystal can join us for dinner tonight. But I want to do it when we're alone. Fortunately, Crystal and Judy have struck up a conversation ahead of us. And Tom is walking just behind them with Mr. Alton. Here's my chance.

"All of this is pretty amazing," I say. Small talk first. Then I'll spring the question.

Sally keeps up her pace. "Uh-huh."

"Do you think we'll find the Hillbrook stash today?"

"I doubt it. I think we've still got a lot of work ahead of us."

"That Judy is really something, isn't she?" I'm running out of things to say. Small talk is hard.

Sally stops, letting everyone move further ahead of us. "I've known you long enough, Steve Jones, to know when you're up to something. What is it?"

"Well… The thing is…" I stammer. "My mom wants you guys to come over for dinner tonight. She wants to meet you and Crystal."

Sally's cheeks turn red. "She does? Why? How does she know…"

"Mrs. Latimer," I interrupt, "a customer of Mom's saw the four of us walking together. And then the other day Tom and I let it slip that we knew what happened at school after Tom was taken to the police station. We had to tell her how you and Crystal told us that Mrs. Hinkle took her kids home."

I stop talking, thinking that I've explained enough. But Sally still looks confused. I guess I just have come out and say it. "She thinks Tom and I have girlfriends. And she wants to meet them."

Now I'm the one who's blushing.

Sally smiles. "Well, do you? Have a girlfriend, I mean."

Her question surprises me. "Well... Uh... No... I mean yeah, ah... kind of, if you like me... I don't know...."

Sally laughs. She obviously enjoys watching me squirm. "Don't worry, Steve. I understand. And in case you were wondering, yes, I like you. I'm sure Crystal and I can come to your house for dinner. I just have to ask my dad to make sure we don't have anything else planned."

Suddenly I feel as if I'm hovering. Did Sally just say she liked me? As a boyfriend?

I float the rest of the way to the trap door. I don't remember going down the slide. The next thing I know, we're in the kitchen.

Tom immediately goes for the table. He and Mr. Alton turn it over and find nothing beneath it. They look under the chairs with the same result.

Judy points toward the cabinets. "You don't think it would be in one of those, do you?"

Emptying all the cabinets will take a while. And it will make a mess.

"I hope not," Tom answers.

Mr. Alton turns to Tom. "Read that verse again."

Tom pulls out the poem and reads the verse aloud.

*Next you must wander to where I eat*
*Be sure to rest there just take a seat*
*If you look around I am sure you will find*
*The next item you'll need though you won't think it kind*

Sally goes to the table. "This is where he ate, right? He says 'just take a seat'." She sits down.

Crystal sits down in the other chair, facing Sally. "He says we just have to look around when we're seated to find it." They begin scanning the room.

"There!" Sally points to an object sticking out of the wall above the table. It's milky white, matching the crystalline stone all around it. I have to look very closely to see it. It's nearly invisible to anyone standing up.

Tom pushes Crystal out of her chair and moves the table away. He brings the chair to the wall and steps up for a closer look.

"What is it, Tom?" Crystal asks.

Tom scrutinizes the object. "I think it's a knife. Just a minute. Let me see if I can pull it out."

Tom grunts as his arm jerks back. When the knife comes out of the rock, something drops to the floor with a thud. Whatever fell must have been held in place by the knife.

"Now there is a hole in the rock where the knife was stuck." Tom reaches into the hole. "Nothing more here."

Sally bends down to pick up the fallen item. It's a small cardboard box about four inches square and an inch thick. It's a small Fannie May candy box. The top is sealed to the bottom with yellowing clear tape.

And the top is glued to a piece of crystalline rock that matches the size, color and shape of the hole in the wall.

Tom steps down from the chair. "It sure was camouflaged. Only the white handle was showing."

We bring the knife and box to the library and place them on the desk.

Mr. Alton is first to inspect the knife. "I think the handle is made from ivory. But what is this coating on the blade?"

He passes the knife around and I see what he's talking about. There's thick black stuff on the blade.

When Crystal sees it, she shivers. "You don't think it's dried blood, do you?"

Actually, it does look like dried blood.

Mr. Alton takes the knife back and uses it to slit the tape sealing the box. Inside there's only one oil cloth bag. He opens it to reveal an envelope containing a note from Old Man Humphrey. After taking out the note, he starts reading aloud.

*The item you have removed from the kitchen wall fills me with regret. I shudder to think of this unhappy episode in my life. The coating you see on the blade is exactly what you think it to be. I could not bear to clean it for fear that doing so would also wipe clean my memory of the dreadful event. For as much as it pains me, I must never forget. And now, neither must you.*

*You will learn more of this sorrowful incident when you dig. Ah yes. You must dig again. For not only will you will learn the circumstances of the knife's use, you will also acquire another item needed to achieve your goal.*

213

The map below Old Man Humphrey's words is as simple as the last one. It directs us to a spot twenty-three paces due south of the trap door. Judy gets on her cell phone to Michael to give him an update.

* * *

This time Sally doesn't use the iPhone. I don't think she's in any hurry to find the spot indicated by the X on the map. None of us are. We count off the paces and scrape the ground for only a minute or so before Crystal points at the familiar stones. She doesn't touch them.

Tom doesn't want to dig this time so Mr. Alton plunges the shovel into the ground. Five minutes later, we hear the thud. A little more digging and the use of the hand shovel exposes another toolbox wrapped in oil cloth. For some reason this toolbox is in much better condition. There is no rust or corrosion.

Since it's only nine fifteen, we decide not to go back to Michael's hotel to open it. Instead, we head for the library. Judy's on her phone with Michael as we start back to the dwelling.

Tom doesn't offer to open it the toolbox this time. And Crystal doesn't comment. So Mr. Alton does the honors. Judy is still on the phone with Michael and describing all the action.

The latch opens easily and Mr. Alton flips open the top. My stomach turns as I see the familiar contents. Another homemade wooden cross is in the top tray. Mr. Alton carefully fishes it out and turns it over.

*RIP   CECILIA ROBERTS   1899 – 1925*

Judy Shivers at the realization that it's not Aunt Judith. But it could have been. She gives Michael the news.

In the top tray there is also a oil cloth bag. It contains an envelope with another newspaper clipping. Just like the one found with Penelope's grave marker. There is also a letter addressed to Jeremy Humphrey. This time it's from an editor at the Denver Post. It's dated November sixteenth, nineteen twenty-one.

Mr. Alton reads them both aloud, but there's nothing worth mentioning. We've seen all of this before.

Mr. Alton then removes the top tray and exposes two packages wrapped in oil cloth. The first is a stack of letters from Cecilia to Jeremy. They start in December of nineteen twenty-one and end in April of nineteen twenty-two. No one wants to read them just now.

From the letters and cross, we know Cecilia corresponded with Jeremy for four months before she came to Clear valley. She lived with Jeremy for about three years before she died.

The second package contains another thin oil cloth bag and an odd looking metal hook. It is about a foot long and made from one long piece of metal. The hook is on one end and a ring is on the other. It looks much like a hook used to hold a screen door closed, but much larger. A short piece of round wood is taped to the hook. It's about ten inches long and it looks a lot like a large drum stick. The kind used to play a musical instrument. Since they are taped together, they must be used at the same time, right?

Mr. Alton opens the thin oil cloth bag and finds an envelope containing two more pieces of yellowed paper. We see the upper-right quarter of the map right away. Tom pulls out other map piece we found yesterday and hands it to Mr. Alton. He holds them up together and they match perfectly. Tom was right about the heading at the top of the page.

## THE HILLBROOK STASH

Piecing the two halves together doesn't help much to decipher the map. We still can't see any recognizable markers, nor can we tell where the starting point is located. And there's no X.

As expected, the other piece of yellowed paper is another note from Old Man Humphrey. Mr. Alton reads it to us.

*I will now elucidate the events involving the item you found in my kitchen. You already think me evil, and I assure you, this explanation will effect no change of heart.*

*Cecilia was a dreadfully delicate flower, even before she came to me. I recognized this peculiarity during our courtship as you will when you read her letters. But I pursued her anyway, much to my everlasting shame and regret.*

*Like Annabelle and Penelope before her, she traveled a long distance to reach me. For Cecilia, having never ventured beyond her own town's city limits, this was a tremendous undertaking. One that caused her great anxiety and extracted from her a permanent toll.*

*Her previously frail countenance upon arrival was further diminished. I cared for her as best I could, but my labors could only pertain to her physical health. And improve in this regard she did. But her mental health was wholly a different matter. Try as I might with anecdotes and pleasant conversation, she did not improve.*

*She ate, she drank, she slept. But after her first month with me, she uttered not word. I readily accepted her unwillingness to converse but worried that it was but a symptom of a more serious ailment. Indeed, time proved me correct.*

*For three years I cared for her. She rarely acknowledged my presence, yet there were times when I could tell that there was something still alive behind her inert eyes. A sudden movement. A gasp. A hand gesture. So I continued to hope that one day she would come back from her frightful journey into oblivion. Alas, it was not to be.*

*One terrible morning in December of nineteen twenty-five did I come upon her lifeless body. She had used the knife. That is all I will say on this matter. God forgive me. And God rest her soul.*

*As with Penelope, you now have information that will allow you to contact Cecilia's people. Assuming you survive my final challenge, which is fast approaching, you will also have the means.*

Tom doesn't wait to speak this time. "This just keeps getting better and better."

Mr. Alton gives a nervous chuckle. "That's not quite what I'd have said, Tom, but it'll do."

Crystal is hugging herself. "Does anyone else think we should call the police?"

"I've been thinking about that too, Crystal," Mr. Alton replies. "But what do we really know? Jeremy lured women here, true. But if he's telling the truth, they all came of their own free will. One killed herself. A suicide, not a murder. And all of this happened over sixty years ago. Talk about your cold cases."

I think of how the conversation would go with Officer Grant. He'd have squad cars and ambulances out here in no time. And the area would be swarming with reporters. I agree with Mr. Alton. There's nothing to report. Yet.

Judy puts Michael on the speaker of her cell phone. "I don't think we should call the police either. The bodies have been buried for over sixty years. Forensics evidence will probably be minimal. And it will not diminish further during the next few days or even weeks. When we're finished, we can turn everything over to the police. But for now, it wouldn't accomplish anything. But it would put an end to our quest."

\* \* \*

It's only one thirty so we decide to carry on. We're emotionally drained from what we just learned about Cecilia, but we're determined to do more today. Tom grabs the poem and reads the verse pertaining to our next challenge.

*Where you go next will surely depend*
*On which side of my dwelling you consider its end*
*Look for a hole that does not belong*
*Rest assured that it's there I won't lead you wrong*

Tom wiggles the poem in the air. "Any ideas?"

"I guess we have two choices, right?" I say. "The slide and the exit room. Why don't we split up so we can search both at the same time."

Mr. Alton nods. "Good idea Steve. Judy, Sally, you're with me."

They take off toward the slide while Tom, Crystal, and I head for the exit room.

Tom and I start walking. Crystal moves quickly to join us and takes Tom's arm. "I hear we're coming to your house for dinner tonight,"

Tom gives me a confused look. Obviously he hasn't been thinking about dinner. Or Mom. Or asking the girls to come.

218

I shrug. "I asked Sally on the way here this morning, Tom. She said yes, as long as it's okay with her dad."

Crystal doesn't wait for a response from Tom. "Oh, it will be okay with him. I guarantee it. He likes you two. So what are we having, Tom?"

"I wouldn't get my hopes up. Mom's not much of a cook. We may be ordering pizza."

Crystal pokes Tom in the side. "Sally told me your mom thinks we're your girlfriends."

I've already been through this. It's Tom's turn to squirm.

"Well," Tom says, "we said you were our friends. Mom added the 'girlfriends' part on her own."

"So we're not your girlfriends?" Crystal puts on a pout.

"I didn't say that," Tom responds. "Do you want to be my girlfriend?"

Tom's much better at this than I am.

"Heck yeah! What about you Steve. Are you Sally's boyfriend."

I take my cue from Tom. "If she'll have me."

Crystal winks at me. "Oh, I don't think you have to worry about that, Steve."

\* \* \*

Once in the exit room, we carefully walk the entire perimeter. We inspect all of the walls. Clear and milky white stone is all around us. If there's a hole here, it shouldn't be too hard to find. But after ten minutes of searching, we find nothing. We continue to look for another ten minutes or so. Still, we can find no unusual hole.

Tom's been in the lead but now he turns back to Crystal and me. "Maybe the others have found something."

We head out of the exit room and along the path that follows the creek. Mr. Alton is leading Sally and Judy toward us. We meet where the path breaks off toward the sink.

Mr. Alton looks anxiously at Tom. "Did you find anything?"

"No. We were hoping you did."

"We may be thinking too literally," Judy says.

"What do you mean?" Crystal asks.

Judy thinks for a moment. "I think I have an idea. But Tom, let's hear that verse again."

Tom pulls out the poem and reads the verse.

*Where you go next will surely depend*

*On which side of my dwelling you consider its end*

*Look for a hole that does not belong*

*Rest assured that it's there I won't lead you wrong*

Judy looks at Sally. "Sally, get out your iPhone out and look up the definition of *end*."

Sally does as commanded. It only takes her a few seconds. "Wow. There are several ways to use the word end. It can be taken to mean finish, as in *to end a sentence*. It can mean to stop, as in *to prematurely end a race*. It can mean extremity, as in *the ends of the earth*. It can also mean a purpose, as in *what end are you trying to achieve?*"

"The purpose meaning might apply in the verse," Crystal suggests.

Judy smiles. "That's exactly what I was thinking."

"So what side of this dwelling do we consider its purpose?" Tom asks.

"I can only think of one thing," Sally says. This is a cavern. It must have been carved out over time by water. Maybe its 'end' is to let the water drain out."

"That would be a double meaning," Crystal agrees. "The purpose for the cavern is to drain water. And the water drains at the end of the cavern. I like it."

We walk along the path toward the slide. The creek exits the cavern just ahead on our left. It flows through a hole in the crystalline rock.

Upon close inspection, we find that up and to the left of the water draining hole is a second hole. It's smaller, only about seven inches in diameter. Maybe the creek flowed through this hole many years ago.

Crystal points at the second hole. "Doesn't that look like "a hole that does not belong' to you? It sure looks like one to me."

Tom has to step over the creek to get close to the second hole. He reaches in. "I think I've got it!"

His arm is in the hole almost to elbow depth. After fishing around for a bit he pulls out a oil cloth bag and hands it to Crystal. He puts his arm back in and feels around some more. "That's strange. I can feel something farther in, but it won't come out. It feels like a handle. I can pull it about two or three inches, but it snaps back when I let go."

Mr. Alton steps over the creek and pulls out his flashlight. He peeks into the hole. "That's odd. It does look like a handle of some kind, but I have no idea what it's for. I don't think it's part of the challenge."

We're all puzzled by the handle but no one can come up with its purpose. In the end, we give up trying. We head for the library with our new possession.

At the desk, Mr. Alton finds two items in the oil cloth bag. A book and an envelope. The book is a diary. Mr. Alton opens it and Judy gasps.

Inside the front cover is the owner's name. Judith Maxwell. Judy gets on her cell phone to tell Michael.

The diary is pretty big. It's about five inches wide by seven inches long and well over an inch thick. Mr. Alton thumbs through a few pages, but there's too much to read right now. He hands the diary to Judy, who takes it slowly and hugs it lovingly to her heart.

Mr. Alton opens the envelope and pulls out the note. He reads out loud.

*Previously you have had only my words to guide you. I have done my best to be forthright, but you probably doubt my honesty. And I cannot blame you for that. Another's words may provide you with a more complete understanding of my true nature. Oh, do not think me vain, for I did not know of these words until after her demise. Indeed, she kept her words to herself. I include them now only for your enlightenment, not for my salvation in your eyes.*

*This woman whose words you now can read was my life. I have loved no other as I did her. You will hear more of her story, and mine, after you dig. You know what you will find, but still you must dig. This be the last time you must dig such as there were no others after her. Jeffrey Hillbrook saw to that.*

The map is again a simple one to follow. Out we go to the exit room and back to the trap door.

We walk the specified number of paces in the given direction and search the ground. Again, Crystal is the one to find the familiar stones. And Mr. Alton digs.

We pull the oil-cloth covered toolbox from the ground and bring it to the library.

Judy is in tears as Mr. Alton opens the toolbox. We all know what's inside. The wooden cross is carefully removed. As expected, the back is inscribed.

*RIP   JUDITH  MAXWELL   1899 – 1937*

Sally points at the inscription. "Does anyone else notice anything special about the year Aunt Judith died.

I'm so worried about Judy, who is sobbing now, that I'm not even looking at the cross.

Mr. Alton answers. "That was the year that Jeffrey Hillbrook was killed."

As expected, there is a thin oil cloth bag in the top tray. It contains a newspaper clipping and a letter to Jeremy Humphrey. The clipping has the same title as the others we've seen. The letter is from an editor from the Lubbock Avalanche and is dated July seventh, nineteen thirty-four.

Judy gasps. "Look at that date. Aunt Judith disappeared in May of nineteen thirty-five. Ten months later."

The letter and newspaper clipping provide no new information, so Mr. Alton picks up the top tray to reveal what is beneath.

Again there are two packages wrapped in oil cloth. The first contains the stack of letters that Aunt Judith wrote to Jeremy. Judy picks them up and hugs them with the diary to her breast. Tears are still flowing and she sobs as she quietly describes the events to Michael.

The second packages contains another thin oil cloth bag and a hammer. The hammer is like one used by carpenters. It has a claw on one end and the hammer head on the other. In the oil cloth bag is an envelope containing two sheets of paper. The first is the lower left portion of the map. We glance at it and quickly discover that there is no X. But there is something of interest. A stick figure is lying on the ground. Where eyes should be in the head are two X's. It's obvious that this person is either sleeping or dead.

Small dots lead away from the character. They are the same dots as Old Man Humphrey used for footprints to get us from the Hillbrook Memorial Pillar to the water tower in our second challenge. They move up and away from the figure to the upper left portion of the map. They continue to the upper right portion. Finally, they move to the torn edge of the page and will continue in the lower right portion of the map. When we find it. We've found the start point, the stick figure. But where is he?

Jeremy's note is much longer than his others. Mr. Alton reads aloud.

*You may think me evil to pursue another after hapless Cecilia, but pursue her I did. Nearly ten years had passed since Cecilia took her own life, and my need outlasted my conscience. It is a thing about which I am not proud.*

*From the moment she arrived, Judith loved me wholly. Even though I had deceived her about my age and youthful appearance, as I had the others, she never once commented. If ever a woman was blinded by love, it was Judith Maxwell. She treated me as she would a man of her own generation. In her presence I felt young and alive. Though we had no carnal knowledge, many a day was spent with her in total bliss.*

*Judith was a woman to me unlike any other. Annabelle despised me from the moment she saw me. She never forgave my deceit. Though I was young then as I proclaimed to be, I had misled her about my status in life. She thought me to be affluent, owning much property and well thought-of by my peers.*

*Upon her arrival in Clear Valley, she only married me because she felt pressure to honor her betrothal. This was at a time in my life when prying eyes were always watching and judging. Annabelle was compelled to marry me, even though she did love me.*

*Her concern for decorum was short lived. Within one month of her sacred vows, she left.*

*I did not know she was with child. In truth, I cannot be sure she did either. But when the child came, I wanted no part of him. And she did well to keep him from me. Only once did I strike him, but the desire to do so occurred on many occasions.*

*That wretched brat took to following me. And in the days when Cecilia was at her worst, he came upon her in the woods. She had long since taken leave of her senses. On that day while I was in town, she exited our dwelling. I was unaware that she could use the exit mechanism. The sight of her terrified the boy, as it would anyone who did not know her circumstance. Later came talk of witches in my woods.*

*While Penelope tolerated me, she did not love me as I loved her. Her desire for solitude was of utmost importance to her. Since I honored her desire as no other would, she endured my presence and never attempted to leave her new home. Indeed I believe she actually enjoyed her time here. She did often seem to me to be content with her surroundings. But not with me.*

*Penelope came to an accidental end. I do not know the details of her demise because I was not present. As was her norm, she had gone for a walk in the woods by herself. She stayed out for a very long time and I began to worry. It was drawing close to dusk when I went looking for her. I came upon her broken body under the cave of your first challenge. She often climbed up there to be alone. To read. To think. Or just to be away from me. She must have lost her footing from quite a height, for her neck was badly broken. I know not whether she was on her way up or her way down when she fell.*

*You know the story of Cecilia and I do not care to discuss her again.*

*But Judith. Oh sweet Judith! My time with her was short, less than two years. But they were fine years indeed. Her violent end crushed me. It was then that I too should have died. Indeed I did stop living on the day of her end.*

*You will learn the details of Judith's death soon enough.*

Judy has been holding the phone close to Mr. Alton so Michael can hear the note being read. Her tears are finally drying up. "It seems Jeremy was involved in a series of four tragic love stories. If he's guilty of anything, it's of caring too much."

Mr. Alton grunts. "I think you're being a bit too kind, Judy. Are you forgetting that he lured them all here with lies to newspaper editors and lies about himself? And what proof do we have that he's not making all of this up?"

Judy holds up Aunt Judith's diary. "We'll know soon enough."

* * *

It's after four o'clock and we're all exhausted. Mr. Alton says we should stop for the day and nobody argues. Judy wants to get back to the hotel and read Aunt Judith's diary. Tom and I should get home to get ready for dinner tonight.

We agree to meet tomorrow morning, Saturday, at Michael's hotel room. Seven o'clock. We'll have another whole day to continue our adventure. Judy puts her cell phone away as we head for the exit room. Crystal is a real trooper and goes up without so much as a whimper. There's no hug for Tom. I think he's disappointed.

On the way home, I ask Sally whether she asked her dad about coming to dinner. She did. And we're on. Tom calls mom at the pawn shop and lets her know.

Tom slides the cell phone into his pocket and looks up at the girls. "We're set for six o'clock. Do you want us to pick you up?"

Crystal chuckles. "My, aren't you the gentleman. Thanks, but I think we can manage to walk a few blocks by ourselves."

Sally has a worried look in her eyes. "I never met your mom, Steve. What is she like?"

"Mom can be a little rough sometimes."

Crystal is listening. "Should we be worried?"

Tom answers. "I don't think so. But just be prepared for lots of questions."

"What kind of questions?" Crystal asks.

"I don't know," Tom replies. "She's pretty nosy when she's curious. But Steve and I have been getting along with her pretty well lately. I don't think she'll grill you. Too much."

* * *

The doorbell rings at six oh two and Tom opens the door to let the girls in.

Mom's been busy in the kitchen but comes into the family room just as Tom closes the door. Her blond hair is out of its bun and nicely frames her face. She's in jeans and a light green top. Her clothes and makeup make her look younger. She brushes her hair back and extends a hand to Sally. "I know you're Sally," she says as Sally takes her hand. "I've seen you with Steve."

She turns her extended hand to Crystal and says, "So you must be Crystal. I hope you girls are hungry."

Crystal ignores Mom's hand. She walks right up to Mom and gives her a big hug. "Thank you for having us over, Mrs. Jones. And yes, we're starved. Aren't we Sally?"

Crystal doesn't know Mom isn't the hugging type.

Sally looks almost as surprised about Crystal's hug as Mom is. She gives a soft gasp. "Yes. We haven't eaten all day."

Mom backs away, eyeing Crystal. "We're having lasagna with meat balls. And I've got a chocolate cake for dessert," she says.

"It smells delicious," Crystal says, extending her nose toward the kitchen. "Do you like to cook?"

Mom's face brightens at the compliment. "Yes I do. But I don't have as much time as I used to."

Crystal taps her head. "Oh yeah. You manage *House of Pawn* over on Ammunition Avenue, right? That's got be a fun job. I bet you get all kinds of people coming into your shop."

No one warned Crystal about talking shop with Mom. We may talk about nothing else for the rest of the night.

Mom chuckles. "It's funny you should mention that, Crystal. Just yesterday a woman came in trying to sell a deck of cards. She wanted a hundred bucks for it."

Crystal brings her right hand up to cover her mouth. "Really? How could she think a deck of cards was worth a hundred dollars?"

Mom is laughing and it's infectious. I find myself smiling. And I never smile when Mom talks about work.

"She said it was signed by a world famous poker player," Mom answers. "Then she pointed out the signature on the box. *The Cincinnati Kid*."

"Wow!" Crystal interrupts. "Was it real?"

"No," Mom struggles to say. She can hardly talk through her laughter. "There was no such person. *The Cincinnati Kid* was a fictional character in a movie. When we told her it was fake she actually argued with us. She said she paid forty bucks for it at an estate sale. We had to go on-line to prove The Cincinnati Kid wasn't real. She left the store cussing up a storm."

Crystal laughs until she snorts. Then Mom laughs even harder.

The rest of us are laughing too. Even Tom.

Mom eventually calms down and catches her breath. "Not everybody that comes into the shop is crazy though. Some people are really nice, down to earth people. They just need a little help making ends meet."

Here comes my mother, the humanitarian pawn shop manager.

Crystal blinks back her surprise. "So do you give them money?"

"Well, not all of them." Mom leans on a chair. "But if they have something valuable, we can give them a loan on it. Or if they want, we can buy it outright."

"That's got to make you feel good," Crystal says. "Helping people. That's what I want to do when I get older."

There's no doubt that Crystal will end up in a job where she's helping people. But probably not working in a pawn shop.

Mom sniffs and wrinkles her nose. "I think something is burning."

There's a worried look on her face as she hurries back to the kitchen. "Come on in and sit down while I finish getting dinner ready. Tom, get them something to drink."

The kitchen table is a little cramped. After Tom gets drinks for all of us, he takes a seat next to Crystal on one side. Sally and I sit on the other. Mom's chair is at the head of the table.

Mom pulls the lasagna out of the oven and it smells wonderful. I look at the size of the baking pan and wonder if we'll have enough. I try not to look worried. I'll have to restrain myself in front of the girls. I hope Tom will too.

The meatballs are baking in another pan. Mom gets them out of the oven and pours sauce all over them. She puts everything on the table.

Mom serves Sally first. "So Sally, are you still walking with your dad every Saturday."

Sally had picked up her fork but now sets it back down. "No, Mrs. Jones. We haven't walked at all this year."

Mom places a large helping of lasagna on Sally's plate. "I used to see you two when you were little. I'd watch you from the front window as you'd walk by. You looked so cute holding your daddy's hand. You couldn't have been more that five or six. My how time flies. It seems like just yesterday."

Mom is rambling on but Sally must feel the need to reply. "Yeah, I know. Every adult that hasn't seen me in a while tells me how much I've grown. I think time must go faster as you get older. Being six years old seems like a really long time ago to me."

Mom hands the bowl of meatballs to Tom to start passing. "And Crystal, you've been living with Sally for what now, a year?"

Crystal's expression darkens slightly. "Just over. I'm so lucky to have an aunt and uncle who could take me in."

Mom sees the change in Crystal and hesitates before she speaks again. "Well, you're a great kid, Crystal. They're lucky to have you."

Mom sits down just as the bowl of meat balls gets to her. "So what have you kids been doing that keeps you guys together so much?"

I'll answer that one. "We just like hanging out Mom. Sally and Crystal are really cool. You know, for girls."

Sally pokes me under the table.

Mom's not satisfied with my answer. "But seriously, where have you been going? I know a lot of people in this town and most of them come into the store from time to time. No one has seen you. Other than

Mrs. Latimer over on Shooter Street. And she has eyes in the back of her head."

"Are you checking up on us Mom?" Tom's voice contains a combination of hurt and anger.

Mom hesitates again. "Well… I guess I am Tom. That's what parents of teenage kids do."

Crystal looks at Tom. Her expression tells him to back off. "It's okay Mrs. Jones. Parents should always do what they think is right for their kids, even if the kids don't like it. I just wish my parents were still around to worry about me."

Mom's expression softens as she faces Crystal. "I can't imagine what you've been through, Crystal. But you seem to have handled it very well. I meant what I said about the Alton's being lucky to have you. You're a joy to have around."

I think Mom is off the subject of why we've been with Sally and Crystal when she drops one of her bombs. "Sally, your dad called me the other night."

Sally chokes on a bite. Tom and I stare at Mom. Even Crystal is silent, waiting for whatever's coming.

"What? I mean, he did?" Sally asks.

"Yes," Mom teases. "We had a nice long conversation."

This is agony. "What did he say, Mom?"

Mom looks at Crystal as she answers, "Well, let's just say he shares Crystal's view about parents doing what they think is right for their kids, even if the kids don't like it."

Mom has known about our little adventure for two days. Mr. Alton told her all about it on Wednesday night. We had just met Michael and

Judy, so there's still a lot she doesn't know. But the funny thing? Mom's not the least bit interested.

"This is your adventure guys," she says after we all stop choking on our food. "I won't try to muscle in as long as I know you're safe. And Mr. Alton gave me his word that he would keep you safe."

Even Crystal is speechless.

I find myself hoping Mr. Alton can keep his word.

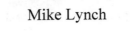

## Saturday

On Saturday morning we're up at six thirty. Tom remembers to throw some apples into his backpack. It's a good idea. I got pretty hungry yesterday. We leave for Michael's room at six forty-five. When we arrive, everyone else is already there.

Judy is talking about the diary. "There is no doubt that Aunt Judith loved Jeremy. And she sure didn't see him as a fifty-five year old man. Her writing makes him seem young and hansom. A man no older than thirty."

Mr. Alton's forehead wrinkles in concern. "Did you read anything that makes you think she was forced to stay with him against her will?"

Judy shakes her head vigorously. "Not one thing. All I saw was a woman who very much loved her man. I did, however, find two significant things. First, Aunt Judith wrote in her diary almost every day. And every entry is dated. Look at the date of her last entry."

She holds the page open so we can see.

*Sat. Jul 10, 37*

Her abbreviation means Saturday, July tenth, nineteen thirty-seven. That was the day Jeffrey Hillbrook was killed.

Mr. Alton raises his eyebrows. "That *is* significant. Do you think she was involved in the shooting?"

"I'm not sure," Judy replies. "But here's the second thing. Listen to her last entry."

*Jeremy seems to regret taking the stranger in. The man was badly injured, but with our help the last three days, his health has much improved. Jeremy thinks him to be a dangerous man but all I see is a poor soul in need of our help.*

"She must be referring to Jeffrey Hillbrook," Mr. Alton says.

We all agree. Who else could it be?

We leave Michael's hotel room and head for Jeremy's dwelling at seven fifteen. Along the way, Tom reads the next verse of the poem aloud.

*One more item is needed to reach your goal*
*It resides in a room that is more like a hole*
*Look closely don't worry and never fear*
*Be patient don't hurry it will surely appear*

Tom nods at me. "It must be hidden in that little room off the bedroom. You know. The room that was totally dark."

I shake my head. "But it was empty when I looked in there. And the last two lines in the verse make it sound a bit more complicated."

We walk in silence for ten minutes. I tap Sally's shoulder to get her to slow down so I can talk to her alone. "Did you talk to your dad about last night?" I ask.

Sally bites her lower lip. "Yes."

I wait for more but she remains silent. "Well, what did he say?"

"Oh, he admitted telling your mom all right." Her jaw set. She stares straight ahead.

"And you're mad at him for that? I'm sure he thought that telling my mom was the right thing to do."

Sally finally looks at me. Her expression is cold. "I'm not mad at him for telling your mom, Steve. I'm mad at him because he didn't tell me that he told you mom."

Sally turns away again and runs to catch Crystal, who is walking with Tom. Why is she mad at me?

* * *

In the cavern I start to lead the group straight to the bedroom, but Sally stops at the kitchen. "Wait. Let's get some candles."

Mr. Alton retrieves a cigarette lighter from his backpack. But surprisingly, the matches we find in the cabinet still work. We light five candles and carefully carry them through the library and into the bedroom. Crystal carries five more unlit candles just in case.

Once we're in the bedroom, Tom hops up onto the bed. He opens the shutters and exposes the pitch black room. Crystal puts a lit candle on the sill as Tom squirms through the window and into the little room.

Tom takes the candle and holds it up. The room lightens a bit, but it's still very dark in there.

Crystal crawls through the hole to join Tom. Once in, she asks for more candles. We hand her the four lit candles. Still the room is pretty dim. We end up lighting the rest of the candles and passing them through.

With all the candles lit, it finally brightens enough to see the entire room. The rocks are still crystalline, but they are much darker than anything in the rest of the cavern. They're nearly black. That's probably why it's so hard to light up the room.

There's not space enough for all of us to get into the room. We'll have to depend upon Crystal and Tom. But even with the room sufficiently lit, neither of them can find anything unusual.

"So what do you see in there?" Judy asks.

"Not much," Crystal responds. "Like Steve said before, it's empty. The floor and walls are solid rock. There's a huge stone in one corner. It's coming out of the floor. I think it's part of the cavern."

I read the last two lines of the verse out loud again.

*Look closely don't worry and never fear*
*Be patient don't hurry it will surely appear*

"I don't get it," Tom says, frustration is rising in his voice. "Are we just supposed to sit here and wait?"

"I don't know," I respond. "Maybe you're supposed to take your time and study everything carefully."

"But what's there to study?" Tom retorts. "It's an empty room."

"Go around the perimeter slowly," Sally says. "Look for anything out of the ordinary."

Tom does as ordered. Five minutes later he still hasn't found anything unusual. "Any other suggestions."

Mr. Alton removes the hammer from his backpack. "I know this isn't where we're supposed to use this, but I have an idea. Tom, take this and tap around on the walls. Listen for any differences in sound."

Mr. Alton passes the hammer through the window and Tom starts tapping. He seems to be tapping pretty softly, but I'm amazed by how loud it sounds. The bedroom seems to vibrate with each little tap.

*Ping. Ping. Ping.*

He slowly makes his way around the room, tapping everywhere. So far, there is no difference in the pinging sound.

When he taps the big rock in the corner, the pitch of the sound drops.

*Pong.*

"Listen!" Mr. Alton says.

Tom taps it several more times. "It sounds like the rock is hollow. Crystal, bring more candles over here."

Crystal brings all but two of the candles to the rock.

"Look!" she nearly screams.

"What do you see?" Judy asks

"Wait a minute," Tom says as he takes a close look at the rock. "I think there's a crack along the top."

We hear Tom grunt. "But I can't get it to move."

Mr. Alton leans in to look. "See if you can use the claw of the hammer to pry apart the crack."

Tom does as he's told and we hear a grinding sound as stone slides along stone. "I got it! It's a lid!"

"It sure looks heavy," Crystal adds. "Don't get your fingers caught in there."

Mr. Alton passes the pry bar in to Tom. "Here. Use this too. Maybe you can lift the lid up with the pry bar and tap it with the hammer."

It takes Tom ten minutes. Eventually he makes the lid slide far enough to confirm that there is a cavity beneath. The sounds he makes tapping the stone lid are deafening. It takes him another ten minutes to slide the lid far enough to see what's beneath. By the time he's done we're all holding our hands over our ears.

Crystal is looking over Tom's shoulder as he works. "Wow! Look at that! It's a gun! Just like the ones in those old black and white movies."

Mr. Alton's expression shows alarm. "Hold it! That sounds like a Tommy-gun. Don't touch it! It may be loaded. Let me get it out of there."

Tom backs away from the stone chest and makes way for Mr. Alton in the cramped room.

Sally's forehead is wrinkled in worry. "Do you know anything about guns, Daddy?"

"Not really. But I do know enough not to touch the trigger."

Tom has moved the lid far enough to safely take out the gun. But Mr. Alton stops as he begins reaching in. "Well would you look at that?" He's pointing at something in the stone chest.

Tom leans over and sees what Mr. Alton is pointing at. "Wow!"

"What?" Judy and I call together.

"There's a note stuck to the gun," Tom replies. "It says *The gun that killed Jeffrey Hillbrook*."

Mr. Alton carefully reaches in again and this time carefully removes the gun and note. He gently places them on the floor near the window.

"Check to see if anything else is in their," Judy says.

Tom is way ahead of her. He's already retrieved two more items. An oil cloth bag and some kind of metal object.

Tom hands the metal thing to Mr. Alton. "What do you think this is?"

Mr. Alton takes it. "It's some kind of hand crank. Like one used to start the engine of a very old car.

* * *

Back in the library, Mr. Alton sets the gun on the desk. No one can't tell if it's loaded. There is an engraving on its side that says *Thompson Sub-Machine Gun Model 1928.*

Mr. Alton points to a round thing in front of the trigger. "This is the drum magazine. If I can get it off the gun, it shouldn't be possible to fire it."

There is a lever that runs above the trigger mechanism. Mr. Alton pulls it with the thumb on his right hand. This releases a latch that's holding the magazine in place. With his left hand, he carefully slides the magazine out of the gun. All the while he's keeping his fingers away from the trigger. We all feel safer as he sets the two pieces on the desk.

Tom hands Mr. Alton the oil cloth bag. Inside are two items. The first is an envelope that contains the lower right corner of the map. Tom has already removed the other three map pieces from his backpack and has placed them together on the desk. Mr. Alton positions the fourth one and it fits perfectly. The dots lead from the sleeping figure in the lower left corner through the upper left corner and upper right corner and finally into the lower right corner. They end at an X. But we still have no idea where the sleeping figure is located. So the map is of no use.

The second item is an envelope containing another note from Old Man Humphrey. It's several pages long.

Tom wants to spend time studying the map but Mr. Alton wants to read the note. Tom slides the map pieces to a corner of the desk so he can study them. Mr. Alton begins reading aloud.

*If you have read My Love's diary, you have surely concluded that Judith came to her end soon after her last entry. And unless you be daft, you have realized that she died on the same day that Jeffrey Hillbrook met his maker. This, of course, is no coincidence. And now you will learn the circumstances of both their deaths. Oh! It is a woeful tale indeed!*

*Even though Judith and I were in love, we were not married in the eyes of God. This was of great importance to Judith, and the reason we lived separately. One year before we began to correspond, I had come upon a second dwelling. You will be directed there shortly. It was in this dwelling that Judith lived.*

*As you will discover, her dwelling is not far from the exit of my home, just a short walk away. It was during one such walk that Judith came upon a stopped motor car in the woods. She was curious but frightened. In the end, her fear won out and she chose not to investigate alone. Instead, she rushed to me and told me of her discovery. Together we went to investigate.*

*From a distance, the motor car appeared empty. But as I approached, I could see a man slumped over sideways in the front seat. He appeared to be dead. I waved Judith to me for she had been hiding behind some nearby tree.*

# The Hillbrook Stash

*Upon further inspection, we found that the man was breathing. I tried to convince Judith to leave him, but she would hear nothing of it. She demanded that we help the man. I agreed to do so. I have regretted this decision ever since.*

*We endured his moaning and dragged him back to my dwelling. We placed him into my bed. Bleeding was profuse from his left shoulder so we made effort to stop it. And stop it we did. He was unconscious for over thirty-five hours. Judith was by his side every minute of that time, nursing and comforting. What a loving woman she was. With her urgings, he quickly grew better.*

*During his unconscious period, I learned of his situation by making several trips to his motor car. I discovered it to be a burgundy colored nineteen thirty-six Buick. I was astonished that such a fine vehicle could navigate such rough terrain as these woods. But here it was.*

*Inside the vehicle I found a large canvas bag containing several guns, including the one you have just discovered. There were also four very large duffle bags. One by one, I brought the five bags home. But even the smallest was too large to fit through the trap door entrance to my dwelling. So I hauled them up to the ledge adjoining the exit room and stored them there, out of sight from the ground.*

*I learned his name from papers among his belongings. Jeffrey Hillbrook. I had never before heard of him, but concluded as any sane man would that he was a wanted man. I tried to convince Judith that we should restrain him for surely he would be dangerous. But she refused saying he was a child of God and he would not hurt people who cared for him so earnestly.*

*On his second day with us he regained consciousness. He was confused, but came to understand his surroundings.*

*He soon began inquiring about his belongings. I tried to put his mind at ease, explaining that his possessions were close by and in a safe place. During our first such encounter, he easily relented. But as he grew stronger, he became more agitated during our exchanges. But in his weakened state, he still grew tired quickly and yielded.*

*But on the third day, his last on this earth, he was much stronger and would not relent. He demanded to see his possessions. Judith and I tried to calm him, explaining that he was still too weak to make even the short journey it required.*

*He was not to be quieted and became uncontrollable. To my amazement, he reached to his ankle and pulled out a small gun he had hidden there. You have seen this gun. It was included in the cigar box with my first correspondence. Pointing it at Judith, he looked at me and demanded to be taken to his belongings.*

*At this shocking turn, we quickly surrendered our efforts to dissuade him. His step was slow but steady and he became stronger as we moved to the exit room. Once there, I tried pointing to the duffle bags above, but in truth, they were barely visible from our position below. He insisted that we go up to them.*

*He was wary of the contraption that I had created to exit my dwelling so he forced Judith to go first. Seeing that it was safe, he went second, demanding that Judith haul him up. This she easily did. He kept the gun pointed at me until he was closer to her. Then he trained it on her.*

*Once he was on the upper landing, he kept the gun pointed at Judith until I made the trip up.*

*I thought he would relax at the sight of his belongings, but this was not the case. He opened each in turn, becoming more agitated until he came to the bag containing his weapons. He settled down somewhat at the sight of them.*

*At this moment, the most terrible of my life, a sound came from close by in the woods. A gunshot. I later learned that over twenty armed federal agents were combing the woods in search of Jeffrey Hillbrook. They had found his motor car and were following his blood trail. This trail, of course, led to my dwelling. One incompetent agent had fired his gun at a near-by squirrel.*

*It was easy from my position to discern that the gunshot was at least fifty yards away, too far to be of any threat to us. But in his distressed state, the gunshot startled Jeffrey Hillbrook. He whirled around and blindly fired his gun. His shot found Judith and she dropped.*

*Not knowing how many bullets were in that little gun, I lunged at its shooter. Though his countenance appeared strong, my blow easily knocked him from the ledge and he fell down the fifteen feet to the rocky ground below. There he remained still as I rushed to Judith.*

*It took only a glance to know she was dead. The bullet had pierced her forehead leaving her face with the horrified expression it found when her life was ended. I hugged her in agony until I noticed movement from below.*

*Jeffrey Hillbrook was getting to his feet. It was obvious that he was badly injured from his fall. And blood was flowing from his right shoulder again.*

*Hatred overwhelmed me. I rushed to the bag containing his guns and pulled out the one you now have in your possession. Having never fired a gun of this kind I simply pointed it in his direction and pulled the trigger. Bullets sprayed everywhere as the recoil from the gun forced my shoulder back. From the marks left by bullets hitting the ground, I eventually brought him in line with the gun's fire.*

*It was at this moment that the gun stopped firing. The gun had run out of ammunition. But I had accomplished my intent well enough. Jeffrey Hillbrook staggered a few steps and was about to fall down dead when the sound of over twenty firearms could be heard from the nearby trees. Some bullets hit rock above me and I quickly dropped to the floor of my ledge.*

*The federal agents had been drawing near the clearing between the trees and the rock face. They thought that my gunfire was Jeffrey Hillbrook shooting at them. Indeed my aim was so bad at first that a few bullets probably did fly in their direction.*

*From my vantage point I could see Jeffrey Hillbrook held up by the repeated thrusts of bullets entering his body. It was an eerie sight indeed. His feet seemed to be taking backward steps as his body disappeared from my sight and up against the rock face below me.*

*When the shooting finally stopped, I heard his body slump to the ground. With agents cautiously approaching, I crawled back to Judith and took her in my arms, out of sight of the people below. I remained thus for over two hours, listening to the agents below argue about who fired the shot that killed Jeffrey Hillbrook. No one seemed to notice that Jeffrey Hillbrook had no gun.*

*So now you know my story. My true nature. Do you still judge me evil?*

Judy has had Michael on her cell phone listening to Mr. Alton. She's the first to speak. "This is amazing guys. I know we only have Jeremy's word for what happened. But I for one believe him. I think he loved Judith and he was destroyed by her death. That, and the fact that no one left him alone after her death. Can you imagine grieving for someone you love while having the whole world pestering you?"

"It is an amazing story," Mr. Alton agrees. "And it sure explains a lot."

Tom, who started out studying the map ended up as captivated by the story as the rest of us. "I can't believe I fired the gun that killed Aunt Judith."

* * *

It's after one o'clock and Tom pulls out the apples from his backpack and passes them around. One for Mr Alton and one for Judy. Sally and I share one as do Tom and Crystal.

We turn our attention to the map. Sally points out the obvious. "It is now pretty clear where the starting point is."

"And it shouldn't be too hard to follow the footsteps to entrance of Aunt Judith's home," Crystal adds.

Mr. Alton has a concerned look on his face. "But we have to be very careful. Even though Jeremy hasn't said so, we know it's booby-trapped."

247

"Grandpa has the drawing that shows the safe entry procedure back at the hotel," Judy says. "We better study it carefully before we try to go in."

Everyone agrees. We'll find the entrance, but just look around. Then we'll go back to the hotel.

We exit the dwelling and walk the short distance to the exit room. One by one, we use the exit mechanism. After climbing down the rope ladder, we stand on the rocky ground below the ledge. We're at the very spot where Jeffrey Hillbrook died. Crystal points at the rock face. "If you look carefully, you can see where the bullets hit."

Actually, you don't have to look all that closely to see where the bullets hit. Now that we know what happened here, evidence of gunshots pepper the rock face for twenty feet in both directions. I wonder if there are any bullets embedded in the rock. I half expect to see bullets on the ground and blood on the wall.

Judy looks up at the hidden ledge. Tears are in her eyes again. "You can almost *feel* him up there, can't you? Holding Aunt Judith in his arms while the federal agents investigate down here."

The thought makes the hairs on the back of my neck stand up.

As Crystal said, it is pretty easy to follow the footsteps on the map. They stick to the contour of the rock face. We get close to the spot marked by the X on the map. It now seems likely that that the dwelling is going to be another underground cavern. And it's probably an extension of Jeremy's cavern.

It doesn't take long to find the four small stones in the ground. They are very close to the rock face. They appear to be just like the ones that mark the entrance to Jeremy's home. And as with Jeremy's home, there is no evidence of a trap door.

Mr. Alton gets down on his hands and knees to examine them. "Stay back. We shouldn't get any closer until we're sure we know what we're doing."

Sure enough, they are just like the ones at the trap-door entrance to Jeremy's dwelling. They don't move when Mr. Alton touches them. He gets back up. "I think it's time for us to be getting back."

Sally takes out her iPhone. "Just give me a minute more, Daddy." She begins snapping pictures. Most are directed are at the rock face and the small stones. But she also takes pictures in all directions and from every angle. In all, she takes over thirty pictures.

⁑ ⁂ ⁂

It's almost three o'clock when we get back to Michael's room. The letter that contains the entry mechanism sketch is on the table.

Mr. Alton pulls out the four items we collected for the final challenge. He arranges them on the table around the letter. They include the pry bar, the hook and stick, the hammer, and the hand crank.

Michael wrinkles his brow. "I've been studying the entrance mechanism sketch and instructions. I understand what the pry bar and hand crank are for. But I'm not sure about the hammer or the hook and stick."

Michael points at the sketch. "See here. You step into this square formed by the stones on the ground. They're just like the ones around the entrance to Jeremy's dwelling."

Michael moves his finger on the sketch from the ground to the rock face. "While standing in the square, you use the pry bar to open this hatch in the rock face wall. It looks a little awkward, but easily doable."

Michael moves his finger again. "Your weight holds down this lever which allows the hatch to be opened."

He then moves his finger back to the hatch. "With the hatch open, you step out of the square and attach the hand crank to the top bolt under the hatch. Turning the crank clockwise a few turns opens the trap door. With the trap door open, you remove the hand crank and close the hatch."

Michael points at another part of the sketch. "Now you climb down this ladder just 'til you get beneath the trap door. Then you use the hammer and tap right here."

Michael points at a spot on the cavern wall next to the ladder and frowns. "That's' my first problem. I have no idea what the tapping does."

He moves his finger again. "Then you use the hand crank on this upper bolt right here. The trap door is spring-loaded. A quarter turn clockwise causes the trap door to snap shut on its own.

"Here's another thing I don't understand." Michael pulls out Jeremy's letter and reads out loud.

*Once I know you are entering your dwelling, I will ensure that the explosive charge is disabled. I will let you know when it is safe to proceed. Do not continue until you have this confirmation!*

"Later in the letter," Michael continues, "Jeremy also says that he can disable the explosive device from his dwelling so they can enter Aunt Judith's dwelling together. But he doesn't say how it's done."

Michael moves his finger again. "To get out, you climb up the ladder to right here. It's the same place you stop when entering. You then tap the hammer right here again."

Again Michael frowns. "I'm assuming you have to wait for some kind of confirmation again. But I don't know what it is or how it's given. You then turn the hand crank on the lower bolt clockwise a few turns to open the trap door. Once you're outside, you open the hatch in the rock face with the pry bar. The hatch isn't locked shut while the trap door is open.

"Then you use the hand crank on this lower bolt under the hatch to close the trap door. Again, just a quarter turn clockwise is all that's necessary and the trap door will snap shut. The last step is to close the hatch. I think that re arms the system."

Michael points at the sketch again. "Anything you do wrong could result in these explosives being detonated. So I don't think we should try any of this until we figure out what the hammer and hook do."

We've all been listening intently to Michael's evaluation of the entry mechanism and the explosive device it contains. It sure sounds to me like he knows what he's talking about.

Crystal looks confused. "What's to keep Aunt Judith from being killed herself if someone tries to enter her dwelling while she's in it?"

Michael rubs his forehead. "I don't know. Maybe her living quarters are protected somehow."

Mr. Alton has a better question. "What if the mechanisms have been damaged over time? It's been at least sixty years since they were used."

"Well, we know the explosives will probably work," Michael replies. "Tom proved that during the first challenge. We can only hope that the rest of Jeremy's mechanisms held up as well."

I think of the trap door entrance to Jeremy's dwelling. "The mechanism to enter Jeremy's dwelling held up just fine. So did his exit mechanism. And they're even older than the mechanisms in Aunt Judith's dwelling."

"You're right, Steve," Mr. Alton admits.

Sally points at the hatch. "You said closing the hatch with the trap door closed probably re-arms the explosive device. There's nothing you've shown that disarms the device. Maybe that's what the hammer does."

Michael is still rubbing his forehead. "I don't see how. There are no mechanisms under the place on the wall where you tap. And Jeremy said in his letter that he can somehow ensure that the device is disarmed from his own cavern."

Wait a minute! I think of how loud the tapping sounded when Tom was using the hammer in the little room next to Jeremy's bedroom. "Maybe tapping the hammer against the cavern wall sends a signal to Jeremy."

Michael doesn't understand, but he wasn't in Jeremy's bedroom. Mr. Alton, on the other hand, knows exactly what I'm talking about. "So you're saying that Aunt Judith was using the hammer to let Jeremy know when she was ready to enter and exit her dwelling. And for him to disable the charge?"

"Yeah. Uh-huh." Though I don't sound too sure. Not even to myself.

"We could easily test the idea," Sally says. "It would just take one of us staying in Jeremy's dwelling while someone else taps the rock outside the entrance to Judith's home. If the tapping can be heard in Jeremy's dwelling, we may be on to something."

Michael's still confused. "Assuming the tapping is a signal, how could Jeremy hear it from so far away?"

We explain how Judith's dwelling appears to be an extension of Jeremy's cavern. And if we're right, the distance between the two dwellings could be as little as twenty feet.

"But what could Jeremy do from inside his dwelling that would disarm the charge?" Michael asks.

"That's what we have to figure out," Sally answers.

We decide to quit for the day and sleep on it. We'll meet again in Michael's room tomorrow morning at seven.

Michael wants to take us all out for an early dinner. This time Crystal speaks up. "You treated last time, Michael. Let me treat this time."

Michael's expression transforms into one of astonishment. "Well little lady, that's mighty kind of you. But what kind of man would I be if I allowed a beautiful woman to buy me dinner?"

Crystal's freckles fade as she blushes at his response. I wonder if it's the first time she's been called beautiful. Or a woman. Either way she's speechless. And the look on her face is priceless.

"I'll take that pretty smile as consent," Michael quickly says.

"Call your mom," Sally tells Tom. "See if she wants to join us."

\* \* \*

Mom meets us at the Clear Valley Café a half our later.

Crystal makes a bee line to her and gives her a hug. Surprisingly, Mom hugs her back. "I'm so glad you could join our little band of thieves, Mrs. Jones." Then she whispers something in Mom's ear. Mom nods. Tom is watching too.

We introduce Mom to Michael and Judy.

It's not very crowded so we gather three tables together to have enough room. The tables are a bit small to accommodate the eight of us. Mom is sandwiched between Sally and Crystal. Michael is at one end next to Crystal, but looks uncomfortable in his wheelchair. I'm sitting opposite Sally, Judy sits opposite Mom, and Tom is opposite Crystal. Mr. Alton sits at the other end of the table near Tom and Crystal.

My eyes drift to the table where we sat when Sally pointed out the water tower. That seems like years ago. Hard to believe it's been less than a week.

Mom looks across the table to Judy. "I hear you're from Texas. What do you do there?"

"I work for a company that installs and maintains wind mills. We maintain one of the largest wind farms in the world there. I help schedule service and maintenance calls."

"That sounds interesting. Is it right there in Lubbock?"

"No. It's in Roscoe, about two hours away."

Mr. Alton has been listening. "I saw a show on *Nova* about Roscoe. I was amazed at how much the farmers get for leasing parts of their fields to the power industry."

Judy faces Mr. Alton. "Don't get me started or I may never shut up. Communities around Roscoe have been suffering for many years. Lots of people have left because there's no work. The reason why they left was the wind. It blows away the top soil and dries everything out fast. Farmers have all but given up trying to grow any crops.

"It's ironic, but now the wind has become a natural resource and created new jobs. So what drove people away is now bringing them back. With jobs to be had, people are coming back and communities are flourishing again."

At the other end of the table, Crystal turns to Michael. "You've pretty much learned what you wanted to know about Aunt Judith, haven't you?"

Michael nods. "Yes. It sure is nice to know that she wasn't murdered or abducted. Or worse. I only wish she'd have left word about where she was going so Grandma Meredith wouldn't have worried so much. I think Grandma Meredith was the only person who really cared about Aunt Judith."

"Will you be going back soon?"

"When this is all over," Michael answers. "There's really not much for me at home any more. And I can't wait to see what you find in Aunt Judith's dwelling. And I don't mean… well, I don't mean what *you're* looking for."

Crystal seems confused, so Michael explains. "Well, the dwelling was her home, Crystal. There must be some personal belongings in there."

"Oh." Crystal's eyebrows go up. "I wasn't thinking about that. So there's still more you can learn about Aunt Judith."

"I hope so."

The food comes and we eat in near silence. We're all pretty hungry.

Tom leans over the table to Crystal. "What did you say to Mom when we first came in."

"Are you worried that we were talking about you?" Crystal teases.

Tom smiles. "No. Not really."

"I just asked her not to ask about our adventure here in public. She agreed."

* * *

In Tom's room later that night, he brings up our current puzzle. "I was thinking about the signal Aunt Judith would send with the hammer. And what Jeremy would do when he heard it." Tom pauses.

I think he wants a response. "Uh huh."

"Well," he continues. "It could have to do with the handle I found inside that hole near the creek. You know, the one where we found Aunt Judith's diary."

I agree. "That sounds likely. The stream flows in the direction of Aunt Judith's dwelling. And the handle must be connected to something, right?"

"So when Jeremy hears the tapping, say he pulls the handle to disarm the explosives," Tom says.

But when does he let go?

256

Sunday

Tom and I get to Michael's hotel room on Sunday morning slightly before seven and find everyone there. It seems Tom wasn't the only one to think of the handle in the hole where we found Aunt Judith's diary. Mr. Alton and Michael are talking about it.

"From what I'm seeing in the entrance mechanism sketch," Michael is saying, "something during the entrance procedure triggers the explosion. But I think the handle Tom found in that hole disarms the device. If the handle is being pulled, the device will be disarmed even if the trigger is tripped."

"Are you sure of this?" Mr. Alton asks.

"I'm not positive, but it makes good sense."

Judy interrupts. "Tell him what you did when you were in Viet Nam, Grandpa."

It's hard to judge the look that Michael gives Judy. But he doesn't look pleased. "I worked with explosives."

"So you know what you're talking about," Judy observes.

"Yes, but as Jim here suggests, I have no idea how Jeremy rigged his load."

Mr. Alton's respect for Michael seems to have grown a bit. "Assuming you're correct, what action do you think would trigger the explosion?"

Michael must have been thinking about this because he replies immediately. "Since Aunt Judith taps the hammer just before she closes the trap door, closing the trap door must be the trigger. Remember. It's spring loaded. It would be easy to make the spring do two things. Close the door and blow the charge."

It's Sally's turn to interrupt. "But what if something went wrong. Like maybe Aunt Judith doesn't move quick enough or she gets stuck somehow?"

Michael's hand goes back to his forehead. "I'm not sure, Sally. But they may have created a whole set of signals by tapping the hammer in different ways, or different places."

Michael pauses for a moment and then continues. "There is another reason I think holding the handle will disarm the system. Jeremy said that he was able to enter Aunt Judith's dwelling *with* Aunt Judith. And he had to be able to get in there by himself. Like before she came to Clear Valley and after her death. So there's got to be a way to disarm the system with only one person present. If I'm right, he must have been able to rig the handle so that it would stay pulled, keeping the charge disarmed. I think that's what the hook and stick are for.

"I'll say one more thing. But you may not like it. If you determine that the hammer is indeed used as a signal, you should be able to safely proceed to the point in the procedure when the hammer is used without triggering an explosion. I'm convinced that triggering the explosive device occurs after that point in the entry procedure."

Now Mr. Alton rubs his forehead. "There's a lot of ifs in our logic. We're not even sure the hammer is used to signal yet. But whatever we find, we've got to come up with a foolproof way to safely enter Aunt Judith's dwelling. That, or we're going to have to call in the authorities."

Everyone agrees with Mr. Alton's assessment.

* * *

Once in Jeremy's cavern, we head straight for the hole where we found Aunt Judith's diary. Mr. Alton retrieves the hook and wooden stick. "Let's see if this works."

He slides the hook into the hole and attaches it to the handle within. He pulls on the hook and the handle comes with it. When fully extended, the hook comes out of the hole just far enough to expose its loop. Sally, who's been holding the wooden stick, slides it through the loop. When Mr. Alton releases the hook, the wooden stick keeps the hook from retracting. It contacts the rock on each side of the hole. Mr. Alton removes his hands and the hook and handle stay put.

Crystal claps her hands. "I guess we know what the hook is for."

We wait near the hole in Jeremy's cavern while Mr. Alton goes to the entrance of Aunt Judith's dwelling. Sally is using her iPhone and Mr. Alton has borrowed Judy's cell phone. They have been talking to one another since Mr. Alton left Jeremy's cavern.

While waiting for Mr. Alton, Crystal notices something that could be important. There is a portion of rock near the hole that has been flattened. All of the rock in the cavern is coarse and jagged. But in this small square section, the rock is much smoother. Crystal points at the flat spot. "You know what I think? I think that's where Jeremy used his own hammer to signal back to Aunt Judith."

Crystal looks around and spots a baseball-sized stone. She picks it up and hands it to Tom. "This should do the trick. Use it to signal back to Uncle Jim."

Sally waves her free hand. "Hush!" She puts her dad on speaker.

Mr. Alton's voice comes through loud and clear. "Okay, I'm approaching the square stones. I can see cracks in the rock where the hatch is located. I'll try tapping just to the right of it."

*Ping. Ping. Ping.*

The sound is faint, coming from all around us.

"Did you hear anything?" Mr. Alton asks.

"Yes Daddy!" Sally shouts. "We heard it. Three taps, right?"

"Right, Sweetheart. And I wasn't even tapping that hard. What about this?"

*Ping. Ping. Ping.*

"It's much louder this time," Sally responds. "Tom wants to try something. Listen carefully, okay?"

Tom taps the stone against the wall three times in the flattened area.

"Did you hear anything Daddy?"

"Yes, but it was very faint," Mr. Alton answers. "Three taps, right?"

"Yes!" Sally answers.

"I bet it would sound much louder on my end from inside the cavern," Mr. Alton says.

Sally's voice now sounds nervous. "Daddy wait. Don't take any chances."

"Don't worry, Sweetheart. I won't. For now I'm just going to get the trap door open. Then I want you to pull on the handle to see if I can see or hear anything. Tom. Remove the hook from the handle in the hole."

Tom does as he's told.

Mr. Alton describes his actions. "I'm standing in the square formed by the stones. Now I'm taking the pry bar to the hatch. Yes. It popped open. I'm stepping out of the square now. The crank fits nicely on the top bolt. Turning clockwise now, and yes, the trap door is opening. Still turning the crank. Still opening. There. I think it's open all the way. I'm closing the hatch.

"Now I'm shining the flashlight into the entry. I see the ladder. It looks solid. Off to the right of the ladder are the bolts that open and close the trap door from below. Down below that is a passage way that leads away from Jeremy's cavern. I can't see very far that way. Tap the wall again."

Tom taps the wall with the stone three times.

Mr. Alton continues, "Yes. I can clearly hear the tapping from inside the cavern. Three taps. Now pull the handle. Tell me at the exact moment when you do."

Sally and Tom synchronize their actions. "Tom is pulling it… Now."

"Yes. I heard something click from below. It's not like the hammer tapping. That sounds like it's coming from everywhere. This click is coming from something just below me. Do it again."

Sally and Tom do as ordered.

"Yes, the click is definitely coming from this end," Mr. Alton confirms. "The handle is definitely connected to something in the entry mechanism. I think it's safe to assume it's disarming the explosive device. Use the hook and stick to hold the handle in its pulled position again. That should be the safest condition, completely disabling the explosive device."

Sally's nervous expression tells us she's not so sure.

Tom applies the hook to the handle and pulls it. Then he slides the stick through the loop. He releases them and the hook stays in place. Then he bumps the stick a couple of times with his fingers to ensure that the stick and handle will stay in place. It does.

"All set Daddy," Sally says into the phone.

"Okay, I'm going down," Mr. Alton says.

We're forgetting something! Something about Jeremy's poem has been troubling me and I finally remember what it is. "Wait!"

Sally face turns from concern to fear as she relays my urgent message to her dad.

Everyone is looking at me.

"The last verse of the poem talks about a challenge at the final turn," I say. Are we sure this is it?"

"What do you mean?" Sally asks.

Tom gets out the poem and hands it to me. I read the last verse aloud.

*One final challenge you may not expect*
*Awaits out of sight so please don't neglect*
*Be alert and be ready at your final turn*

*Ignore my warning and surely you'll burn*

"See?" I say.

No one answers so I continue. "*'One final challenge you may not expect'*, Jeremy said. I think it could be after this one. Something out of sight. Something we don't expect. Something at the final turn. Whatever that is."

"The explosives are out of sight," Tom suggests. "And without Michael's help, we sure wouldn't have expected the entrance to Aunt Judith's dwelling to be booby-trapped."

I'm not so sure. "But the verse says we'll burn, not explode."

"Did you hear all of that Daddy?" Sally asks.

"Yes Sweetheart. I'll be very careful."

I'm not sure Mr. Alton can be careful enough. He's too excited about entering Aunt Judith's dwelling. He's getting carried away.

"I'm on the ladder now," Mr. Alton says. "Climbing down. Just a minute while I tap."

*Ping. Ping. Ping.*

"We heard it Daddy," Sally says.

Tom looks at the hook to confirm that it is still holding back the handle. Then he taps back.

"I heard the tapping loud and clear this time," Mr. Alton says. "Closing trap door now. Got to put the phone in my pocket for a moment."

A few seconds pass before he continues. "It's pretty bright in here even with the trap door closed. It's about the same brightness as Jeremy's dwelling. Climbing the rest of the way down now. I'm at the bottom. I see the explosives. Wow. There's a lot of them. There's a thick taut wire going into a hole that must lead to you. It is connected to a switch on the explosives. I think we could rig that switch permanently from this side. But not now. Let me look around a bit."

Seconds pass with no word from Mr. Alton. Sally is nearly gasping. Her expression is wracked with worry.

"I see a path," he finally continues. "It must lead to Aunt Judith's dwelling. It zig-zags back and forth, like a maze. I'm moving into the maze. Moving back and forth. Getting a little darker. With all these turns it would definitely protect anyone on the other side from a blast. There's more light ahead. Getting brighter now."

Turns! Your final turn! "Wait!" I scream again. But I'm too late.

"The light's coming from…" We hear a muffled yelp and then a click.

"Daddy!" Sally screams.

There's no answer.

"Daddy! Answer me!" she screams again.

Her phone is dead.

* * *

Tom and Sally rush to the exit room. I know they want to get to Judith's dwelling, but once they get there there's nothing they can do without the pry bar and hand crank.

"Wait," I say. "Let's all go together."

Tom is almost out of sight when he calls back. "I can get there faster by myself."

"Okay," I respond. "But what can you do once you get there?"

Tom is gone. By the time I get to the exit room, he's already pulling himself up. He disappears out to the upper landing as Sally straps into the belt. Tears are flowing down her cheeks as she pulls herself up. Then she disappears too.

Crystal doesn't seem at all worried about heights right now. She pulls herself up and then sends the belt back. I go next. Crystal pulls me up. Finally Judy makes her way up.

We use the rope ladder to get to the ground and rush the short distance to the entrance of Aunt Judith's dwelling.

The sight that greets us fills me with relief. The trap door is open and Mr. Alton is sitting on the ground, hugging Sally with one arm. He's rubbing the top of his head with the other.

As we approach, I smell an odd, chemical odor. It's coming from Mr. Alton.

Sally is sobbing. "Oh Daddy. I was so worried."

Tears are in Mr. Alton's eyes too. "I knew you would be, Sweetheart. But I couldn't contact you after I broke Judy's cell phone."

Mr. Alton looks up to Judy. "Sorry about your phone."

Judy shakes her head. "Don't you worry one little bit. I'm just so glad you're okay. I would like to call Grandpa though."

Judy is looking at Sally. Sally seems confused for a moment.

"Oh," she says, "here." She passes her iPhone to Judy.

"What happened down there?" Tom asks.

Mr. Alton looks at me. "You were right about the final challenge, Steve. I was coming out of the maze of turns. At the last turn, I could see a large room ahead. I must have set off a trip wire because I heard a click just before a bucket fell on my head. That's when I dropped the cell phone. From the smell, I think the bucket was originally filled with gasoline. But its volatility must have evaporated away years ago. All that was left was a little oil."

Mr. Alton pulls his shirt away from his skin to show us a dark stain. "When I picked up the cell phone, it was broken. So I couldn't contact you guys. I was on my way back when Tom and Sally arrived."

He pulls a cigarette lighter from his pocket. It looks just like the one Tom found in the cigar box. "This was on the floor next to the bucket. I don't know how it was rigged, but it must have been meant to ignite the gasoline."

"Do you think it's safe to go in there now?" Tom asks.

Sally gives him a cross look.

"I think so. Hey! I just thought of something. I wasn't thinking about the exit procedure when I came out. I just did it. And I didn't set off any explosives. That must mean the handle definitely disarms the device. It must have made it safe for Jeremy and Aunt Judith to enter her dwelling together. The hook is still engaged in the hole, isn't it Tom?"

Tom nods. "We never took it out."

"Well then," Mr. Alton says, "I think it's time to find the Hillbrook stash."

\* \* \*

One by one, we follow Mr. Alton down into Aunt Judith's dwelling. I follow Tom, who follows Mr. Alton. Tom helps me with the ladder. Then we help Sally, Crystal, and Judy down the ladder too. Mr. Alton goes back up and uses the hand crank to close the trap door.

Mr. Alton was right about the light. It's a bit dim, but there's more than enough light. He leads the way through the maze. There are lots of turns. We finally come to a larger, even brighter room.

He pauses as he's about to enter the room and points up. "See the wooden platform just above us? That's where the bucket was."

He then looks down, searching the area near his feet. "And look. There's the trip wire."

The wire is now broken, coiled up on the floor.

"Back up a bit guys," Mr. Alton says. "Let me go in alone just in case there is another booby trap."

Tom and I back up, forcing everyone back into the maze.

After a minute or so, Mr. Alton calls to us. "Okay. I think it's safe now."

As I enter the room the sight astounds me. The ten by ten room is obviously Aunt Judith's sitting room. There is an easy chair right in the middle of the room. Next to it is an end table. A small vase with a long-dead wilted flower rests on the table. A silver candlestick holder is next to it. A small sofa is pushed up against the far wall.

But what takes my breath away are the pictures on the wall. Well, not pictures exactly, but pencil sketches. They were obviously drawn by Jeremy Humphrey. I count twelve of them ranging in size from small index-card-sized to as big as about two feet by three feet. They are all neatly placed in home-made wooden frames.

Most depict Aunt Judith and Jeremy doing something together. In the sketches, Jeremy is not drawn as a young man. He looks every bit the fifty-plus years he was when he drew the sketches.

One sketch shows Judith and Jeremy reading together in his library. Another shows them hand in hand in the woods. Yet another shows them eating at the kitchen table of his dwelling. The largest one, my favorite, is a portrait of Aunt Judith. Near his signature at the bottom right-hand corner, Jeremy has written *Judith Maxwell, The Love Of My Life*.

Crystal is the first to speak. "This beats the Spartan accommodations in Jeremy's dwelling. You can sure tell a woman lived here."

There is a doorway on the wall opposite the way we came in. It leads further into Aunt Judith's dwelling. Mr. Alton leads the way, to her bedroom. I stop looking around when I see a huge canvas bag and four slightly smaller duffle bags on her bed. An oil cloth bag is on top of them.

We all stand in awe. All except Judy. She opens the oil cloth bag which, of course, contains a note from Jeremy Humphrey. His last one. Judy reads it aloud.

*Well, my adversary has at last won his prize. If you came through unscathed, accept my congratulations. For I did not believe it possible that you would do so. If you had accomplices, it is likely that some have perished during your quest. If this be the case, accept my sympathy.*

*You can now see just how Judith lived. Her accommodations in their rudimentary form were much like my own. But as you can tell, a woman's touch can breathe life into even the dreariest of places. She gracefully made this cave her palace.*

*And now! You are surely curious about your booty.  Let me save you the trouble of counting it, for I have done so many times.  It was on my mind to use it on countless occasions.  I often considered using part of it to disappear from this wretched little town.  But in the end I could not bring myself to spend a penny of this money.  For this is blood money.  Simply look at the Hillbrook Memorial Pillar in City Park and learn of the 64 civilians and 12 federal agents killed by Jeffrey Hillbrook and his cronies.  And of course, one more beloved that is not noted on that pillar.*

*Your prize totals $536,275.  All of it is in cash.  This accounts for the thirty-seven banks robbed by the Hillbrook Gang, which averaged $15,000 each.  Some rumored that gold was included in this treasure but they be misinformed.*

*You will also find here the bag of guns taken from Jeffrey Hillbrook's motor car.  Be careful.  I know not whether any of them be loaded.  I would assume the are.*

*And now my friend, for it is as friends that I would like us to part, please do me the service of informing the families of Penelope, Cecilia, and Judith.  You can now explain what became of them and how they came to their ends.  And if they wish it, provide them with the locations of resting places.  Some may want their loved ones brought home.  You now have the means to grant my request.  And as for the family of Judith Maxwell, you would do well to present them with a portion of what you have found today.  It can be said that Judith gave her life so that you could have it.*

Mr. Alton opens one of the duffle bags to reveal stacks and stacks of money. A paper band is strapped around each bundle of bills and limits it's thickness to about a half inch or so. There must be hundreds of bundles in this duffle bag alone. All the currency looks new and crisp, as if it were never circulated.

Tom reaches in and pulls out a bundle of fifty dollar bills and holds it up. "Wow! I've never seen *this* much money. Let alone what's in these bags."

Mr. Alton takes the stack from Tom and examines it. He points to the top bill. "Look at this. This is a nineteen twenty-nine fifty dollar bill. All of the money in these bags had to be printed before nineteen thirty-seven, of course. And it all appears to be in mint condition. I'm no expert in coin or currency collecting, but I'll bet that every one of these bills is worth more than their face values. A lot more."

Sally smiles. "So we have more than five-hundred-thirty-six thousand dollars Daddy?"

"Again, I'm not positive, but I think so. I'd bet the actual value is at least double the face value for each bill."

Tom gives my good arm a high-five. "That means we have over a million dollars here! Wow!"

# Epilogue

It's been exactly one week since we found the Hillbrook stash. I had no idea how much our lives could change in such a short time. Just about everyone in Clear Valley has come by for a visit. They've come from neighboring towns too. Many of them just want to see our house. Some set up tents in the front yards of our neighbors. Mom said our neighbors don't mind since they're charging rent.

Television and radio stations have been by for interviews. Some are in vans and have been camped out with the locals. Cameras flash every time we open the front door. Even CNN got into the act.

Someone from the Jay Leno show called and asked if we'd be guests on the show. Mom quickly agreed and I think it's scheduled for sometime next week. Even a movie producer called. She wants to buy the rights to make a movie about our adventure.

Everyone wants to know how we found the Hillbrook stash. So far, we haven't said too much. We don't want anyone to trash Jeremy's or Aunt Judith's dwellings. And there's the little matter of the booby-trap. We also don't want anyone getting hurt or killed. We called a bomb-squad to fully disarm the device in Aunt Judith's dwelling. They're supposed to be here tomorrow. So until now, we haven't told anyone where the dwellings are located.

It'd kind of funny, but we're getting a dose of Old Man Humphrey went through after Jeffrey Hillbrook was killed. It was fun at first, but it's getting old. And it's only been a week. I can't imagine what it would be like to be hounded like this for a lifetime.

It's not like we haven't told Jeremy's story. Everyone now knows how Jeffrey Hillbrook really died. And they know about Jeremy's women. There's quite a controversy brewing over whether he was a good or a bad man. Since Judy took Aunt Judith's diary and most of the sketches Jeremy made for her, we can't offer much evidence in Jeremy's defense.

It took ten trips to get all the money home. Then we made another two trips to collect Aunt Judith's personal belongings. And we made one more trip for the bag of guns. Judy insisted that Mr. Alton keep one of Jeremy's sketches. With Mr. Alton's blessing, she took the rest.

Michael and Judy left for home on Tuesday, two days after we found the stash. The circus that was to become our future had begun, but was not yet in full swing.

"We don't want to steal your lime-light. You guys did all of the work," Michael had said. "We'll just be going on home now."

So Michael was true to his word. He and Judy only wanted to discover what happened to Aunt Judith. They didn't give a hoot about the stash. I think they were satisfied with the result. They now know that Aunt Judith was truly happy with Jeremy. We offered them an equal share of the money, reminding them of what Jeremy said in his last note. But neither of them would take a penny.

Michael made it very clear. "I don't object to you guys spending the loot one little bit. But as for me, and I'm sure for Judy, we agree with

Jeremy. It's blood money, gotten with blood from our family. We couldn't spend a dime of it."

Mr. Alton promised Michael that he'd go on-line and look up the families of Penelope Peters and Cecilia Roberts. When he finds them, he'll offer to explain everything we know. But from what's been happening outside our front door, I'd be surprised if the media doesn't get to them first.

We exchanged email addresses and phone numbers, promising each other that we'd all keep in touch. Crystal suggested that we have a "Hillbrook stash reunion" next year at this time. Judy and Michael quickly agreed. After hugs all around, they were off.

Mom's reaction surprised me. She remained pretty calm when we told her. Maybe she expected us to find the Hillbrook stash all along. "Oh my!" she had said. "Things are sure going to be different around here from now on."

I thought she meant because of the money, but now I know she meant because of our imminent fame.

Before we started hauling the money out of Aunt Judith's dwelling, we agreed to split the money equally between our two families. So Crystal, Sally, and her parents took half and Tom, Mom, and I took the other half. We made equal trips to Sally's house and ours with the money. While the actual split didn't come out perfectly even, it was pretty darn close.

We tried to be stealthy while we carried the loot out of the woods so as not to arouse any suspicion. We varied our route each trip and alternated which house we'd go to. But we underestimated Mrs. Latimer's nosiness. Remember her? She's the one who told Mom about

Crystal and Sally. Mrs. Latimer had seen us walking to or from Bandit Woods a few times during the week. She didn't say or do anything then, but she must have been curious about what we were up to.

During our more frequent trips to haul everything out of the woods, her curiosity overcame her. We made four trips on Sunday right after we found the stash. During the sixth trip on Monday she came out to ask us what we were doing. Everyone, including Mr. Alton, was pretty nervous. This must have made us look suspicious. We made a hasty retreat from Mrs. Latimer. She called the police as soon as we were out of sight.

Officer Grant was waiting in his squad car as we came out of the woods with the last load. The guns. We didn't admit anything right away, saying we'd explain when we got home. He escorted us to my house with his red and blue beacons flashing. At least he didn't use the siren. But even so, we attracted a lot of attention during that last walk home.

It had long been determined that whoever found the Hillbrook stash would own it. The city of Clear Valley, and even the county of Bristol, long ago created special statutes that state as much. No other person is allowed to lay claim to The Hillbrook Stash. Over the years these statutes have promoted lots of tourism since even an outsider could keep the stash if he found it.

Even so, Officer Grant questioned our right to haul the money out of the woods without some kind of approval. Fortunately, we had already carried all the money out. And it was evenly divided between our two families. We only had the guns with us on that last trip out, though Officer Grant didn't know it until we got home.

When Officer Grant voiced his objections, Mom got right in his face. He sheepishly backed off. But just to be sure, Tom went on-line and read him the statutes.

That's when the phone started ringing. Not just at our house but at Sally's too. Apparently Officer Grant had called in our situation while he was escorting us home. He reported six people loaded down with heavy backpacks coming out of Bandit Woods. This, plus Mrs. Latimer's busy-bodying combined to get the rumors rolling. Now everyone was calling to find out if we really did find the Hillbrook stash. With every call Mom casually admitted that yes, her two sons really did find the Hillbrook stash.

That's when the doorbell started ringing. At one point, nearly everyone I know, and many people I don't know, were either in our house or out on our front lawn. Parked cars lined our block on both sides. Eventually they blocked the street.

That's when the local television station's news crew showed up. Someone had obviously called them. People with cameras and microphones lined up on our sidewalk. They we interviewing people in the front yard. I knew they'd soon get to us.

Before long, a crew from CNN showed up. The movie producer called shortly after.

Mr. Alton was right about the cash being worth more than its face value. The total value of the cash came to one million, two hundred twenty-two thousand, five hundred sixty dollars. And there was an unexpected bonus. It turns out that Thompson sub-machine guns are very rare and collectable. The four of them averaged twenty-five thousand dollars a piece. Not bad for just over a week's work!

* * *

Tom and I are anxiously awaiting Dad's arrival. Mom is with us, but I'm sure she isn't nearly as excited as we are. We sent Dad an airline ticket as soon as our house emptied out. It took ten days. He booked a flight for the following Sunday. Two weeks to the day after we found the Hillbrook stash.

We got to the airport a half hour early. We're now in a waiting area near the exit lobby. I wanted to meet Dad at the gate but Mom said only passengers can go to the gates.

"Why don't we buy tickets to somewhere?" Tom had said. "We can afford it. Then we can meet him at the gate."

Mom ignored him, thinking he was joking. I know he was serious, but he didn't push.

We see Dad's head bobbing in a sea of people coming out the exit hallway.

"Dad! Over here!" I call.

Dad sees us and makes his way over. Tom and I both leap to him. I can only hug with one arm but it sure feels good as he hugs back.

We back away a step and I notice that someone is standing next to Dad. A woman.

Dad has a big smile on his face. "Guys, I'd like you to meet my fiancé, Janice Bench."

Tom and I freeze into statues.

Janice is very pretty, but she doesn't look much older than Crystal. And she's fat. No, not fat. She's pregnant!

Janice approaches for a hug. We both shy away.

"Come on guys," she says, "aren't you going to give your new mommy a hug?"

Even Dad cringes. "Don't push it Baby. Give them some time to warm up to you."

Somehow I don't think that will ever happen.

Since Mom didn't want Dad staying in our house, she made us book him a room at the Hideout Hotel. Mom drives us all there and drops us off. No one says a word during the long ride from the airport.

Dad registers and the four of us go to his room.

Janice is the last one in the room and closes the door. "Do they have a pool here?"

Tom rolls his eyes.

Dad patiently answers. "I don't think so Baby. But I think there's an exercise room. Why don't you go check it out while I talk to my boys."

Janice takes a few minutes to gather some things into a gym bag. She grabs a towel from the bathroom and exits the room. "Later."

Dad's room is not nearly as large as Michael's was. There is only one bed. There is no table, only a small desk. Dad turns the desk chair around so that it faces the bed and sits down. Tom and I sit quietly on the end of the bed facing him.

"You guys have been through quite an adventure. It even made the T.V. stations in Dallas," he says. "I couldn't believe I was seeing my two boys on television."

"Uh huh," I say.

Tom grunts.

"What do you think of Janice? She's really something, isn't she?"

Tom looks out the window. "How old is she?"

"Oh, she's old enough."

"She doesn't look much older than my girlfriend," Tom says. "She's thirteen."

"It's really none of your business," Dad says.

Tom keeps staring out the window.

"Are you really going to marry her?" I ask.

"Well… yeah. I wouldn't have caller her my fiancé if I wasn't."

"Where will you live?" I follow up.

"Her family is in Dallas. I guess we'll live somewhere around there."

"What about *your* family?" Tom spits out. "I thought you were only in Dallas to find work. Now that we have money, you can come home."

"Janice would never go for it," Dad responds. "She'll want the baby to grow up close to her family."

"So her family is more important than your family?" I ask as the tears start welling up.

"Of course not," he says. "But I've got to start over. And it can't be here."

Tom looks at me and gets up from the bed. "Well I'm going home too. Where *my* family is. Are you coming Steve?"

Tom is already walking toward the door. His face is red and he's choking back tears. I get up and join him as he opens the door.

Dad doesn't say a word as we leave.

We start down the sidewalk, heading home. We've taken just a few steps when a car horn toots. Tears are blurring my vision, but I recognize Mom's car across the street. The driver's side window is down.

"Over here guys," she calls as she gets out.

I can't help myself. I run to her and throw my arms around her waste. Tom is right behind me. He's sobbing as loud as I am.

"There, there," Mom soothes, gently rubbing her hands on our heads. "You guys have been through so much this last couple of weeks. It's good to just let it out."

"You knew this was going to happen, didn't you?" Tom asks when finally calms down a little. There's anger in his voice but it's not aimed at Mom.

Mom doesn't respond. She seems content to hug.

The End